As Gouda as Dead

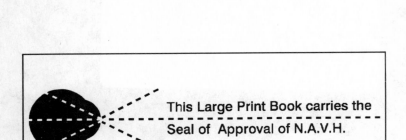

A CHEESE SHOP MYSTERY

As Gouda as Dead

Avery Aames

WHEELER PUBLISHING
A part of Gale, Cengage Learning

GALE
CENGAGE Learning·

Farmington Hills, Mich • San Francisco • New York • Waterville, Maine
Meriden, Conn • Mason, Ohio • Chicago

GALE
CENGAGE Learning

LIBRARY OF CONGRESS CATALOGING-IN-PUBLICATION DATA

Aames, Avery.
  As gouda as dead / by Avery Aames. — Large print edition.
    pages cm. — (A cheese shop mystery) (Wheeler Publishing large print cozy mystery)
    ISBN 978-1-4104-8199-3 (softcover) — ISBN 1-4104-8199-9 (softcover)
    1. Valentine's Day—Fiction. 2. Murder—Investigation—Fiction. 3. Large type books. I. Title.
PS3601.A215A9 2015
813'.6—dc23   2015019962

Published in 2015 by arrangement with The Berkley Publishing Group, an imprint of Penguin Publishing Group, a division of Penguin Random House LLC

Printed in the United States of America
1 2 3 4 5 6 7 19 18 17 16 15

To my loves:
Jackson, Jill, Craig, Kevin,
and your families.
You bring me tons of joy!

ACKNOWLEDGMENTS

"Flaming enthusiasm, backed up by horse sense and persistence, is the quality that most frequently makes for success."
— DALE CARNEGIE

Thank you to my family and friends for all your support. Thank you particularly to my husband, my first reader. I love your insight and enthusiasm. Thank you to my talented author friends, Krista Davis, Janet Bolin, Kate Carlisle, and Hannah Dennison, for your words of wisdom and calm. Thanks to my brainstormers at Plothatchers: Janet B., Janet K., Kaye, Marilyn, Peg, and Krista for all your input. Thanks to my blog mates on Mystery Lovers Kitchen and Killer Characters. Love you all!

Thanks to those who have helped make A Cheese Shop Mystery series a success: my fabulous editor, Kate Seaver, as well as Katherine Pelz and Danielle Dill. Thank you to my copyeditor, Rob Farren, and my cover artist, Teresa Fasolino. Great work!

John Talbot, thank you for believing in every aspect of my work. Sheridan Stancliff, you are an Internet and creative marvel. Kimberley Greene, I appreciate everything you do for me. I am so blessed.

Thank you librarians, teachers, and readers for sharing the delicious world of a cheese shop owner in a quaint, fictional town in Ohio with your friends.

And last but not least, thanks to my cheese consultant, Marcella. May your new direction in life bring you years of fulfillment.

Chapter 1

"Where are you taking me?" I asked. "And don't 'Hush, Charlotte' me again." I hate being blindfolded, hate not being able to see. Even as a girl, I despised it. I remembered one time when my oh-so-sly cousin coerced me into following him into a cave. We encountered shrieking bats and spiders and — *ick* — something creepy-crawly with a long tail that skittered across my foot.

"Hush, Charlotte," Delilah said. The moment I'd arrived home from work, she and Meredith, my other best friend, had kidnapped me.

"It's Thursday night, for heaven's sake. I've got to open Fromagerie Bessette early tomorrow. We have so much to do to prepare for next week's Lovers Trail event before I —"

"We're going to a party."

"A bachelorette party," Meredith added.

"Yours." Delilah pushed me at the small of my back. "Now, move it."

"Look." I tried to dig in my heels, to no avail. "I'd be game for whatever you have up your sleeves if I didn't have things to do."

Tons of things: decorations to put up and gift baskets to create for the Lovers Trail event. Not to mention all the things I needed to do for my impending nuptials: a hem to stitch, boutonnieres to fashion. Did my sweet friends care? Not a whit. They were giggling too hard to care about anything.

A brisk gust of February wind attacked me. I shivered from the cold. "Where are we?" I demanded. Delilah had escorted me out of her car a minute ago; we were on foot. On cement. A sidewalk, I was pretty sure. I heard light traffic. I detected the faint smell of cinnamon and coffee. Were we near Café au Lait, a delicious coffeehouse designed with a French flair? I could use a cup of coffee. "At least take the blindfold off. It's tugging the back of my hair."

"No, ma'am," Delilah said.

"Ma'am," Meredith sniggered. "That's right. You're going to be a ma'am soon. Maybe we should continue to call you *Miss Charlotte* for a while longer." More giggles

erupted from Meredith. How had Delilah talked her into this escapade? Meredith was usually the reliable and sane one. Sure, back in high school, she had been sneaky, but now? "Sounds like something right out of *Gone with the Wind*," she continued. "*Miss Charlotte.* Hmm. Which do you prefer, *Miss* Charlotte or *Mrs.* Jordan Pace?"

I didn't know who, where, or what was on the agenda for tonight, but in three days, on Sunday, I was moving forward with my life and marrying the man of my dreams — Jordan. A sizzle of desire shot through me just thinking about him. Prior to moving to Providence, Jordan had been the chef and owner of an Italian restaurant in upstate New York. One night outside the restaurant, he saw two thugs attack a third man. Without hesitating, Jordan, a former military man, sprang to the third man's defense. Days later, Jordan entered the WITSEC program to testify against the survivor, whose buddies had been the lynchpins of a gambling ring. Entering WITSEC had landed him in Providence, Ohio. Lucky me.

"This way, Miss Charlotte." Delilah steered me to the right.

A door opened and I breathed easier. I recognized the jingle of the chime above the door. We were entering Fromagerie Bessette.

The aroma of a potent Irish Cheddar cheese — our last sale of the day — hung in the air. I detected a hint of the quiche I'd made in the morning, too — apple bacon Gouda. It had been rich with a smoky, savory flavor.

"Let me go and tell me which way to go."

"Uh-uh," Delilah said.

"C'mon." I could navigate blindfolded through the shop without their help. I often dreamed about Fromagerie Bessette — or as the locals called it, The Cheese Shop — and its displays of cheeses, honey, mustards, and specialty crackers. Yes, I was a major cheese geek. Being a cheese shop proprietor was a dream job. I had inherited the shop from my grandparents, who had migrated from France to the States after World War II and had raised me to love the shop as much as they did.

Delilah joggled me. "Oops."

Although I would have been safe if I'd been allowed to grope along on my own, with Delilah as my guide, I instinctively reached out in front of me. Good thing I had. My foot hit something hard. "Ow." I grasped what had attacked me — a display barrel, the old oak cask kind with metal struts. "You did that on purpose."

"Did what?" Delilah guffawed.

"Shh," Meredith cooed. "Charlotte, just a

few more feet."

Gingerly, I shuffled across the hardwood floor praying I wouldn't wind up with ten stubbed toes. At least I was wearing a pair of Ugg boots; they were padded and perfect for the winter. I still couldn't understand a girl wearing them in the summer, but I wasn't a fashion guru.

"Where are we headed?" I asked. "The annex?" The wine annex, which my cousin managed and stocked with some of the finest wines this side of the Rockies, was situated to the right through a stone archway. "Ooh, are we having a wine tasting?" I was always up for one of those.

"Sort of," Meredith said.

I had known Meredith and Delilah since I was in grade school. The two of them were like night and day. Meredith was blonde and sun-kissed with freckles; she had a rosy disposition. In contrast, Delilah had dark curly hair, striking features, and a wicked sense of humor. Meredith was an elementary teacher and soon would run the Providence Liberal Arts College. She was married to my cousin, and stepmother to my pre-teen twin nieces — I referred to them as my nieces; they were really my first cousins once removed. Delilah ran The Country Kitchen diner across the street.

She had returned to Providence after her career on Broadway stalled. Weekly, the three of us and a few other women went out for girls' night. I imagined tonight's bachelorette soiree was going to be an entirely different kind of event.

"What are we going to do at the party?" I said.

"It's a secret," Delilah answered.

"How many people?"

"Just a few of us."

"All girls?" I asked.

"No boys allowed," Delilah said.

"Well, almost no boys." Meredith snorted. What had gotten into her?

A chilly wisp of air tickled my nose. Abruptly Delilah pivoted me and ushered me in the direction of the cold. Good thing I'd worn a cashmere sweater and corduroy trousers. I knew where we were headed. Downstairs, into the cellar. My cousin and I, with Jordan's help, had installed a wine and cheese cellar. It was one of the best investments we had made. Even after cheese makers shipped wheels of cheese to us, we preferred to age some of them a tad longer.

I stepped down the stairs, drinking in the luscious perfume of cheese. The temperature in the cellar ranged from a cool fifty-five degrees to a toasty fifty-eight. Heat affects the speed with which wine and cheese age. We had painted the cellar white and had fitted it with wood racks. In addition, we had commissioned a local artist to paint a faux window with a view of the rolling hills of Providence in the eight-foot, semi-round alcove. Below the painting stood an oak buffet as well as a mosaic-inlaid table with chairs. Perfect for a small gathering.

My left foot touched the cellar floor. "C'mon, ladies, out with it. I smell something nutty with a hint of charcoal and fresh herbs. Are we having a cheese tasting party?"

I heard more tittering. Not from my guides. From other party members already in the cellar.

"Please say something," I pleaded. "Wait, do I also smell . . . suntan oil?"

Meredith brushed my arm with something furry.

I recoiled. "Ew, what is that?"

"It's a paintbrush, silly."

I moaned. "We're having an art party?" I'd heard about them. They were very au courant. "I'm not an artist," I protested. "Isn't this supposed to be all about *me*?"

"No, you goon," Delilah said. "This party is about all of *us* giving you a fabulous sendoff into married life. Get with the program."

"Don't worry," Meredith reassured me. "None of us are artists."

"You are, Meredith," Delilah chimed.

"I'm not sure about *this* kind of art." Meredith pinched me.

"What do you mean 'this kind of art'?" I cried, truly hating being in the dark . . . about anything. "Take off my blindfold. Now!"

"Don't get snippy." Delilah released my hand and moved behind me. She started to untie the scarf she had slung around my head. "One, two, voilà."

"Surprise!" the other party guests yelled.

When my eyes adjusted to the light, I realized each was wearing a cream-colored artist's smock over warm winter clothing, and each held a glass of sparkling wine. A gorgeous spread of appetizers was laid out on a long table behind them: biscuits stuffed with ham, mini quiches, and one of my all-time favorites, a cranberry crusted cheese torte.

"Turn around," the women said in unison.

When I did, I couldn't believe what I saw.

CHAPTER 2

In the nook with the faux window that held a view of Providence stood the handsome yet darling Deputy O'Shea . . . wearing nothing but boxer shorts. The kid — okay, he wasn't a kid, he was pushing thirty — blushed. He reminded me of something right out of a Calvin Klein ad. His skin was bronzed. His abs were perfectly formed. His hair hung rakishly across his forehead.

Rebecca Zook, my slim assistant, traipsed to me and gave me a hug. "Hooray! You really *are* surprised. I was so afraid I would spill the beans. An art party!" Before coming to work at Fromagerie Bessette, Rebecca had lived a sheltered life in an Amish community. She left the fold to explore the world, and though she now considered herself worldly, she was still the epitome of innocence. She swooped her long golden hair over her shoulder. "Don't you love it?"

A flood of emotions — love wasn't one of

them — rushed through me. I did my best to curb a fit of giggles. We were going to paint a semi-nude man. My artwork would no doubt turn out looking like a glob. I could bake. I could sew. I could sculpt cakes made out of cheese. I could even refinish furniture. But paint? Most of my creations turned out to be bad Jackson Pollock imitations — splatter with no substance. Nope. I had no talent.

Rebecca said, "Charlotte, cat got your tongue?"

"It's . . ." What could I say? When Delilah said we were on our way to a bachelorette party, I had expected a simple party. Chitchat. Cake. Nothing too extravagant. This? Every single woman in the cellar, including Meredith, Delilah, Rebecca, and four of my other friends, looked ready — no, *eager* — to sketch the deputy. My cheeks warmed; my heart thrummed with anticipation. I wondered what Jordan was doing at his bachelor party, kicking back a beer and watching sports? I couldn't imagine any of his friends hiring a stripper. Perhaps I was too naïve for words.

"C'mon, Charlotte," Delilah said. "This will be fun. Here's a smock. Put it on."

I shrugged off my coat and purse and threw the smock on over my sweater. The smock billowed around my corduroy slacks.

"There," Delilah said. "Georgia O'Keeffe, eat your heart out. Party time!"

The deputy drew near, and the aroma of suntan oil grew stronger. Had he just left the tanning parlor? "Sorry, Charlotte," he whispered, using my first name instead of the more formal Miss Bessette. "I hope you're okay with this. I got wrangled into the gig."

"Who wrangled you?"

"Who do you think?"

"Your uncle Tim?"

"Yep." O'Shea's uncle, who owned the Irish pub where my girlfriends and I occasionally spent our girls' nights out, was a bit of a prankster. "Uncle Tim suggested it to Tyanne."

He nodded in Tyanne's direction. Tyanne, a part-timer at The Cheese Shop and the town's premier wedding planner, was currently dating Tim. They made a cute pair, he with his burly ruggedness and she with her Southern femininity. She caught me looking her way and buffed her fingers on her smock. I mock-glowered at her.

O'Shea added, "The two of them thought it would be a gas."

"And you?"

"I said, 'Go for it.' Granted, this is a one-time deal. If word gets out, it might . . . Well, you understand."

"Undermine your authority. Got it. It's our secret." I nodded. "Aren't you cold in this chilly cellar?"

"Nah. I go ice fishing and winter swimming. I can take it."

"Well, deputy —"

"Tonight you can call me Devon."

"Devon," the women in the cellar sang in unison. Exactly how much liquor had they imbibed already? Had all of them promised to keep the secret, too?

"Devon, it'll be my pleasure to attempt to sketch you."

A telephone rang insistently. O'Shea looked toward a gym bag that was sitting on the floor by the door.

"Uh-uh," Rebecca said. "No phone calls. It's a rule."

He said, "But it could be business."

"And business could mean bad news. No." She folded her arms. For a slight thing, she sure could look tough. "You're officially off the clock. Stay right there. I'll fix this." Without asking his permission, she hurried to his bag and rummaged through his things. She swiped her finger across the face of the cell phone and dumped it back into the bag.

She returned and drew me off to one side for a tête-à-tête. "Isn't the deputy the yummiest?" For the past few months, Rebecca had been sitting on the fence, deliberating whether to choose her former fiancé or Devon O'Shea as a full-time boyfriend. In the end, she didn't have to decide. Though her former fiancé had protested to the gods above, at his parents' directive he had sold his honeybee farm and returned to Hawaii. Poor guy. Now Rebecca and O'Shea were an item. I had to admit they were cute together. "Well, isn't he?"

"Definitely. Yummy. You don't mind him doing this?"

"Why would I?"

I had no answer for that. I would have been uncomfortable if a half dozen women were ogling my boyfriend with downright lust, but apparently she wasn't. Maybe I needed to grow up.

"All right, everyone." Meredith clapped her hands. "Let's get this party started. Maestro, music."

Jordan's sister, Jacky, a willowy, dark-haired beauty who had given up her former life to live near her brother, was in charge of the iPod. She pressed a button and the Eurythmics' "Sweet Dreams (Are Made Of This)" started to play through a portable speaker.

"Turn it off," I yelped as a shiver shimmied up my spine.

Jacky switched off the song. "What's wrong?"

"She doesn't want Councilwoman Bell to hear the noise," Delilah chirped. "You know how she can be. She complains so much, you'd think she could hear every single sound in town."

"No, that's not it. I —" I hugged myself as a painful memory flooded my senses. I was back in the car with my parents. Pre-crash. "Sweet Dreams" was playing on the radio. The wind. My parents laughing. Then the screams. "Just pick another song, okay?" Talk about a mood killer.

Jacky whisked her finger across a playlist, and sultry Latin music started to play. "Better?"

"Thank you."

"That Mrs. Bell," Rebecca groused. "I swear, I thought she was so nice when I first met her, but she complains more than our not-so-favorite dress shop owner."

Delilah tangoed to me with a flute of sparkling wine and a platter of cheeses that included one of my all-time favorites, Big Rock Blue, a creamy, teal-veined cheese with the texture of fudge. "Drink up,

22

everyone, and have some cheese to fortify yourself," she announced to all. "It's party time." Then she whispered to me, "Are you okay? Bad memory?"

How well she knew me. "My parents," I said.

"I'm sorry."

"I'll be fine." I took a sip of the wine. It was ice-cold and luscious, with hints of peach and apricot. The bubbles tickled my nose.

Meredith waltzed up with a paintbrush in hand. She thrust it at me and gave me a nudge. Easels had been set up around the cellar. "You get to pick first. Deputy O'Shea, take your position."

"Call me Devon," he said.

"Devon!" the ladies chimed again like a group of giggly chorines.

I laughed. Despite my earlier trepidation and the momentary upset with the music, the party was going to be fun.

Devon moved to the center of the cellar and perched on a short ladder with one foot propped on the lowest rung.

"Arms up," Delilah ordered.

O'Shea raised his arms overhead and offered a muscleman pose. His biceps flexed; his abs tightened. The women cooed their appreciation. After a moment, O'Shea

23

shook his head. "Uh-uh, not a chance. I can't hold this pose for longer than a minute." He shook out his arms and squared his shoulders. "How's this?" He angled his elbows and gripped his hands in front of his torso. If Jordan wasn't twice as handsome, I might have found myself salivating.

For over an hour, while my friends and I sketched, they plowed me with questions about Jordan and the wedding plans. Although neither Jordan nor I had been married before — both of us had been engaged in our twenties; my fiancé, let's just say, turned out to be a bad apple, and Jordan's fiancée had died tragically of a heart attack — we weren't doing anything overly dramatic for our nuptials. We had planned a low-key ceremony at his farm. I would walk down the aisle to a solo French horn, to honor my father, and we would have Irish music and an Irish prayer to honor my mother. I'd also requested that a swarm of butterflies be released after we said our vows. I'd considered having Jordan come to my grandparents' house and pick me up — it was an old French tradition — but we had decided against it; we were way beyond being kids.

"What're you wearing?" Rebecca said.

"You've been so hush-hush about it. And what is Jordan wearing?"

Freckles, a pint-sized, sunny woman who owned Sew Inspired Quilt Shoppe, waved a hand. "I can answer that." She had designed my simple ecru dress, which was in need of hemming, and she had tailored Jordan's light brown suit. She described them in detail. Bridesmaids were going to wear shimmering gold cocktail dresses.

"I've advised Charlotte to keep her hair just as it is," Tyanne said. She may have relocated from New Orleans a few years ago, but her Southern accent was still intact. "It's very sassy."

I had touched up my hair with extra blonde highlights and had cut it shorter to frame my face, very much like Tyanne's current hairstyle. Ever since she had started an exercise regimen, her entire look had changed. She had lost weight and toned up. Divorce, in her case, had been good for her overall well-being.

In addition to the ceremony requirements, I had two other traditions that mattered to me. I would wear my mother's pearl earrings, the same she had worn when she married my father, and I would carry a handful of daisies — my mother's favorite flower. How she and my father would have loved to see me walk down the aisle.

"How many people are coming?" Freckles asked.

"Jordan and I have invited a few friends, including all of you and our immediate family." At the last, my cousin had strong-armed us into inviting his ex-wife Sylvie; otherwise, she would crash the party. So be it. Who needed the aggravation? Fortunately, she had not been invited to the bachelorette party. I could only imagine what she would have been saying to taunt me.

"And the menu," Tyanne said. "Tell them about the menu, Charlotte. Y'all, it's so delicious, you'll die."

"I want the whole affair to be romantic," I said. "We'll have a winter salad with chocolate-dipped strawberries, roasted chicken with chocolate mole sauce, and a decadent chocolate cheesecake for dessert."

"That's my recipe," Delilah boasted. "I've been working on it for weeks. It's got chocolate swirled throughout, and there will be a mound of whipped cream topped with shaved chocolate curls on top."

The others *ooh*ed their appreciation.

Tyanne said, "Isn't it thrilling? And how much more romantic could it be? The wedding is set during our town's Lovers Trail festivities."

The Lovers Trail celebration was my septuagenarian, go-getter grandmother's creation. She served as mayor of Providence. The festivities started tomorrow and would run for ten days, through the following Sunday. The celebration would feature sleigh rides, moveable feasts, and more. Many places, like the wineries, the ice-skating rink, and Nature's Preserve, were hosting daily events. Otherwise, the town was divided up by main streets: east and west, north and south. On a specific day, shops and restaurants in town were to honor good old St. Valentine's by offering candy, wine, and meals with a lovers' theme. Fromagerie Bessette was preparing lovers' baskets complete with heart-shaped cheeses. Next Thursday, in the wine annex, we were throwing a cheese and wine soiree. Tickets were required.

"What could be more romantic than Providence in February?" Tyanne said. "The whole town is ablaze with twinkling lights. Everyone is in love or pretending to be."

"Some are totally in love." Rebecca flushed pink as she ogled Deputy O'Shea. He did his best not to break his pose, but he couldn't prevent a transcendental grin from spreading across his handsome face.

I tried to capture that grin with my

paintbrush, but I failed. Miserably. I wondered whether I could convince everyone who looked at my artwork that I was trying to emulate Picasso in his cubist period.

"Why isn't your grandmother here, Charlotte?" Freckles asked.

Delilah answered, "She's busy with preparations for the weekend's festivities."

Rebecca said, "Also, she has purchased the rights to the play *Love Letters* for the Providence Playhouse, so she's busy building sets."

In addition to serving as mayor, my grandmother dedicated her life to making the Providence Playhouse a must-visit theater. *Love Letters* was a Pulitzer Prize finalist that focused on two people. The actor, who played a staid lawyer, and the actress, who played an unstable artist, sit side by side onstage. Though they are worlds apart, they read letters and cards that pass between them over the course of fifty years, in which they express their hopes, dreams, and bitter disappointments. Grandmère had asked me to read the play before she purchased the rights. By the final scene, I was a sobbing, hiccupping mess. During the play's twenty-plus-year run, Hollywood stars like Kathleen Turner, Jason Robards, and Colleen Dewhurst had performed in it. Grandmère suggested that Jordan and I take on the roles, but I nixed that idea. I am not an actress in much the same way that I am not an artist. Yes, I acted in high-school plays, but I fumbled lines and generally stunk. Lately I'd heard Grandmère trying to cajole our local chief of police into taking on the male role. I would never reveal, not even after drinking sparkling wine with my dearest friends, that I was the one who had suggested him to my grandmother. Heaven forbid he discover I had. He and I could go head-to-head on occasion.

Delilah instructed O'Shea to change his pose. At the same time, a cell phone buzzed. Everyone's gaze flew to Deputy O'Shea's gym bag.

Rebecca huffed. "Sheesh. Didn't I switch it off? No —"

"That's a message. Let me take a look, Rebecca." O'Shea didn't wait for her okay. He dashed to his gym bag and pulled out his phone. Crouched low, he pressed a button and listened. "What the —" He glanced at the readout.

A shiver snaked up my spine for the second time that evening. It wasn't related to my parents' crash. Why was I on edge?

What was going on? I'd been feeling so confident and settled lately. Was it just pre-wedding jitters?

I rushed to O'Shea. "Is everything all right?"

The deputy had the phone planted against his ear. He jammed a finger into his other ear. A few seconds later, he snapped to a stand. "Dang."

"What's wrong?" I said.

O'Shea didn't answer. He stabbed in numbers on the cell phone and pressed Send.

"Devon, talk to me."

"Uncle Tim —"

"Is he okay? Did something happen?"

"I'm not sure. He sounded flustered. He said he heard, no, he *saw* something."

"What are you talking about?"

"He left a message." O'Shea looked worried. "His voice cut in and out. He didn't sound good. He sounded . . . scared. He said he was going to contact Chief Urso. Just as the call ended, something crashed in the background."

CHAPTER 3

While apologizing, Deputy O'Shea threw on his shirt, trousers, and shoes. He seized his bag and dashed upstairs. Needless to say, my celebratory good vibrations flew out the window. I tore off my smock, asked everyone to clean up the cellar, grabbed my coat and purse, and raced after him.

Luckily yesterday's snow had melted and the streets were dry. The cold air stung my cheeks. "Where are you going?" I called.

"To the pub." O'Shea didn't slow down.

"Why are you so worried?"

"It's not like Uncle Tim to —" He shook his head once. Hard. "You know him," he yelled over his shoulder. "He's not the kind who panics. About anything."

"And he sounded freaked out?"

"That's the thing. I'm not sure. But I'm going to find out."

"When did he leave the message?"

"An hour ago."

Timothy O'Shea's Irish Pub was located at the north end of the Village Green, about a block from Fromagerie Bessette. Deputy O'Shea entered first. I trailed him.

Invariably, O'Shea's was crowded. The pub was the only place at night that had multiple televisions airing sports or highlights, nonstop. When it was time for the three-piece band to play, like now, all the televisions were switched to closed-caption mode. The walls were bare. Tim wouldn't put up the St. Patrick's Day decorations until March; they would stay up until May.

The deputy and I bypassed the hostess's station and headed toward the antique bar. The leader of the band announced that the upcoming song would be their last for a while, and then the band launched into a rousing rendition of "The Irish Rover."

Deputy O'Shea strode to a red-haired waitress at the far end of the bar. Like all the waitresses, she was fit and bright-eyed. Tim insisted that his waitresses be able to handle any person, drunk or sober. Rowdies, he called them.

O'Shea said, "Where's my uncle?"

"No need to shout, Devon, my darlin'. I can hear just fine, music and all." The waitress planted a hand on her hip. "Last I saw him, he was shuffling toward the kitchen." She gestured with a thumb toward the kitchen door.

"When was that?"

"An hour ago. Maybe more. Why?"

"You're not concerned that he's gone?"

"Why would I be? He often leaves and comes back at close of business. He takes walks. It's good for his heart, he says." She thumped hers. "I figure he stayed out for some fresh air. I wouldn't blame him. It's hot in here." She loosened the red bandanna around her neck and mopped her forehead with a white bar towel. "I hate when we crank up the heat because it's cold outside. People dress warmly. There's no —"

"Hush." O'Shea held up a hand.

The waitress grimaced. "What's eating you?"

"Tim called me."

"That's because you're his favorite nephew. He always has a soft spot —"

"Stop talking. Listen to me. I'm not kidding. I think something might be wrong."

The waitress, realizing O'Shea was earnest, tried to apologize, but O'Shea didn't respond. He marched ahead. I trailed him through the kitchen to the rear of the restaurant.

"Has anyone seen Tim in the last hour?"

O'Shea said to the kitchen staff. He pushed through the back door. I peeked over his shoulder. The alley was empty. No sign of Tim. O'Shea made a U-turn. "Anybody?"

"He went outside a while ago," said a female sous-chef who was in her mid-thirties, about the same age I was. She continued to stuff potato skins with whipped potatoes. "I don't remember seeing him return. He likes to —"

"Stroll," a whip-thin waitress said while filling a basket with Parmesan breadsticks.

"Did somebody drop a tray of glassware in the last hour?" O'Shea asked.

A timid dishwasher in a dirty white apron raised a hand. "Me."

"That means you were outside when my uncle was calling me on his cell phone."

"No."

"I heard the glasses shatter."

The guy blanched. "I mean, yes, I dropped the glasses, but I didn't see Tim. I wasn't outside. I was just inside the door."

"Where was Tim?"

"I don't know. We had the door wedged open. We just needed some air. I . . ." He shrugged. "I was clumsy. I think I heard him crank up his truck, though. It's got that sputter sound. Like it needs a good tune-up."

Tim had owned his truck since high school. He loved working on the engine. That didn't mean he was any good at fixing the darned thing.

"Did you see him drive off?" O'Shea asked.

"No. I just heard —"

O'Shea didn't wait for the rest of the guy's explanation. He strode back into the pub and stood with his hands on his hips while scanning the place. Picking a target, he stomped off to talk to a pair of regulars.

Believing that the more news we gleaned the better — especially before anyone left the bar — I chose another twosome to question. Violet Walden, the woman who ran the upscale Violet's Victoriana Inn, was sitting with Paige Alpaugh, a pert, forty-something single mom who reminded me of a show pony with her big jaw, big teeth, and plume of caramel-colored hair.

With no introduction, I slid onto one of the chairs at the women's table and said, "Hey, Violet, I've got that Fromager d'Affinois you like in stock." The cheese was a delicious French double-cream, similar to Brie in taste, and in my personal opinion, creamier.

"Mmm." Violet, also mid-thirties, who had a classically pretty face but dyed her shoulder-length hair a ridiculous marshmallow-blonde color, hummed without looking up. She was rummaging in her purse. Out came a lozenge, a folded piece of blue paper, a receipt, and a pack of cigarettes. The latter must have been what she was after. She jammed everything but the pack of cigarettes back inside and began tap-tapping the pack on the tabletop. "I'm off of cheese for a while."

"Why?" I assessed her. Had she lost weight? Despite the fact that her B&B offered spa cuisine, Violet usually appeared thick. Perhaps it was because she wore clothes that were one size too small. Tonight, however, she looked downright trim in her chic sweater and jeans. "Has Paige ordered you to change your eating habits?"

"It wasn't me," Paige said, holding her hand up like a Girl Scout ready to take the pledge. "I adore cheese." A divorcee and mother of two, Paige made her living as a farmer. She was also a foodie blogger who wrote passionately and tirelessly about a well-balanced diet. I couldn't get over the amount of hours she put into her blog. She posted recipes daily and showed every step of preparation. Each post had a chatty story and sometimes a moral or warning to go along with it. "Dairy in the diet is a good thing," she said. "It's the sugar you have to watch out for. Candy, sodas, pastries."

"Amen." Violet gestured with a V sign.

"And the cigarettes."

Violet threw Paige a nasty look.

"Eat right and you'll make pretty babies," Paige went on with authority. I was sure she believed what she professed, but, honestly, genetics had a lot to do with beautiful offspring. Paige's eldest daughter had turned out as attractive as Paige; the younger girl had her father's features.

I turned to Violet. "Are you pregnant?"

"No. I'm single. I would never —" She huffed. "I hope to have kids one day. Soon. Paige is just being . . . Paige. In other words, annoying."

Paige hiccupped a laugh.

"What's up with the deputy?" Violet eyed O'Shea. "He looks like he's on the warpath."

"His uncle Tim called him."

"So?" Violet, who was a head taller than I was, shimmied in her chair until she was sitting straight and, I was pretty sure, could look down on me. I wouldn't necessarily call her controlling, simply in need of the upper hand.

"He left a message, which sounded urgent," I said. "But the reception cut in and out, so the deputy didn't catch all of

Tim's message. Now he can't reach him."

"Typical around here," Paige said. "All the rolling hills. What we need is a good cell tower."

"Oh, yeah, right." Violet gave her the evil eye. "Talk Councilwoman Bell into that. Can you spell eyesore on her precious landscape?"

Not only did the councilwoman dislike noise in our fair town; she disliked any change whatsoever. She owned Memory Lane Collectibles, which was wedged in between the pastry shop and the Revue Movie Theater. Her shop reflected who she was: a woman who wanted things in her life and town to remain quaint and unchanged.

"If she had her way," Violet went on, "we would return to pioneer days, as long as the showers and plumbing worked."

Paige let out with a high-pitched whinny of a laugh.

"Have either of you seen Tim?" I asked.

"The last I saw, he was pouring a pitcher of beer for that table over there." Paige pointed to a group of four. I recognized them. They were California tourists who had come into The Cheese Shop earlier and had bought out my entire assortment of New England cheeses.

"When was that?"

"Over an hour ago." She snorted again. "We've been here awhile." She ran a finger along the rim of her glass of beer. "I'm nursing my one and only. A girl's got to party, just not too hearty, don't you think?"

"How about you, Violet?" I noticed the pack of cigarettes she was toying with. A cigarette was missing. Perhaps holding the pack helped her over the hurdle of needing to smoke another. I knew a man who would suck on an unlit cigar all day. Years ago, I'd suggested trying a lollipop, but he wouldn't go for it. I said, "Did you happen to see Tim when you went outside for a smoke?"

"Aha!" Paige *tsk*ed. "That's why you snuck out." The disappointment in her tone was heavy-handed.

"No. I mean, yes. I had one. Only one." Violet tucked the cigarettes into her purse, and then leaned toward me. "I'm trying to quit."

I said, "The kitchen staff said Tim went out back, by the garbage."

"I wasn't out there. I was in the parking lot."

"So you didn't see Tim."

"No." Violet tapped her manicured fingertips on the table.

"One of the staff thought Tim might have driven off in his truck."

Violet's eyes brightened. "You know, now that you mention it, I did see Tim. In his truck. Driving away. And I noticed someone else. Jawbone."

"Jones?"

"How many Jawbones can there be?" she quipped.

The first time I'd met Jawbone Jones, who was the owner of a gun shop, I felt scared down to my toes. His appearance wasn't the typical look people sported in Providence. He shaved his head, he wore a goatee, and he had the word *king* tattooed on his neck. However, over the past year, I had grown to enjoy him. He was a true aficionado of hard cheeses. I remembered how he would wax rhapsodic about Vermont Shepherd Invierno cheese, a sublime mixture of cow and sheep's milk with a mushroomy taste. He would also purchase a huge portion of Jordan's Pace Hill Farm Double-cream Gouda whenever he came in; he said it was his mother's favorite.

"Why did you notice him?" I asked.

"Because he peeled rubber and sped off in his truck, too. Maybe he was chasing Tim."

"Which way did Jawbone go?"

"He made a right turn."

That would mean he had headed north.

"Did Tim drive the same direction?"

"I think so." Violet linked a finger into the hair at the nape of her neck and twirled. "You know, Ray Pfeiffer might have seen him, too." Ray was the latest owner of The Ice Castle, the rink where I'd learned to skate ages ago. "He was outside fetching something from his car." She gazed toward the ceiling, as if picturing something in her mind. "Jawbone was definitely in a hurry."

I scanned the pub. "Is Ray still here?" Maybe he had seen more than Violet had.

"No, he and Dottie left a while ago. You know how it is with Dottie. She's got to hit the hay so she can get up early to make all those pastries of hers."

"Those sugar-loaded fattening pastries," Paige said under her breath.

Those *delicious* pastries, I thought, but kept my opinion to myself. Dottie was the owner of the Providence Pâtisserie, from which our shop purchased many of the breads we used to make sandwiches.

I hurried to O'Shea and tapped him on the shoulder. He whipped around.

I apologized to the pub regulars for interrupting. "Violet saw Jawbone Jones tear off in his truck. He headed north. She wasn't sure, but he might have been chasing your uncle. You said Tim wanted to talk to Urso.

Maybe he drove to Pace Hill Farm. That's where Urso is. At Jordan's bachelor party."

Chapter 4

O'Shea raced out of the pub and nearly flew to the precinct parking lot. I made it into the passenger seat of his SUV seconds before he tore off. As he zoomed toward the farmland in the north part of the county, I pulled my cell phone from my purse. Following the first wild turn, I was forced to grab the bar above the passenger side window. So much for being able to dial Urso. Where had the deputy learned to drive that way? Had he trained with NASCAR racers, or had the academy taught him the skill? His teeth looked cemented together.

"Deputy, please slow down."

"Roads are dry."

"We can barely see the pavement." The sky was pitch-black. There was no moon. The pastoral areas beyond the town's main roads weren't lined with street lamps. "All it takes is a patch of ice kicked up by one of the sleighs to make us spin out."

"Don't worry."

Easy for him to say. My fingers were tingling from gripping the bar. I didn't dare let go.

We rounded the bend by Windmill Crest. The ancient windmill at the top was doing its level best to fight off a blustery wind. A Camaro whizzed past us. I couldn't see the driver's face, but I recognized the car. Its owner was a young man who worked at Providence Pâtisserie and often delivered the bread we purchased. Right after he zoomed past, we came upon a sleigh moving along the side of the road, just beyond the buildup of old snow.

"Do you see the sleigh, Devon?" Saying his name made me think of the bachelorette party and the way the girls had hooted after uttering his name. How long ago that seemed.

"I'm not blind."

He slowed ever so slightly as he passed the sleigh and then resumed speed. I glanced back. The couple, draped in blankets and lit by the glow of hurricane candles mounted on either side of the driver, looked happy and totally oblivious to our plight. If only I was riding in a sleigh with Jordan and not a partner on this wild adventure.

"There's the Bozzuto Winery," I said. Torchlights lit the winding road that led to the winery. It looked so inviting. All week long, expressly for the Lovers Trail festivities, the winery was having a wine tasting, twice daily and once nightly. "Pace Hill is beyond."

"I know," he grumbled.

Don't shoot the messenger, I thought.

Pace Hill Farm is an artisanal farm that raises its own cows and turns out about eighty thousand pounds of cheese a year. Seasonally, tourists are encouraged to walk the hiking trails and visit the cheese-making facility. On a typical day in spring, the drive to Pace Hill Farm would have taken us through brilliant green swales and knolls dotted with oak. We would have smelled the sweet aroma of grass wafting through the open windows of the SUV, but today, following a week of snow and temperatures hovering in the teens, all we smelled was the car's interior, and all we saw were white hills and dales framed by the dark of night.

The deputy hit the brakes and made a sharp turn onto the road leading to the farm.

"What if your uncle didn't come here?" I asked. "What if he thought better about whatever he was setting out to do and went home? We should have gone there first."

"But we didn't. We're here."

"I'll try to call him."

"His cell phone glitched out. Don't you remember?" Venom filled the deputy's tone.

I refused to buckle. "What's his home number?"

O'Shea rattled it off. I dared to release my hold on the overhead bar and dialed Tim's number, but it didn't ring through. I glanced at the readout; my cell phone had lost its signal. I reflected on the conversation with Violet and Paige back at the pub. We really could use another cell tower in the area. What if we decorated it with those fake trees to mask it? Would Councilwoman Bell get on board then?

My cell phone trilled. Heartened, hoping it was Tim — maybe he'd glimpsed that I had called him at home, and he was returning the call; crisis averted — I answered.

"Charlotte," Rebecca said. She sounded out of breath. "Where are — Where's Dev —" Her words kept cutting off. A wheeze of what sounded like air but had to be electric static echoed in the background. "I'm at the pub with Delil — We came looking for — We got worr—What's going on?"

My insides felt cinched tight. "We're on our way to Jordan's place. Urso's there."

"Why do you —" More dead air. "Urso?"

"I can barely hear you, and I can't talk now. Tim's missing. I'm hanging up. I'll call you when we learn something. It's probably nothing." Another icier-than-all-get-out chill coursed through me. I chalked it up to me channeling the deputy's worry. Nothing was wrong. Nothing.

At the top of the drive, O'Shea swerved around the many cars and trucks parked in front of Jordan's ranch-style house and screeched to a halt. We bounded from the SUV at the same time.

"Look!" He pointed. "That's my uncle's truck."

At the far left of the driveway, a blue 1995 Chevy Silverado stood at an angle. I remembered when Tim bought it. I was still in high school, but my grandparents took me into the pub for a burger. Tim was behind the bar bragging about the truck and how he was going to rebuild the engine and upgrade the radiator from a single-core to a three-core because the lesser wasn't good for towing. Like he towed anything, his conversation mate had teased. Now I recalled a more recent boast by Tim; the Silverado had over two hundred and fifty thousand miles on it. He claimed it was the most reliable buddy a guy could ever have.

My grandfather said Tim would make a great spokesman for Chevrolet.

O'Shea darted to the truck and peeked through the driver window. "He's not inside. Follow me."

Not one to argue with the law — okay, sometimes I did, but I wasn't about to tonight — I obeyed.

O'Shea sprinted to the main house and up the triplet of steps to the porch. He lifted the lion's-head-shaped doorknocker and rammed it against the wood. From inside, I heard men laughing.

When Delilah and Meredith had *kidnapped* me, they hadn't let me grab my gloves. I rubbed my fingers to warm them. Not good enough. I cupped them and blew into them. "Deputy . . . Devon . . ." Were my teeth chattering? "I think we might be overreacting. I'll bet your uncle came here to join the party. He and Jordan are friends. Maybe he was trying to tell you he saw an invitation. He forgot to RSVP. He was going to call Urso to tell him he was on his way. Maybe this party was a surprise like mine was. Maybe —"

"No." O'Shea was adamant. "Uncle Tim refuses to go to bachelor parties. He hates them. He hates all celebrations."

"You're kidding. He owns the most rousing place in town."

"I know."

"And he was the one who talked you into posing at my bachelorette party."

"*I* can celebrate. *You* can celebrate. Not him."

"I don't get it. Why does he hate celebrating so much?"

"You don't know?" O'Shea rammed the doorknocker into the wood again. "He got dumped at the altar twenty years ago."

"Wow. I had no idea. I barely knew him then. I was in high school."

"Yeah, of course. Dumb me."

To the deputy, I would bet anyone over thirty was ancient.

"Tim was the youngest brother," O'Shea continued. "After all of his older brothers got married, he was feeling the pressure to follow in their footsteps. So he got engaged to a girl he didn't love. Respectable, but, well, you know." O'Shea grimaced. "Sometime before the big date, he decided to quit farming and buy the bar. I guess he forgot to tell his intended. On the morning of the wedding, she called it off. She didn't want to have anything to do with someone who supplied liquor to people."

"Who was she?"

"Maggie something."

"Does she still live in town?"

"No. She moved away about a year later. Tim told me she never married. He swears he ruined her for everyone. Some couples aren't meant to be, I guess."

I wondered how Tim tolerated Tyanne's career as the town's premier wedding party planner. Tyanne had never mentioned his loathing for celebrations.

O'Shea knocked a third time. His boot drilled the porch while he waited. "C'mon, open up," he grumbled.

"Try the knob. It's not breaking and entering."

He did. It was unlocked. He pushed the door open. "Uncle Tim?"

Jordan's home was very male, filled with leather and wood furniture. The aroma of beer and ribs drowned out the normal aroma of pine and musk. The party appeared to be made up of about fifteen males. A couple of them were playing darts. A few others were seated at tables playing cards. I don't know what I had expected Jordan's bachelor party to be, but this wasn't it. The word *tame* came to mind.

I didn't spy Tim among the group, but I caught sight of Jordan, who was standing with his back to the door chatting up another farm owner. Despite the tension of the moment, my insides did a happy dance. In three days, I would be his bride. But that wasn't why we were here. "Jordan!" I yelled.

Jordan pivoted. His mouth turned up in a quick grin. He set down his glass of beer and strode toward us, rolling up the sleeves of his work shirt as he approached. Call me nuts, but whenever I saw him saunter toward me, I thought of hunky cowboys in romantic movies. He grasped my elbow and leaned in for a kiss. "Hello, my love. What a nice surprise, but you know you're not supposed to be here." In an exaggerated way, he glanced surreptitiously over his shoulder and back at me. "You might see something you don't want to."

"A stripper perhaps?"

"Alas. None to be found," he teased. His jocular mood quickly disappeared when he took in Deputy O'Shea. "What's up?"

"Is my uncle here?" O'Shea asked.

"No."

"His truck is." He pointed.

Jordan peered beyond us. "Huh. The devil." He swung around and surveyed the room. "Tim!" he bellowed.

Tim didn't emerge from the pack.

Jordan yelled to the crowd, "Has anyone seen Timothy O'Shea?"

Like a big bear, Umberto Urso, our chief

of police, muscled his way through the group, a can of beer in his hand. He and Jordan had the same dark hair and the same lover-of-the-outdoors tanned skin, but that was where the match ended. Urso stood a good four inches taller than Jordan and outweighed him by at least fifty pounds. "Deputy, why are you here?"

"I think my uncle came looking for you. He called me. Did he call you?"

"No." Urso withdrew his cell phone from his pocket and scanned the readout. "I see a missed call. No message, though." He pocketed the phone. "What's this about?"

I had known Urso since we were kids. He was an expert at separating business from pleasure. He urged the four of us to move to the porch, and he closed the door.

"Tim called me. He sounded upset." O'Shea replayed the bits and pieces he had gleaned from Tim's voice mail. "At first he said he *heard* something, but then revised that to say he *saw* something. I'm not sure what he saw, but it sounded urgent. He said he was going to track you down. I've got to find him."

O'Shea didn't wait for a command from his superior. He turned on his heel and strode to Tim's truck. He crouched down and clicked on the flashlight application of his cell phone. Peering at the surrounding ground like a seasoned tracker, he pointed and said, "I see a boot print pointing this way." He strode toward the cheese-making facility, about fifty yards from the main house, where Jordan's staff made the farm's specialty — Pace Hill Farm Double-cream Gouda.

While Jordan's house was designed in the American Western style of a working ranch, the cheese-making facility was state-of-the-art. The exterior was streamlined. It only had one long window near the top of the building to allow in light.

O'Shea went to the front entrance, put his hand on the doorknob, and twisted. The door opened. He stepped inside.

Jordan, Urso, and I crowded in behind him. No lights were on. A sense of gloom hung in the air.

"Uncle Tim, are you in here?"

No response. I didn't even hear the hum of machinery.

"Out of my way, deputy." Jordan hurried to a panel of switches and flipped on the overhead fluorescent lights.

The facility was as cold as a morgue. The room wasn't vast, measuring about forty-by-twenty feet. A large stainless steel vat, a third of the size of the room, stood in the

53

middle of the linoleum floor. Long whisk-like prongs were attached to a metal arm above the vat; the prongs, when swirling, assisted the cheese makers with the coagulation process. Paddles, ladles, skimmers, and sieves hung on hooks on the far wall.

At the far end of the room —

I looked at the vat. It was filled with milk, ready for cheese making. "Jordan!" I pointed. "Milk."

"Oh no." His hushed tone matched mine.

Urso said, "What's odd about that?"

"There's not supposed to be any milk in there," Jordan said.

Urso shook his head. "I still don't get it."

"It's too soon," I explained. "The staff doesn't release the day's draw of milk from the refrigeration tanks until four A.M."

"Here's how it works." Jordan used his hands to describe the method. "The cheese maker pours the milk into the clean vat. Next, because we vat pasteurize the milk, we heat the milk to one hundred and forty-five degrees for thirty minutes, and then add starter culture to kick off the process. Then" — Jordan struggled to catch his breath — "rennet is added and so forth. The milk thickens. After a time, we separate the curds and whey, and . . ." He rolled his hand to signify the rest of the lengthy procedure.

"But the milk shouldn't be there right now," Urso said.

"Correct. This is wrong."

Urso squinted. "Are you suggesting —"

"No," Jordan cut in.

"Couldn't be," I chimed.

"Wait a sec," O'Shea nearly shouted. "You don't think my uncle tripped and fell in the vat, do you?"

I wasn't thinking that he tripped. The floor was flat; there was no way for Tim to have tripped. And the vat was filled with milk. I doubted Tim had filled it.

"If he's in there, we've got to get him out!" O'Shea rushed toward the edge of the vat. "He must have come looking for you in here and —"

"Why would he have done that?" I said. "It's obvious the party was in the house."

But O'Shea wasn't listening to me. "Where's the drain? There's a drain, isn't there?" He squatted and stared beneath the vat. There were a few inches between the bottom of the vat and the floor to allow for drainage.

"Hold on, kid." Urso tapped O'Shea on the shoulder. "This is all conjecture. Maybe the milk-filled vat is a prank." He turned to Jordan. "It's your bachelor party night. I'll bet Tim stole in here and pulled the chain to release the milk purely to mess with you. He's planning to tell you there are ghosts on the farm."

"Pretty expensive prank," I said.

Jordan spun around. "Tim, are you here? Come on out. You got me."

But Tim didn't appear. The lights started to buzz overhead. Other than that, nothing made a peep.

I perused the room for some telltale sign that might reveal that Tim had been in the facility. Why would he have come in here instead of Jordan's house? Violet Walden claimed that both she and Ray Pfeiffer had seen Jawbone Jones tear out of the pub's parking lot. Had Jawbone caught up with Tim? Had the two fought? What beef could Jawbone have had with Tim? I hadn't noticed two sets of tire tracks outside, but I hadn't been looking. The road and parking area had been recently plowed by a snowplow; the pavement was clear.

"Where's the plug for the drain?" O'Shea repeated.

Like the young deputy, I dropped to my knees and searched beneath the vat for the drain. Something small and shiny glinted on the floor. "Hey, look." I reached for it but couldn't quite grasp it. My arm wasn't long enough. "Urso, help me out."

Urso squatted beside me. He extended his arm and nailed the object. He rocked back on his heels and opened his palm to reveal a silver-tooled button.

O'Shea gasped. "That's . . . that's from my uncle's shirt." Tim liked to wear plaid shirts, especially ones made by a seamstress in town. "He's in there. C'mon. Do something."

Urso raced around the vat. "Let's empty this."

CHAPTER 5

Jordan said, "That'll take too long." He dashed to the wall and seized three cheese-making tools that looked like rakes. He handed one to Urso and one to O'Shea.

Working together, they propelled the rakes through the vat of milk. It didn't take long to locate Tim. When they drew him out of the milk, I gagged. He was dead, of course.

Jordan fetched a large plastic tarp from his barn, and Urso and O'Shea hauled Tim onto it. I saw the deputy wipe his eyes a couple of times with the back of his sleeve. Jordan and Urso did, too. None of them lost total control. Me? I was a mess of tears. What was Tyanne going to do when she heard? She would be devastated.

While waiting for the coroner to arrive, Deputy O'Shea and Urso moved to the side to chat. I caught snippets of the conversation. The deputy was making the case that Tim was murdered. He ruled out the release of the milk as a prank, reiterating what I'd said, that it was an expensive practical joke, and his uncle wasn't into waste. Secondly, the bruise at the back of Tim's head. Thirdly, Tim had called the deputy, upset. And lastly, two witnesses, Violet and Ray, had seen Jawbone drive off in his truck when Tim left the pub.

Moving to join them, I said "U-ey," but quickly revised it to "chief." In a professional setting, he preferred that I not use the nickname he'd been given back in grade school, because his name, Umberto Urso, had two capital *U*s. "Jawbone owns Lock Stock and Barrel."

"What's your point?"

"He has all sorts of guns at his disposal. Maybe he forced Tim at gunpoint to go into the cheese-making facility and climb into the vat. Or maybe he sneaked up behind Tim, butted him on the head, and pushed him in."

"Jawbone is a former Olympic biathlete hopeful," Urso said. "He's good with guns. An ace shot. Why go to the trouble of filling the vat and putting Tim in it when he could just shoot him? And what motive would Jawbone have to kill Tim?"

"I don't know yet, but —"

"Charlotte, go home. Try not to think

about it. I'm on the case."

Dejected, I retreated to Jordan's porch. I couldn't go home. I'd come with the deputy. And, honestly, how could I put the murder — I was certain it was murder — from my mind? Tim was a friend. He was killed on my fiancé's property. Jordan stood at the front door. His face was flushed, his eyes glistening with tears that he refused to let fall. One by one, he informed his bachelor party guests what had happened. He advised each of his friends to head to Urso for questioning. According to what I could overhear, no one had a clue that Tim had arrived on the property. No one had seen a thing.

A half hour later, a chill took residence in my back. I shivered and shuddered. I kept picturing Tim's body, his clothes drenched with milk, and all the life — the vitality — drained from his face. Before I knew it, a series of gallows humor jokes ran roughshod through my mind. *Death was not Gouda; it was bad. Tim got creamed. Tim met with a cheesy death.* I pinched myself to make my wicked mind quit while it was behind.

A screech ended my mental tirade.

Urso's other deputy, Rodham, who reminded me of the Road Runner with his spear of red hair, leaped from the cab of his truck. As he approached Urso, another notion came to me. I raced toward them. Rodham whipped around, hands ready to strike. He was clearly on tenterhooks, not because of a fresh murder, but because his wife was due any minute with baby number two.

Urso swung an arm out to keep Rodham in check. Urso looked weary. His eyes were red-rimmed in the same way that Deputy O'Shea's were. He and Tim had been good friends. They hadn't been contemporaries; Tim was — *had been* — older. But Urso had appreciated a good beer, and Tim had appreciated a man who liked to fish.

"What are you still doing here, Charlotte?" he asked.

"I came with Deputy O'Shea."

"I'll get you a ride back to town."

"No. Listen." I touched his sleeve. "I don't mean to overstep. I know you've looked for tire tracks and footprints by the truck."

"There's a muddle of prints," Urso said, "all of which could belong to any number of people in town. Most people around here use the same snow tires. They wear the same boots."

"Right." That was one of the notions that had struck me. "But did you check the linoleum in the cheese-making facility? A telltale print on the smooth surface might show the way the killer walked. Heavy on the inside or outside of his foot."

"The killer must have considered that. The linoleum was mopped clean."

"Are you kidding? While everyone was here at the party?"

"Pretty bold, I know."

"Urso, Tim said he saw something. What if he saw the guy —"

"The *guy*?" Urso's mouth twitched. "Charlotte, usually you're an equal opportunity amateur sleuth. A murderer can be a he or a she."

"I believe this killer is a man." A few months ago, after helping solve the murder of a stranger in town, I had begun to feel confident about my ability to process information. I wasn't a policeman. I wasn't a professional detective. But I had good instincts, which I relied upon. "Here's why. I doubt a woman could have overpowered Tim, who was a pretty big man, and hurled him into that vat."

Urso smiled wearily. "True."

"What we have to find out is what Tim saw."

"We —"

I held up a hand. "Don't fight me on this. You're tired; I'm tired. Hear me out. What if Tim saw a crime outside or near the pub?

Like a robbery or a beating?"

"Or he saw a bear roaming the streets or a missing kid whose face is on a milk carton."

"Don't tease."

Urso sighed. "Please, I beg you, don't think about this. It's my job."

"And Tim was my friend. *Our* friend. Jordan's friend, too." Tim and Jordan had knocked back more beers than Urso and Tim had, and they'd talked about their mutual affection for the restaurant business. And music. Both men loved jazz and the blues. "Tim deserves swift justice. You need everyone's input to get this solved."

"I'll consider whatever you say. Fair?"

I nodded.

Urso scrubbed his dark hair with his fingertips then beckoned Jordan. "Would you mind taking Charlotte home? I need my deputies to remain here, and I don't think she should stay the night, in case —"

"In case what?" I asked. "In case I have more theories? In case I —"

"Hold on," Urso snapped. "Don't get defensive. I just said I'd take your hunches into account. But I don't want you here in case the killer decides to come back."

I threw a panicked look at Jordan.

"Don't worry." Jordan ran a hand along

my arm. I'd never seen him look so shattered. His jaw was tight, his right cheek twitching. Obviously finding a dead body — not just any dead body; a friend's body — on his farm was sapping him of his usual verve and focus. "Whoever killed Tim is not coming back, not with all these cops around." Jordan glowered at Urso for even suggesting the idea. "But the chief is right. You should go home." He steered me toward his Explorer.

On the drive, we didn't talk about the murder. We didn't talk about our bachelor and bachelorette parties. We kept silent, the hum of the heater and my occasional involuntary moans the only sounds to disturb the night.

After he checked out my place to make sure all the windows and doors were secure, my cat Rags trailing us and chugging his concern, Jordan drew me into his arms.

"Jordan, I'm scared."

"I told you, with the police at the farm —"

"No. Not for you. Not for me. For Providence. How many murders can this town handle before the tourists are convinced to stay away and the locals are compelled to move? There's already one Providence in Ohio that's a ghost town. I don't want there to be a second."

"Sweetheart, you know our town is no more dangerous than the next one. We've just had our bad luck of it lately."

"What about your farm? What's going to happen to it?"

He ran his hand along the back of my head and sighed.

"One day at a time?" I whispered.

He forced a tight smile. "That's my motto." He kissed me gently. "Get some sleep. Things will look brighter in the morning. In fact, tomorrow, why don't you put Rebecca in charge of the shop? Then pick up some of those pastries I like, and come back to the farm. I'll whip you up breakfast, and we'll make a new memory."

Chapter 6

After Jordan left, I called Tyanne. I didn't want her to hear the news from anyone else. The poor thing burst into heaving sobs. I asked if she wanted company, but she begged off. She would rally, she said. A Southern belle always did. Next, I called Rebecca to fill her in. She, too, broke down. When she regained her composure, I asked her to man the shop in the morning. Her response was so spirited, you would have thought I'd asked her to defend her country. I made two more calls to Delilah and my grandmother, and then I crawled into bed and allowed Rags to cuddle me. However, I didn't sleep more than a total of fifteen minutes, because I kept having horrid dreams of my wedding day becoming a shambles, or cows attacking trucks, or rivers of milk flooding and destroying Providence.

And I dreamed about finding Tim. Who

had killed him and why?

On Friday morning, I awoke feeling parched and irritable. Realizing Jordan was right, we needed time together to mourn, the first thing I did after I went to Fromagerie Bessette to prepare a batch of Bosc pear and ham quiche, was head to Providence Pâtisserie to buy pastries for Jordan and me. The shop opened an hour before we did.

I neared the front door and spotted Dottie Pfeiffer and her husband Ray inside. He seemed to be trying to take a tray of baked goods out of her hands; Dottie was resisting. I remembered my conversation with Violet at the pub last night. She said the Pfeiffers were also at the pub. She claimed Ray could have seen Jawbone Jones chase after Tim. What else might Ray have noticed?

If only I knew what Tim had seen. A pickpocket? A runaway starlet? A drug deal going down? Yes, even in quaint Providence, drugs existed.

I opened the door and entered. Ray, who reminded me of a fitness guru with his ropy muscles, angular features, and thick wavy hair, quickly backed away from Dottie. It never ceased to amaze me how insufficiently dressed he was. Year-round, he only wore jean shorts and a white T-shirt. Brrr. Maybe working in a virtual icebox like The Ice Castle skating rink inured him to cool temperatures. On the other hand, he always wore gloves. I would imagine he donned them to protect his fingertips from what was known as cold burn.

"Ray, hon," Dottie said. "C'mon."

Where was Dottie's assistant, Zach Mueller, the kid that had sped past Deputy O'Shea and me last night?

"Need some help, Dottie?" I asked.

"I'm fine, Charlotte. Thanks." Prior to buying the pâtisserie, Dottie had owned a modest shop near the grocery store northwest of town. Though her product was always good, she hadn't had the best location. When she moved and started offering free tastings at her current shop as well as supplying fresh product daily to the police precinct, she won the hearts and minds of Providence.

Ray shuffled away while muttering something that sounded like he wasn't happy with his wife's exercise regimen. He added: *A woman your age.* Dottie, who was a doughy woman with unruly red hair that she kept tucked into a hairnet, couldn't be much older than forty-five. She looked miffed, but I supposed if she was running shorthanded, she couldn't shoo away free help.

"It's so nice to see you, Charlotte. What can I get you?" Dottie asked. "Prune Danish? Cherry?" Deep crevices, created from years of smiling all the time — other than a few seconds ago — formed in her cheeks. "Or have you come in for some of those goat cheese Danishes that Jordan likes? I've added a touch of rosemary to switch it up. Think he'll mind?" Sometimes Dottie and I shared recipes. She was the first to figure out that I added white pepper to the pastry shells for the quiches we made at The Cheese Shop.

"I'm sure he'll devour them."

"Ray, fetch me a set of waxed pastry bags, would you? I'm fresh out. That darned Zach."

"Where is he?" I said.

"He quit on me, the thankless, no good —"

Ray returned and muttered something that sounded like *lying thief.*

"Now, hon, we don't know that." Dottie caressed his bare forearm.

Ray cut Dottie a snide look. To all appearances, he did know, or he certainly wasn't going to be dissuaded. He tossed a packet of pale-pink waxed bags to her and started to leave. "If there's nothing else . . ."

"Ray, wait," I said. "I don't know if you've heard, but Timothy O'Shea was found dead late last night."

Ray looked stunned.

Dottie covered her mouth. "Heavens."

Ray said, "Poor guy. What happened? Heart attack?"

"No." I didn't think it was my place to go into details. "The police will be forthcoming."

"The police?" Dottie gasped.

"Was he murdered?" Ray asked.

I nodded. "Sometime between nine and ten P.M."

"Did Belinda Bell do it?" Dottie asked. "She had a beef with him."

"Dottie, don't go spreading rumors," Ray said.

"She did!" Dottie sliced the air with her hand. "The noise. She couldn't stand it. She was all over Tim, exactly like she is with us."

"You," Ray said.

Dottie glowered. "She also didn't like the over-imbibing and the drunken behavior on the street."

I cleared my throat. "I heard you two were at the pub last night."

"We were." Dottie blinked back tears. "We

70

saw Tim. He was always so happy, teasing the customers the way he did. Oh my, his poor family."

"He doesn't have a family," Ray said.

"Does too. All those nephews. His brothers."

"But no wife."

"Ray, don't be insensitive." Dottie bit out the words. "Not everyone is meant to be married. And he was dating that darling Tyanne. Why, she must be distraught."

"She is," I said, wondering how my friend had survived the night.

Dottie fluttered her hand in front of her mouth. "Charlotte, what did you want to ask? We'll do anything to help."

"Violet Walden was at the pub with Paige Alpaugh, and they said —"

"Paige," Dottie sniffed. "She should keep her health tips to herself. 'Sugar is the devil,' she says. What is wrong with her? Sugar is no worse than anything else in this world. My, oh my, but she's a nosy-nose sometimes, like that Belinda Bell."

"Dottie, don't be mean-spirited," Ray cut in. "Stay on topic."

"Yes, hon, of course. Charlotte, I apologize. Do go on. You were talking about Violet and Paige."

"Violet said Tim drove off in his truck.

71

Not long after, she saw Jawbone Jones speed away in his. She wasn't sure if Jawbone was chasing Tim. She thought you, Ray, might have seen something, too."

"Me?"

"You did, hon," Dottie said. "Remember? When you went outside to get my overcoat." She punched him lightly and then addressed me. "Ray told me to leave it in the car. It would be warm enough in the pub he said, and I, like an idiot, listened to him. Then, of course, I got cold." Snuffling, she quickly pulled out a tissue that she'd tucked inside the sleeve of her dress. She blew her nose and promptly spritzed her hands with sanitizer solution. "Charlotte, you said the goat cheese pastries, right? Of course you did. Anyway, hon," she addressed her husband, "remember when you came back inside a few minutes later?"

Ray scratched his ear and shook his head.

"Yes," Dottie persisted. "You told me Jawbone confronted Tim or something. Tim tore off, and then Jawbone ground that truck of his into gear. Maybe you don't remember because we left right after."

"No, I remember. Sure I do."

"Now who's the one that's dotty?" Dottie jibed, making light of her name.

"Jawbone confronted Tim?" I asked.

"Finger to his chest, that's what Ray said."
Dottie mimed the gesture. "Typical boorish
male behavior. Where do they learn to be so
aggressive? If I had boys, they'd be little
gentlemen."

Ray grunted.

I regarded him. "Did you hear what they
were arguing about?"

"Nah. I was too far away."

Using tongs, Dottie lifted two pastries
from a tray and set them into a waxed bag.
"Charlotte, just so you don't get the wrong
idea and think we have a bone to pick with
Jawbone —" She hesitated, apparently realizing the play on words she had made:
bone, Jawbone. "He's a nice enough man.
A Good Samaritan, I'd imagine. He donates
to the Providence Children's Fund every
time he comes in here." She pointed to a
red donation pot sitting on a table by the
exit. The fund benefited kids who needed to
attend afterschool programs. "Not that
you'd be able to tell by Jawbone's looks.
Scruffy." She shuddered. "No matter." She
wiggled her fingers. "Like I said, he's nice
enough. He's always humming whenever he
comes into the shop. Yes sirree! He's a hum-
mer. Come to think of it, maybe he wasn't
poking Tim. What do you think, hon? Maybe
Jawbone was giving him something, like a

business card. Your eyes aren't the best, you know."

"Then why would Jawbone chase Tim?" he asked.

"Got me."

"What direction did he head, Ray?" I said.

"Jawbone turned right out of the lot."

Exactly like Violet claimed.

"Huh," Dottie said. "Doesn't he live south of town? Not far from your grandparents, Charlotte."

If Jawbone did live south of town and he went in the other direction, maybe he'd had a reason to follow Tim. Had Jawbone apprehended Tim at Jordan's farm? Had he confronted him with a gun? Had he forced Tim into the cheese-making facility, knocked him out, and drowned him?

My stomach started to churn. Tamping down the anguish that was climbing up my throat, I thanked Dottie, paid for the pastries, and headed toward the exit.

"If there's anything we can do," Dottie added.

"There is. Tell Chief Urso what you saw."

"Will do." Dottie nudged Ray. "One last thing, Charlotte. Not that it means anything, but Violet was flirting with Tim something awful."

"She wasn't flirting with him," Ray

countered.

"Sure she was, hon. She's sweet on him. A woman knows." Dottie gave me a shrewd look. "You might ask her what was bothering Tim. And, in the meantime, you might ask Frank Mueller how he feels about Violet putting the moves on Tim." Frank Mueller, Zach Mueller's father, owned Café au Lait. "Frank and Violet, well . . . everyone knows. They've been lovers for years."

"Not true," Ray said.

"Just saying." Dottie winked.

CHAPTER 7

Driving to Pace Hill Farm, I was struck by how peaceful the scenery was. Sunlight glistened on the crystalline snow. A few cows, braving the cold, huddled near a stand of trees. A number of tourists had parked alongside the road to take pictures of the rolling hills. A steady stream of sleighs filled with happy travelers passed by me heading in the opposite direction, toward town.

When I arrived at the farm, the place looked normal. No police cars stood in the parking area. No investigators roamed the grounds. However, the yellow crime scene tape was still in place around the cheese-making facility.

I approached the front door of Jordan's house and saw a handwritten note addressed to me posted to it. Jordan had filled the note with loving phrases. In closing, he directed me to come to the cheese cave. To get to the cave, I had to head past the house to another building located at the foot of a hill. The building's reception area was brick and cement. The caves themselves were carved deep beneath the hill. The temperatures within were perfect for aging cheese, naturally staying between forty-two and forty-four degrees Fahrenheit. I remembered the first time I'd entered the caves, thinking how large they were and how marvelous it would be to throw a Christmas party there with carolers and candles.

Jordan must not have heard me enter. I found him rotating wheels of cheese on the shelves.

I set the bag of pastries down on a tasting table and said, "Where's that breakfast you promised me?"

He turned to face me and my heart wrenched because his cheeks were streaked with tears. I hurried to him and enveloped him in my arms. He wrapped his arms around me, too, and we stood like that, without kissing, without talking, for a long while.

When we broke apart, I said, "I'm so sorry. I know how close you and Tim were."

Jordan winced. "When he said he didn't want to come to last night's party, I'd brushed it off. It was Tim. He had his quirks. If only I'd insisted."

"He wouldn't have come." I explained about Tim's loathing for celebrations. "It's not your fault he's dead." I traced a finger from his ear to his throat and rested my hand on his chest.

He swallowed hard. His eyes searched mine. Finally, he said, "I think we should postpone the wedding."

During the few minutes that I'd slept last night, one of my dreams had been about our wedding. The daisies were wilted; the music off-key; people I didn't know were lying lifeless in the aisles. I'd awakened thinking the dreams — nightmares — were an omen, and I'd wondered whether the Fates were against Jordan and me becoming a permanent couple. Back in October, right when I was ready to set a wedding date, we'd learned that his WITSEC trial had been moved up. I hadn't thought anything negative about postponing the wedding at that time. When the trial ended in November and Jordan was free to live his life again, we'd set this date: Valentine's Day, a day we would remember forever.

"Postpone?" I whispered. My throat felt too thick with emotion to say more, but I forced myself to continue. "Yes. You're right. We — our nuptials — should not be the focus of attention right now." I swallowed hard. "What do you think Tim's murder will do to the rest of what's going on in Providence? Will it cast a pall over the Lovers Trail festivities? This is supposed to be a special time. People have come here as a destination place to get married during the event."

"Others will go on with their lives. They aren't us."

"Us . . . stumbling over dead bodies."

He sagged; his shoulders curved inward.

I caressed the back of his neck. "What else is going on?"

"I think this might be a sign that it's time to move on."

My breath caught in my chest. "You don't mean move on as in move *away,* do you?"

"No, we'll stay in Providence. This is our home."

I exhaled as energy pumped back through me. He had used the words *we* and *our.* We were still a couple. This tragedy was not going to put an end to *us.* I said, "Then what do you mean?"

"I'm thinking of selling the farm and going back into the restaurant business."

Anxiety flooded through me. "Won't becoming a restaurateur put you in jeopardy?"

"How?"

"In WITSEC, don't CPAs give up doing taxes and singers give up singing? You know, to keep a low profile."

"Sometimes."

A lump crept up my throat. I urged it to retreat. "If you return to the restaurant business, won't that put a target on your back?"

"Charlotte, sweetheart." He stroked my arms. "Calm down."

"I'm calm. I truly am." *Liar.*

"Could have fooled me." Jordan stretched his chin and worked his jaw in a circle. "I heard the La Bella Ristorante might be up for sale." Delilah's former boyfriend, who owned La Bella Ristorante, was considering moving to California to be with his grandchildren.

"But you love this farm."

"True, but a farm must be worked daily."

"Which you do."

"It isn't for the weak of spirit, and having a murder on the property —"

"Especially the murder of a friend —"

"Can dampen the spirit."

Embarrassment flooded through me. How could I have been so insensitive? Of course he needed change.

Jordan took my hands in his. "The food at La Bella Ristorante is right up my alley. The place has an established clientele. And I have fond memories from there." He and I had met at the Italian restaurant while taking a cooking class. Ever since Jordan had moved to Providence, he had been aching to get back inside an industrial kitchen.

"Okay," I said. "If you need to start anew, tackle whatever your heart desires. I'm on your side." I rolled my lower lip under my teeth, hesitant to ask the next question. But I had to know. "What about us?"

"What do you mean?"

"Will we set another date?"

He kissed me on the forehead. "We'll discuss that soon, okay? I can't talk about it right now. Do you understand?"

I nodded, but I didn't understand. His words made my heart go pitter-pat, and not in a good way. Despite my earlier feeling that we, as a couple, would come through the tragedy unscathed, I was worried.

CHAPTER 8

Canceling the wedding would take a bit of work. There were so many vendors. Neither Jordan nor I were worried about the cost; we could take the financial hit. But the burden for Tyanne . . .

On the way back to the shop, I phoned her and reached her voice mail. I left a message for her to call me. The moment I entered Fromagerie Bessette, I drank in the aroma of cheese and drew strength from the fact that this was what I knew; this was my past and my future. Jordan and I would figure out what was in store for us, given time. I weaved between the display barrels, greeting customers as I passed before moving behind the cheese counter.

Fridays at The Cheese Shop can be hectic. Everybody is getting ready for the weekend, stocking up on platters and buying cheese to use in recipes they'll have time to make.

Rebecca, whose cheeks were rosy red from

working so hard, was designing one of the many Valentine's baskets that customers had preordered. "Morning," she said as if last night hadn't happened. I could tell by her tight jaw and sharp focus that she was keeping up appearances for the customers. She jutted a pair of scissors. "Check out the decorations I put up."

The walls of the shop were a Tuscany gold. Hardwood floors and rustic shelving enhanced the shop's old-world charm. Rebecca had hung strands of sparkling gold hearts across the glass-enclosed cheese case and had set a foot-high gold Cupid on top of the granite tasting countertop.

"Nice," I said.

"Do you like what I did in the display window?" She had set three baskets in the window, each filled with jams, honey, crackers, and a pretty cheese-cutting board. She'd attached gold and silver helium balloons to each.

"Very nice."

"What about the cutouts?"

In each of the windows, she had hung silhouettes of hearts, flowers, and lovebirds.

"It all looks great," I said. "By the way, thanks for covering this morning."

"You bet." She looked as if she wanted to corner me and ply me with questions, but a fresh flow of customers entered the shop.

When the customers dwindled to six, Rebecca ushered me toward the kitchen. I stopped short of entering.

"Spill," she rasped. "What happened? Who did it? You found Tim? It's so horrible. I can't believe it." Tears pooled in her eyes. "By the way, everyone in town is talking about it. You don't need to keep it a secret. The word is out. Do you know that farmer who makes the baby Swiss cheese? He attended Jordan's bachelor party. He came in earlier and was blabbing."

Swell. Now tales would spread all over town.

"I called Devon. He hasn't returned my call." The tears leaked down Rebecca's cheeks. She wiped them off. "I sensed something was wrong. Last night. When you ran out with Devon. Delilah and I went to the pub after you did. That's where I called you from. Nobody would say anything. But I knew." Rebecca sighed. "Poor Tim. He was such a nice guy. I can't imagine anyone wanting him dead. C'mon, tell me, what happened? Who did it?"

Before I could answer, she pelted me with another string of questions. I pointed out that we had to attend to our customers, but she couldn't be deterred. She assured me our hushed conversation wouldn't squelch their excitement. None were standing at the cheese counter or by the register. They were roaming the new displays of cheese platters and wineglasses. My cousin Matthew suggested that if we increased the amount of giftware we sold in the store, we would boost the sale of our edible goods, not to mention that selling wineglasses would encourage customers to mosey into the wine annex. The wine-and-cheese-pairing event set for Thursday was nearly sold out. Thirty couples and a few singles would come for an education.

Rebecca gestured to the customers. "Look at them," she whispered. "Everyone in town is lit up with love. Those two over there" — she pointed at a man standing with a woman who looked younger than him by a good ten years — "did a Valentine photo shoot at Snapshots & More." Snapshots was a boutique photography store that offered all sorts of cute memory gimmicks, including photos and ceramic handprints of children and pets. "And those two?" She pointed toward an elderly couple. "They renewed their vows beside the tower in the Village Green, exactly at the strike of noon, which is when they got married sixty years ago. Grandmère presided over the ceremony.

How cool is that? I'm telling you, nothing — not even murder — is going to throw a wrench into the town's festivities. Now, talk."

Quickly I summarized what we had discovered at Pace Hill Farm. Tim's truck, the button from his shirt, and Tim dead in the vat of milk.

"Does Urso have a suspect?"

"Violet Walden —"

"She did it?"

"No. She was at the pub with Paige Alpaugh. Violet saw Tim drive off in his truck. She said Jawbone Jones chased him. Ray Pfeiffer, who was also at the pub with his wife, backed that up. He claimed Jawbone and Tim had an argument. He saw Jawbone poke Tim in the chest. Ray doesn't know what they might have been arguing about, but like Violet, he saw Jawbone take off after Tim."

"Hmm." Rebecca toyed with a strand of hair.

"What?"

"Do you know Jawbone very well?" she asked.

"I've only interacted with him here. I know, in addition to Vermont Shepherd Invierno, he likes Fiscalini Bandaged Cheddar." The cheese was a product of Fiscalini

Farms in Modesto, California, and literally sang with the ripe notes of butter and sweet grass.

"I went into his gun store once."

For some reason the notion that my darling, formerly Amish assistant had ventured into a gun shop shocked me. I always thought that the Amish didn't bear arms; they won't serve in the military or law enforcement or any kind of career that requires them to use guns.

"Don't look so stunned," Rebecca went on. "Guns are not *verboten* to the Amish."

"They're not forbidden?"

"Heavens, no. We have them to kill pests. I know a farmer who uses a gun to get rid of groundhogs. They can ruin a crop. And I even know some Amish who like to hunt for sport. The Amish simply won't shoot people."

Wow. I had no clue. "So you've fired a gun?"

"Me? No!" She shook her head vehemently. "My father never let me handle one, but a few months ago, I was concerned about what I was seeing on the news, you know, all the attacks on schools and at airports, and I was curious to know more about guns."

I tried my best not to watch the news

except around voting time. I admit, it wasn't a very enlightened way to approach life, but hearing about world tragedies and political nonsense often made me sick to my stomach.

"I wanted to see how it felt to hold a gun," Rebecca said. "I wanted to understand the allure. So I went to Lock Stock and Barrel. It's real clean and spare. There were a few people there, shooting in the gallery. Jawbone — he told me to call him Jawbone — fitted me with a Remington and said, 'Remember, little lady, guns don't kill people; people kill people.' "

"And . . . how did it feel?"

"Cold." She shivered. "Jawbone was really nice about it. The rifle was empty, so it was safe, he assured me. He wedged it against my shoulder and placed my hands in the right position, and then he helped me aim it at a target. He has narrow, long fingers, by the way. Like a musician."

"Did you pull the trigger?"

"No. I couldn't. I froze."

I gawked at her, wishing I could swaddle her in bubble wrap to shield her from harm forever. She was such an innocent. "Well, for now, I'd keep a wide berth from Jawbone. He is the number one suspect in Tim's murder."

"Why would he want Tim dead?"

"Good question." I recalled Urso asking about Jawbone's motive. If not him, who else might have wanted Tim dead? Dottie had hinted that Councilwoman Bell complained about the noise at the pub. She had also suggested that Frank Mueller, jealous over how Violet was flirting with Tim, might have lashed out. I didn't know that side of Frank. He seemed an even-tempered man, kind to his employees and welcoming to customers, but lots of people could put on a good face for the public.

If only I knew what Tim had seen.

Rebecca said, "Do you think the killer dumped Tim in the vat, hoping no one would find him until the next day's cheese making began, so it would throw off the time of death?"

"What TV show did you learn that from?"

"That's a classic forensic assumption." Soon after Rebecca had left her community, she became a mystery and crime show aficionado. She watched them on television and streamed them on the Internet. "Maybe it was a crime of passion. Maybe Tim and Jawbone were both in love with Tyanne."

At that exact moment, Tyanne entered the shop. She looked frazzled, her hair messed and her cheeks wan. She hadn't put on any lipstick, and she wasn't wearing hot pink, the color she'd declared she would wear the entire Valentine season. Instead, she was dressed in a drab black suit that did nothing for her skin tone or sassy figure.

I hurried to her and put my arm around her. "I'm so sorry for your loss."

"Oh, sugar. My sweet Tim. Murdered. I can't believe it." She sucked in a dry breath while fanning herself with a fistful of flyers. "I loved him, Charlotte."

"I know."

"We were good together. He told the funniest jokes. He said he adored the sound of my laugh."

"He did. I could tell you two were meant to be."

Could Dottie Pfeiffer have been mistaken about Violet flirting with Tim? Perhaps I could forget about Frank Mueller attacking Tim in a jealous rage. However, what if Violet, feeling rejected because Tim was so obviously in love with Tyanne, had lit into Tim? No, she couldn't have killed him. She had a solid alibi. She was at the pub with Paige.

"What're those?" I asked, pointing to the flyers in Tyanne's hand.

Tyanne sighed as if the anguish of the world continuing in Tim's absence were cutting out a piece of her insides. "There's going to be an event at All Booked Up on Tuesday afternoon."

My business-savvy grandmother, by divvying up the center of town into four districts, had ensured that all of the businesses would benefit from the flow of tourists. The shops and restaurants on Cherry Orchard would make merry on Monday. Honeysuckle businesses would revel on Tuesday. The places on Main Street would share Wednesday. My neighbors and I on Hope Street would celebrate Thursday, hence why we were having the wine-and-cheese-pairing event.

"It's called the Lovers Lane reading," Tyanne went on. "Octavia is so excited about it." Octavia Tibble owned All Booked Up, one of the most prestigious independent bookstores in Ohio. I could always rely on her to suggest good books to read. Like I, she enjoyed a great mystery. "She's serving tea and scones. People can dress for the occasion, if they desire." Octavia had turned the shop into a destination spot. It didn't hurt that she was also the town's librarian and had enticed a few of her elderly readers to donate some very special first-edition books that made all sorts of people come to town for a peek. Tyanne heaved another pain-filled sigh. "I was planning on going with Tim, but now . . ." Her voice trailed off.

I took her hand and ushered her to one of the stools by the tasting counter. "Have you eaten today?"

"How could I? My appetite is nonexistent. It's a happy, blissful time in paradise," she chirped, though, clearly, her spirit was not in it. "That's what I'm saying to all my clients. Fake it, you own it, right?" Her voice caught. "Can you believe I have four weddings in the next eight days? Four. Count them. And there are sure to be some spur-of-the-moment occasions. Ah, me." She set her elbow on the counter and rested her forehead in the cup of her hand, and then her reserve broke. She sobbed.

I stroked her back until she regained control, then I spread a cracker with a luscious amount of a creamy goat cheese from our local Emerald Pasture Farms, and handed it to her. "Eat. You need to keep up your strength. For your kids." She had two; a boy the twins' age, and a younger girl. "For your clients, too. They deserve your undivided attention."

"You're right." She bit into the tidbit. "Do you know when the funeral will be for Tim?"

"I'm sure the family will put it together

once the coroner releases the body."

Tyanne nodded. "Of course."

"This cheese is laced with lavender," I said. "Did you know lavender is rich with aromatic esters? It's good for healing as well as anxiety."

Rebecca joined us, carrying a partially filled glass of sparkling wine. "Drink this, Tyanne." She thrust the glass at her. "It's barely two ounces. You won't get soused. Matthew tells me it pairs perfectly with the cheese and calms a whole passel of nerves."

Tyanne obeyed. After taking a sip, although her color didn't improve, she did sit straighter in her chair. "Why did Tim go to Jordan's farm, Charlotte?"

"Tim called his nephew. He left an urgent albeit muddled message. He said he saw something. When he couldn't reach Deputy O'Shea, he went in search of Urso."

"I don't understand. Tim wasn't the impulsive type in any way, shape, or form. Not in business. Not in life." Tyanne finished her morsel then wiped her hands on a Valentine-themed napkin. "Following his engagement to that young woman —" She cleared her throat. "You heard about that, right?"

"For the first time last night."

"Tim never wanted to jump into dangerous waters again without knowing all the downsides. That's why we were taking it slowly. Dating. No introductions to family, even though he adored his family. No spending the night at each other's houses. Not yet. What could have gotten him so heated up?"

I told her what I knew of his message to Deputy O'Shea.

"Do you think he saw a crime going down?" she asked.

"Hey," Rebecca cut in. "What if he saw an escaped convict? Don't restaurants and bars receive those printed notices like police precincts do?"

"Whatever he saw," I said, "it made him race off."

"Why didn't he call Chief Urso on the telephone?" Tyanne asked.

"Cell reception was bad last night. What I want to know is why didn't he send a text message?"

"No, no. Tim wouldn't text. Not ever." Tyanne shook her head. "He was a romantic. Words, he said, were meant to be uttered aloud or put into handwriting. Nothing digital. Not even an email." She wrapped her arms around herself and hugged. The effort made her shudder. "Golly, I'm going to miss him."

"Would you like something warm to drink?" I asked.

"I'm fine." She sighed. "Tim said he had a surprise for me on Valentine's Day. I think he'd finally found the courage to ask me to marry him."

A sense of gloom welled up within me. "That reminds me. Did you get my voice mail message?"

"I did. I'm sorry I didn't call you back. What did you want to talk about?"

"Jordan and I —" I swallowed hard. "We're going to postpone our wedding."

CHAPTER 9

"What?" Tyanne and Rebecca shrieked in unison.

I held my hands in a T for timeout while glancing around the shop. None of the customers appeared to be listening in. The pair who had taken photos at Snapshots were still browsing the gift displays. The others were filling their shopping baskets with goodies.

"Don't worry," I whispered. "We're still getting married. We didn't think, what with Tim dying and the murder happening at the farm, and —" A tiny moan escaped my lips. "We'll pick another day; we haven't done so yet, but we will. And Tyanne, you'll be paid for everything to date."

"Sugar, I'm not worried about the money, but shouldn't we keep the date and simply change the venue? I'm sure we could drum up someplace special. That chapel in the hills or the library or even here. We could decorate the wine annex with —"

"No. Thanks. The mood . . ." I shook my head. "No."

Tyanne slung an arm around me. "Now I'm the one who's sorry."

Rebecca joined the group hug.

"It's okay," I said. "Truly. I want to find out who killed Tim first. Then we — all of us — can move on."

"Aha!" Rebecca said. "So you're going to investigate."

"Will you, Charlotte?" Tyanne blurted. "Oh, please, say *yes.*"

"No, I'm not." Okay, I would if I could, but I had nothing. No clues, no hunches. "No," I repeated. "Urso has it handled. He's personally invested, and we all know Deputy O'Shea won't let this rest."

Believing the only way for me to keep myself calm was to get busy, I did exactly that. After Tyanne left and while I waited for customers to finish making their choices, I tidied the cheese cases and created a few new flags to stick into some of them. For the award-winning Hooligan cheese from Cato Corner Farm, I wrote: *So stinky it's got to be good.* For the Hubbardston Blue, a creamy goat cheese with a subtle gray rind and the flavor of truffles, I wrote: *This cheese will chase away the blues and mend a broken heart.* After I added the new flags, I made silver snowflake silhouettes and added them to the others in the display windows.

When customers concluded their business and the store was once again empty, I retreated to the office and set to work on our website. Without my Internet guru to help, it was worse than tedious. I was almost as bad at website design as I was at drawing and painting. I struggled with placing the photographs of the Valentine's baskets in the right place. They kept bouncing from the right margin to the left. If I had enough time, I would put myself through a week-long website design course, but I didn't, so I continued to struggle, one click and drag at a time.

Around one P.M., when I realized noon had come and gone and I was starving, I hurried to the kitchen and fetched the last slice of pomegranate, sage, and crème fraîche quiche. I'd set aside a piece two days ago; it was one of my favorites. The flavors melded together into a delicious mouthful of yum.

While I devoured the quiche at the granite counter and drank a glass of milk, Rebecca joined me. "Guess who stopped in while you were in the back?" she said.

"Meredith?" Soon, all my girlfriends

would come in to commiserate if Rebecca had anything to do with it, the frivolity of last night's bachelorette party a mere mist of a memory.

"No, silly. Jordan."

I gaped. "Why didn't you show him to the office?"

"Because he seemed in a hurry to find Tyanne."

"Didn't you tell him I'd informed her about the postponement?"

"I did, but that didn't deter him. He said he wanted to settle accounts."

A pang of regret gripped me. I thought of all the flowers that would have to be canceled and the food and the cake that we'd commissioned from Providence Pâtisserie. Not to mention all the guests that would have to be alerted. I'd given that task to Tyanne. I thought it might ground her. I told her I'd contact my grandparents and bring them into the loop. I hadn't yet. I knew Grandmère would tend to me like a mother hen.

"Call him," Rebecca suggested.

"I will when I take my next break." I slung on my apron and trudged through the shop to make note of what needed reordering. As I slipped my hand into the pocket of my apron for the pad and pen that I usually kept there, I felt something else — a folded square of paper. I opened it and realized it was a note. Not simply a note; a love letter. From Jordan. Blinking away the instant tears that sprang to my eyes, I read how much he loved and adored me. In closing, he asked if I would like to go on a date soon.

"What's wrong?" Rebecca asked, trying to take a peek.

"Nothing. Nothing at all." I showed her the note.

She applauded. "Oh, yay! What a romantic. He's wooing you all over again. By the way, he has nice handwriting."

"Yes, he does." I chalked that up to the fact that he was a magnificent chef who liked everything to be just so. I eyed the note again and reflected on what Tyanne had said about Tim not writing text messages. If he'd wanted to reach Urso so badly and couldn't get hold of him by phone, why hadn't he at least attempted texting? Had he been worried that whomever he saw doing *whatever* it was the person was doing might see the text and hurt him? Well, too late for that. The person did hurt Tim; he killed him — text or no text.

The front door to the shop flew open. In bustled my grandmother. *"Chérie!"* Had she sensed that I'd been thinking about her?

"There you are. I am so sad for Tim and his family. And for you." She brushed a fresh dusting of snow off the shoulders of her winter coat and gathered me into her arms. We kissed *la bise,* first one cheek and then the other, and then she held me at arm's length. "You look pasty."

"I'm fine."

"I heard you have postponed your wedding."

I skewered Rebecca with a glance. Had she sneaked into the office and called Grandmère? Defiantly, Rebecca shrugged a shoulder.

"You and Jordan," Grandmère went on. "You are as sad as the pair in *Love Letters.*"

"We are nothing like them, Grandmère. Jordan and I will be together." Spoiler alert. At the end of *Love Letters,* the lifelong friends do not wind up together. The bad decisions they make throughout their lives destroy all possibility of a future for them together.

"You must come to auditions tonight," Grandmère said. "It will boost your spirit."

"The auditions are tonight?" Rebecca sounded gleeful.

"*Oui.* We moved them up a week. Why?"

"Because I want to audition."

"*Mais bien sûr.* We would love to have

101

you." Grandmère winked at me. "We have a budding actress in our midst."

"More like a budding ham," I teased.

Urso entered the shop, removing his hat as he did. "Ladies."

Deputy O'Shea trailed him. He looked glum; there was no spark in his gait. Why would there be? I ached at the sight of him. I could tell by the way Rebecca was clutching her arms that she felt the same. I was sure she wanted to comfort him, but now was not the time, not when he was so brittle that he might crack, and certainly not in front of his boss.

"Hello, chief. Hello, deputy," Grandmère said, eyeing them as if they were prey. "You could not have arrived at a more opportune moment. I was telling Rebecca and my granddaughter that we are holding auditions at the playhouse tonight. Both of you should audition."

"No, thank you, Bernadette," Urso said. "I told you before that I'm not an actor. Besides, I have an investigation to conduct. Now, my deputy on the other hand —"

"No, sir," Deputy O'Shea said curtly.

"I have removed you from the case, young man."

I bit back a smile. Young man. Urso barely had five years on his deputy.

"You've got to do something to keep your mind in gear," he continued.

Deputy O'Shea looked as chastised as a wayward puppy. "But, sir —"

"I will not change my mind. That's the end of it. A family member does not work a case."

"And a best friend does?"

Urso scowled.

"Deputy Rodham's wife is due," O'Shea added.

"And I'll *make* do. Got me?"

Rebecca said, "Actually, Mrs. Rodham is on her way to the delivery room right now." She gestured toward the exit. "That last customer told me."

"Sir," O'Shea said.

"No. Rodham will be back on duty in less than twenty-four hours." Urso ended the discussion by spinning around and peering at the selection of sandwiches in the case. On any given day, we put together a few dozen of them. "Charlotte, I'll take the six-inch soppressata with Jarlsburg, spicy mustard, and pepperoncinis."

"Not the foot-long?"

"I'm on a diet." He patted his stomach. I could tell he was lying. He probably didn't have any appetite but knew he had to force something down to keep up his strength.

"Do you want anything, deputy?" I asked.

"The same," he said, sounding defeated.

Grandmère tapped his elbow. "I look forward to having you audition."

The deputy shrugged.

A grave silence fell upon all of us.

I removed the sandwiches from the display case and sliced each in half on a diagonal, then I wrapped them in our specialty paper as I would a present, folding the ends and sealing them with our logo stickers.

Grandmère broke the awkward moment. "Might I ask what is going on with the investigation, Chief Urso?"

"We have no clue who killed Timothy O'Shea, ma'am," Urso said in a no-nonsense manner, the chief of police politely responding to a question put to him by the mayor. "Or why. So far, I can't find anyone that holds a grudge against him. I've questioned everyone who was at the pub. A few contend that Tim raced off in his truck."

"You have one suspect," I said. "Jawbone Jones. Also, Dottie Pfeiffer suggested that Councilwoman Bell might have had reason to kill Tim."

Urso frowned. "Why?"

I explained.

Grandmère said, "No! It cannot be so. Belinda has her moments. She is contentious.

104

But she is a good woman. She is not evil."

"Not everyone who kills is evil," I reminded her. "Some are simply pushed too far."

Grandmère clucked her tongue, doing her best to dismiss me, but I could see she was concerned. Even if she didn't like someone on the city council, she would support him or her as a fellow politician should.

Urso said, "I've contacted every one of Tim's family members."

"You mean I did," Deputy O'Shea muttered. "Uncle Tim left the bar to all twelve of his nephews, me included."

Urso said, "That doesn't imply that any of you had motive to kill Tim."

"How could it? None of us wants the pub. Not that it isn't a great place." O'Shea waved his hand. "It is. It's just . . . we've all got careers."

I placed the sandwiches along with napkins and packages of extra mustard into bags. "This is on the house, U-ey. I insist. No argument." On occasion, I could be as tough as he could be. I addressed Deputy O'Shea. "The other eleven nephews don't live anywhere near here, do they?"

"No, we're spread out in three states. Most of them are up north, near Cleveland. We're close, but we don't talk a lot. We communicate via a social networking site. We share pictures of kids and pets."

"You don't have either of those," Rebecca said.

"Yeah, but you know the drill." He flapped his hat against his thigh. "Two of my other uncles are coming to run the pub until we decide what to do, and my dad and mom are due in town. They'll be handling the funeral arrangements."

My grandmother whispered, "Some people leave this world too soon."

Another poignant silence enveloped us.

Rebecca drew in a deep breath. She looked from me to the deputy and back to me. A sneaky grin spread across her face. "You know, chief, if you need a hand with the investigation, you should deputize Charlotte."

"No."

"Temporarily. You can do that, right? She sees things others don't."

"No," Urso repeated, his tone brusque.

My grandmother seconded his decision.

"I assume you've questioned Jawbone Jones," Rebecca continued. "He's your main suspect, correct?" She snatched the bags holding the sandwiches off the counter and swung one like a carrot in front of Urso. Her pluck — okay, audacity — truly amazed me sometimes.

Urso took the bags. "Mr. Jones swears he didn't race after Tim."

"And you bought that?" Rebecca said. "Two witnesses saw him. Does he have an alibi?"

"He was on his way to a jam session."

"A jam session?" Rebecca eyed me. "I told you he had musician's hands. Strong fingers. I'll bet he plays a mean guitar." She turned back to Urso. "But he wasn't at the jam session, was he? He said he was on his way, which means no one can verify as to his specific whereabouts."

"The other half of his duo said she talked to him on his cell phone," Urso said. "He'd called to tell her he was running late."

Rebecca smirked. "That's a pretty feeble alibi, if you ask me. We all know cell phone reception isn't good around here."

Deputy O'Shea jumped in. "I agree. Uncle Tim's message was jumbled. And Mr. Jones owns Lock Stock and Barrel, right?"

"Your point?" Urso said.

"Can you trust what a gun shop owner says?"

"Are you saying what he does isn't legitimate?"

"I don't know, is it?" A hank of Deputy O'Shea's hair fell onto his face. He brushed it back with force. "Does he do anything off the books?"

"Deputy, don't infer a wrongdoing without substantiation."

"Fine. But what if Uncle Tim saw —"

"Stay out of this," Urso ordered.

"My uncle saw something!" O'Shea shouted. "Why else would he go looking for you?"

"Unless you heard wrong."

"You've listened to the voice mail. Did I hear wrong? Did I? Huh?" Deputy O'Shea leaned forward, the muscles in his neck pulsing with pent up anger.

Urso bit his lower lip. I knew that look. He was doing his best not to level his deputy in front of Rebecca, my grandmother, and me. There was a time and a place.

Rebecca jumped in to defray the tension. "Do you have any physical evidence to go on, chief? You know, like tire track prints?"

Urso glowered at me.

I held up a hand. "I didn't tell her anything."

"No, we don't," Urso said to Rebecca, then added, "We're through here. Deputy, let's go." He gestured toward the door.

Deputy O'Shea mouthed *I'll call you* to Rebecca and, chin lowered, trudged out of the shop.

The door swung shut with a bang. I flinched. I knew I couldn't sit still and do nothing. Urso had looked as defeated as his deputy. I flashed on what Dottie Pfeiffer had said to me about Violet Walden flirting with Tim and wondered again whether her behavior had spurred Frank Mueller to lash out. Should Urso be considering him as another suspect? Even though Urso had said he'd questioned everyone who had gone to the pub and even though he hadn't officially deputized me, I could at least do one thing that might help him solve this case.

Chapter 10

A fine mist of snow splatted the windshield as I made my way to Violet's Victoriana Inn, which was located northwest of the Village Green. Violet liked to call the inn a state-of-the-art B&B, but I thought the terms were contradictory. In my mind, a bed-and-breakfast should be like the one next to my house. Lavender and Lace was decked out with cushy chairs and beautiful antiques, and it was always flavorful with the aroma of tea and scones. Violet's Victoriana Inn was sleek and modern. The furniture was steel gray and firm. Unlike other bed-and-breakfast inns that offered gardens to wander and trails to hike, Violet's Victoriana Inn had a gym filled with stair-steppers, treadmills, and weight machines. And yet the place was popular and regularly sold out.

Idyllic instrumental music was emanating from a variety of speakers as I entered.

Violet, clad in a trim-fitting jogging outfit, her marshmallow-colored hair swept into a dramatic twist with chic wisps falling from the updo, stood behind the registration counter. Without all the makeup she'd worn the other night at the pub, she looked almost plain. She was polishing the chrome counter with a rag while talking angrily on the phone to what sounded like a supplier. I'd used the same kind of no-nonsense, mannish voice on occasion.

A stream of women, dressed to the nines, waltzed into the inn. All were chatting about the high tea they were going to enjoy in the lounge. Violet quieted until the women passed by her and then resumed her gruff timbre. Far be it from her to scare off the customers.

She ended her call with a *slam* and grinned at me. "Hello, Charlotte." She stuffed her dusting rag beneath the counter and checked the readout on the pedometer that was clipped to her waistband. "Got to keep moving to burn the calories." She rocked from foot to foot. "What brings you here?"

For someone who, according to Dottie, had been interested in Tim, she didn't seem in the least depressed. Perhaps she hadn't heard about the murder yet. On the other hand, gossip was rampant, and Urso said he had spoken to everyone who had been at the pub. Maybe he had skipped a few because he knew either Deputy O'Shea or I had questioned them.

"I'm here to talk about Timothy O'Shea."

Violet's cheeks tinged pink. "Of course. I heard he drowned. What a shame. Where? At Nature's Reserve? Aren't all the ponds frozen over?"

"He died at Jordan's farm."

"Jordan's farm doesn't have any ponds or lakes."

"No, it doesn't."

Violet's eyes widened. She wrinkled her nose. "Ick! Do you mean Tim accidentally drowned" — she twirled a hand and sputtered — "in a cheese vat?"

"The police aren't sure it was an accident or that he drowned."

"Are you saying he was murdered? How horrible. And to think it happened while the rest of us were out on the town having fun."

"How do you know that?"

"I'm assuming. I mean, it had to have happened last night, right? That's why you and the deputy were asking questions at the pub, wasn't it?" Violet pressed her hand to her chest. "What will happen to Jordan's farm?"

She often purchased Pace Hill Farm's Double-cream Gouda to serve with the inn's cheese plate dessert. "He'll have to close it, won't he? Such a shame. He employs so many people."

I ached to think what might happen to Jordan's staff if he sold the farm. As it was, their livelihood might be affected simply because of the adverse public reaction to a murder occurring on the property.

Violet retrieved her rag and clutched it like a security blanket. "What do you want to ask me?"

"I saw Dottie Pfeiffer earlier today at the pâtisserie. She said you seemed interested in Tim."

"Dottie." Violet made a *pfft* sound. "She doesn't know her elbow from a pastry tube."

"She said you were flirting with Tim last night."

"Flirting? Me? No way. I barely spoke two words to him. How could I? He was hobnobbing with all the tourists, per usual. You know how he can be." She halted. Her cheeks reddened again. "Could be . . . was." She licked her lips. "Look, Tim and I were friends. Just friends." Violet pulled a strand of hair out of her coif and twirled it at the nape of her neck. Was that the flirty move Dottie had seen her do? "There wasn't anything between us, promise." Violet released the hair. "Besides, Tim was involved with Tyanne. For months. I expected them to get married in the next year. She must be heartbroken."

"She is."

Violet resumed polishing the counter. "You know, Tim's family stays here whenever they come to town. At a discount, because there are so darned many of them. A dozen nephews. Seven brothers." She held up seven fingers. "Whew! How does a mom do that?"

"With lots of love and patience."

"Some of the O'Sheas have already arrived. Others are holding rooms. I don't think they know when they'll be able to have the funeral. What do you hear on that end?"

"I haven't a clue."

Violet stopped buffing. "Want some herbal tea? It's got lots of antioxidants."

"Thank you. That would be nice."

She led the way to an alcove where a glossy silver table was set with two china cups and elegant napkins. "I'll be right back." She returned with a glass teapot fitted with an infuser, two spoons, agave sugar, and a platter of thinly sliced Cobb Hill's Ascutney Mountain cheese, an alpine-style cheese with white natural rind and a sweet, nutty flavor.

She settled into the chair opposite me. "We should let the tea steep. Dig into the cheese, though. I bought it at your shop yesterday. Rebecca is some salesperson." She took a slice and nibbled the corners.

I did the same. "I thought Dottie was wrong about you being interested in Tim. Ray told her she was, too."

"Ray was at the bakery? He doesn't even like her pastry."

"He was helping out. I guess Dottie lost her assistant, Zach."

"That boy. Talk about a bad apple." Violet rolled her eyes. "I wouldn't trust him as far as I could throw him. He sure doesn't fall far from the tree."

"What do you mean?"

"Zach's father Frank is, simply put, a cad."

"Are you and he dating?"

"We did. A long time ago. Not anymore." She sniffed; her upper lip rose in a sneer. "He stepped out on me with a toad of a woman. He said I was getting too trim for him. Humph."

"I'd noticed you'd slimmed down. Are you on a new regimen?"

"For life. My goal, from this day forward, is to be the best *me* I can possibly be. It's about time I get some control. Okay, I'm already *controlling.*" She offered a wink. I guess she was keen to her reputation. "But I have no self-control when it comes to what I put into my body. I'm pushing thirty-five. My child-bearing years will be gone soon. Got to keep healthy if I want kids."

A pang of regret whooshed through me. I was the same age as Violet. Would I miss out on children if Jordan and I waited too much longer to get married? Could I have children? I'd never asked my doctor to do any tests.

I took another slice of the cheese, intent on eating away my worry. Life was great; cheese made it better. "So, if you weren't dating Tim and you aren't dating Frank —"

"Definitely not *him.*"

"Is there someone else in your life?" I asked. If she wanted children, and unless she wanted to go through parenthood alone, I would imagine someone was in the picture.

"We're not officially dating. We're waiting to see where it goes. Oho!" She aimed her index finger at me. "I know what you're thinking. I caught that look in your eyes. No, I'm not pregnant, no matter what Paige hinted at last night. She can be such a royal pain." Violet assessed the tea. "It's ready. May I pour you some?" She didn't wait for a response. She dispensed steaming tea into the china cups. The sweet aroma of almonds and vanilla wafted upward. Violet nudged the natural sweetener in my direction. "Who are the police looking at as a suspect?"

"Jawbone Jones."

"Based on my statement to you?"

"Yours and Ray Pfeiffer's."

"You questioned Ray?" She shook her head apologetically. "Of course you did. You said earlier that you saw him and Dottie. What did he say?"

"Like you, Ray said he saw Jawbone tear out of the lot, heading north. Ray also said he saw Jawbone poke Tim in the chest. He thinks they were having an argument. Did you see that?"

"Now that you mention it, I did."

"So you saw Tim outside of his truck."

"Yes. But I couldn't hear what they were saying." She took a sip of tea.

"What do you know about Jawbone?"

"Not much. He's sort of scary-looking. That bald head." Violet fanned her hand over her own head and fluttered her fingers beside her neck. "Those tattoos. I heard he plays in a band, but I wouldn't know for sure. The only music I listen to is music like this." She twirled a hand; Beethoven's "Pathetique" was playing. "And, of course, whatever I hear at the pub. I love Irish music."

"Speaking of that, Dottie also suggested that Belinda Bell had it in for Tim because of the noise factor created at the pub. Do you know anything about that?"

"Belinda." Violet snorted. "She's all puff and no air. I've seen her lay into lots of people in town. She throws those massive hips around, but she never follows through with her threats. On the other hand, it's exactly those types that surprise us, isn't it?" She took another sip of tea. "Ah, Tim. He'll be missed."

"Yes, he will." For so many reasons. I felt tears brimming in the corners of my eyes and blinked them away.

"In my opinion, Jawbone doesn't really fit in, in Providence," Violet said.

Apparently we had left the topic of Belinda Bell behind.

"He doesn't even try to fit in," she continued. "That gun shop of his does really well, though. He has a ton of customers. We've got a lot of hunters in the area. Many stay here, which surprises me. I usually think of hunters holing up in a rustic lodge, but so many of them are into their fitness programs." Violet leaned forward and whispered, "Between you and me, I think many are trying to prove their masculinity. They act macho. Some even pretend they're big shots in the military." She laughed, the sound reminding me of an orangutan, breathing and panting all at the same time. "You know, that argument between Tim and Jawbone . . ."

I swirled the spoon in my tea, hoping she would continue.

"One night at the pub I heard the two of them talking." Violet hesitated. "Yelling is more like it. Jawbone said he wanted to buy the place. Tim swore he was never going to sell. 'Never!' " She raised her voice, acting out the drama. "Actually, there were quite a few of us there that night. Tim thought Jawbone was way out of line for suggesting it. Jawbone didn't take kindly to Tim's tone. He was lit. He'd had way too much whiskey. He probably wouldn't remember that he threatened Tim."

"Threatened him how?"

"He said that if Tim didn't sell, he'd get him."

"He said those words: *Get him*?"

"Jawbone swore that if he couldn't own the pub, nobody would."

"That sounds like a pretty big threat. Are you sure that's what he said?"

"Maybe not in those exact words."

Was she making up this story? Why? To cast suspicion on Jawbone instead of on someone else, namely herself? *Don't be ridiculous, Charlotte. She was at the pub with Paige.*

"I think he wanted a place in town to perform his music," Violet added.

"When did this happen? Recently?"

"A year ago."

"That's an awful long time to carry a grudge."

"Yes, but when someone says he's going to *get you,* you sleep with one eye open. You know what I mean?" Violet finished her tea and set the cup down with a clatter. "I've seen Jawbone make threats before. At other places. He seems to pop off his mouth as if it were a pistol. Maybe he gets that way when the liquor is talking. Maybe it's idle threats, but still . . ."

I understood what she left unsaid: Maybe this time Jawbone's threats weren't idle.

CHAPTER 11

I left the inn feeling an incredible urge to sprint to the police precinct to bring Urso up to date with my findings. Granted, he rarely appreciated my unsolicited input, but with one deputy benched for the remainder of the investigation and the other unavailable because his wife was giving birth, I was willing to risk Urso's wrath.

Despite the chilly weather, vendors were out in droves along the north edge of the Village Green. They were offering everything from candy to handmade jewelry. One vendor was luring a flurry of people with tastings of hot cocoa. A couple singing a vintage Beatles' love song at the top of their lungs skipped to the end of that line. A group of teens nearly twirled into me while trying to catch snowflakes on their tongues.

I spotted Ray Pfeiffer among the crowd, taping something to a kiosk, most likely a flyer for the ice-skating rink's upcoming Lovers Trail event. When he finished, he joined a few other guys who were standing in line to purchase flowers. One of the guys offered Ray a cigarette. He lit up. However, when he realized Zach Mueller, the rangy young man who'd recently quit the pastry shop, was also in line, Ray dropped the cigarette to the ground, demolished it with his boot heel, and glowered at the kid. If looks could kill.

Zach caught sight of Ray. His lip twitched in a snarl, but he made tracks in the opposite direction, right past a balloon artist at a pushcart. Thanks to the force of Zach's departure, Mylar balloons, in the shapes of wedding bells or hearts, bopped against one another. The balloon artist shouted something at Zach, who made a rude gesture and ran straight at me, almost knocking me down. I *eek*ed. He swooped his shaggy bangs out of his eyes, but he didn't offer an apology. No *oops*. Nothing.

Nice, I mused.

Deputy O'Shea, who was standing in line for a balloon, caught sight of me and yelled, "Are you okay?"

I nodded. He moved ahead to receive a balloon and held a finger to his mouth. I winked, offering my silent pledge that I would not tell Rebecca anything about the gift I was certain she was going to receive.

Inside the Victorian house that served as the Providence Precinct — the Tourist Information Center shared the foyer space — I saw a group of women huddling in the corner. They looked sly, like they were keeping the world's greatest secret. When a toothy redhead spotted me, she tapped another's elbow. I knew the redhead — her name started with an S. She was always complaining, upset with a homeowner's board or the PTA. One by one, her pals turned to gawk at me.

Ah, if only I had the nerve to do something risqué and shock them all.

Instead, I strode to the clerk, a gray-haired woman with a heart-shaped face. I explained my mission and was instantly permitted access to Chief Urso.

I found him in his office, sitting behind his desk. He was outlined by a halo of sunlight that filtered through the Levelor blinds covering the window behind him. The sandwich he'd received earlier at the shop sat uneaten on his desk, the wrapper still sealed with stickers.

Urso rose slightly.

I waved him to sit back down. "Don't stand on my account."

"What's up?" He guiltily eyeballed his uneaten sandwich.

"Don't worry. I'm not offended," I said. "My appetite is at an all-time low, too. I simply stopped in to give you an update on something I learned."

He heaved a sigh. "You're not actively pursuing —"

"No. Well, not on purpose. Rebecca's right. You could temporarily deputize me."

"Charlotte —"

"Tim was my friend, U-ey. I'm going to ask questions." I sat in the chair opposite his desk like an equal. He didn't boot me out, so I continued. "Something Dottie Pfeiffer said made me want to follow up. Did she or Ray come in and talk to you?"

"No."

I told him about Dottie inferring that Violet had a thing for Tim. "She said they flirted that night. So, wondering whether Violet had an inkling about what Tim might have seen, I decided to contact her."

"You *what*?"

"Don't raise your voice. I visited her at the inn. I asked a few questions. Nothing official."

He scowled at me.

I folded my arms across my chest. "She denied flirting with Tim. In fact, she denied any relationship at all."

"Do you believe her?"

"Yes, which means I can cross Frank Mueller off my list of suspects."

"*Your* list?"

I ignored the snarky remark. "According to Dottie, Frank was carrying a torch for Violet, but if Violet wasn't interested in Tim, then —"

"You can rule out Frank either way. He has a solid alibi. He was at Jordan's party. With me."

"I missed seeing him there."

"He was."

"Great," I said. *Case solved.* "Moving on . . . I asked Violet about Jawbone Jones again. Remember, she was the one who had seen him drive off." I filled Urso in on Violet's claim that Jawbone threatened to *get* Tim if he didn't sell the pub.

Urso said, "However, as Violet said, that happened over a year ago, and Jawbone didn't lash out. Maybe she's casting suspicion on someone else to take the focus off of her."

"I thought the same thing, except she was at the pub. With Paige. No matter what, perhaps you should question Jawbone again."

"I will."

"If you'd like me to accompany you —"

"No. You have a business to run, and don't you have a wedding on Sunday?"

I shifted in my chair. "I guess Tyanne hasn't called you yet. We're going to postpone the wedding."

"Really?" Urso raised an eyebrow. He wasn't showing a renewed interest in me. A few months ago, he had finally given up trying to woo me. He realized that I was truly in love with Jordan and would never change my mind about marrying him, the current postponement notwithstanding.

"With Tim murdered at the site . . ." I licked my lips. "A wedding on Jordan's farm didn't feel right."

"I'm sorry."

"I don't want you or anyone to feel pity for me . . . for us. Jordan and I will set another date." I felt the sudden urge to speak to Jordan. I'd forgotten to call him on my break. Would he have time to talk now? He had so many issues to deal with: his employees, his product, and the fate of his farm — to sell or not to sell.

Deputy O'Shea rapped on the doorjamb. His cheeks look blistered from the cold. "Chief." The balloon he'd purchased bobbed merrily beside his head. "I'm going out for some air."

"You do that."

O'Shea disappeared and I said to Urso, "I'm worried about him. He looks frail. Has he eaten anything?"

"I'm watching out for him."

"The same way that you're looking out for yourself?" I motioned toward his uneaten meal.

He opened the wrapper and took a bite of the sandwich. "Happy?" he asked while chewing.

"Overjoyed."

He glanced at the clock on the wall and his eyes brightened. He stood up and pushed the sandwich aside. "Sorry to cut this short. I've got to go."

I rose to my feet. "You know, U-ey, I've been dying to ask you something."

"Can it wait?" He fetched his overcoat and hurried toward the door.

Actually, it couldn't. I followed. "I was wondering whether you've decided to run your brother's campaign in Virginia or not." A few months ago, his brother, a budding politician, had started to pursue Urso. If he took the job, he would leave Providence.

"I have."

"And?"

"I'm staying here."

"You are? That's great." A rush of relief

washed over me. I appreciated my friend and didn't want to see him relocate; not to mention we needed someone with his integrity and wits as our chief of police. "What made you decide —"

"I can't talk now."

Cavalierly, he gestured that I should move through the doorway first. That was when I became aware of something I hadn't picked up on earlier. Despite the tragic loss of a dear friend, Urso seemed lighter and more at ease with himself. Was he, like so many others in Providence, enjoying the season of love?

"Got a hot date?" I teased.

"Maybe."

I nearly cheered. Urso, above all, deserved happiness. He saluted as he exited toward the parking lot. I left through the foyer.

On my way, I sneaked to the buffet table that held the daily delivery of pastries from Providence Pâtisserie. As I plucked a bite-sized raspberry crème fraîche turnover from the tray, I heard some chatter.

Councilwoman Bell, a towering pear-shaped woman in her early fifties with a cap of black hair and a grimace that cut a slash across the lower portion of her broad face, had joined the mix of conspiratorial women. Prudence Hart, a sour dress-shop owner, looking as lean as ever in a lemon-colored winter coat — the color made my mouth pucker — had also linked up with the group.

The ladies strolled toward the clerk, who sat taller in her chair.

Uh-oh.

Bell took the lead. "We have a complaint."

"You always do," the clerk quipped.

"Three things. One. The noise level around town has got to be reduced," Bell said in a booming tone that suggested she could out-*noise* any noise level. "Two. What is it with all of these vendors in the streets? Who authorized them to park helter-skelter? And three. Have you seen the public display of singing and dancing?"

I was astonished that Bell would be upset with general frivolity. Her daughter was an actress in Los Angeles; she had recently won the starring role in a television series. I remembered how the girl, back when she was in high school, would parade around town singing or emoting at the top of her lungs. She had performed at the Providence Playhouse a couple of times. She was very talented, if a bit precocious.

"Now, Belinda," the clerk said. "This is a merry time. People are in love. They're celebrating. Cut them a little slack."

"Cut them —" Bell sputtered. "I . . . *we*"

— she twirled a finger in the air to include her band of complainers — "are standing firm. Claim form, please."

"Councilwoman, be reasonable."

Bell exhaled with force, which caused her entire frame to wobble.

"Fine." The clerk, who had a bit of the devil in her, took a moment to tuck some of her wispy hair back into her bun with a bobby pin, then she rose and shuffled to a file cabinet. Leisurely — could she move any slower? I wondered with amusement — she withdrew a form from a drawer.

"Hurry up," Bell ordered. She looked like a human geyser. Any minute, she would boil over and steam would burst out the top of her head in one long spew. I flashed on Dottie and Violet's assessments of the councilwoman. Could she have seen Tim drive away from the pub and, in a fit of rage, chased after him? Had she caught up to him at Jordan's farm?

"Here you are." The clerk extended her arm and waved the form. "Fill this out to your heart's content. When you're done, put it in my inbox, which you can see is pretty darned full, but I'm sure I'll have time to attend to it in the next century."

"Why, you —"

"Breathe, Belinda." The clerk grinned.

"Inhalation is guaranteed to extend your longevity."

I suppressed a smile.

Bell turned on her heel and pushed her gaggle of friends toward the corner in which they had first convened. Bell whispered something to Prudence, who bobbed her head vehemently. I heard Bell say, "We're doing it. It's settled. She's out. *O-u-t.* Agreed?"

I gulped. If they were intent on getting the clerk fired, I would vouch for her. She had done nothing wrong. On the other hand, if some other woman was the target of the group's wrath, I pitied the poor soul.

Chapter 12

By the time I returned to The Cheese Shop, it was late afternoon. I hurried in, my intent to call Jordan. I wanted to tell him that I'd found his note, and yes, yes, yes, I wanted to go on a date, but I didn't get the opportunity, because Rebecca waylaid me.

She clasped my hands. Hers were clammy and trembling. "I need you to come."

"Where?"

"To the auditions. I need moral support."

"But —"

"Rags can come, too. Please!"

I couldn't believe she was this nervous. Whenever she needed to put one over on someone — like, say, Urso — she was fearless. On the other hand, back in the Amish fold, she had never acted. Sure, she'd played imagination games with the younger children, but the Amish reluctance to be self-promoting or vain — a concept known as *Gelassenheit* — was key to understanding why she had never found the courage to get onstage until now. I looked around the shop for the balloon O'Shea was supposed to have brought her on his break, but I didn't see it. Maybe she had stowed it in the office. If I reminded her about how much he cared for her, perhaps she would have more courage.

"Have you seen Deputy O'Shea?" I asked.

"No. Why? Is something wrong?"

Not wrong, I thought, but curious. Why had he told Urso he was going out for some air if not to visit Rebecca and present her with his whimsical gift? Had he gone on a different adventure? Was he investigating his uncle's death without Urso's approval? Heaven forbid Urso found out.

"Did he say he wasn't going to audition?" Rebecca asked, her voice tight with panic. "Did he say he didn't want me to do so?"

"Stop it." I tried to pry loose from her viselike hold, but to no avail. "You're so edgy you're going to drive yourself mad."

"You're right. I . . . I . . ." She let go and rotated her hand in front of her body in a wavelike motion to encourage breathing. "Inhale for four counts" — she obeyed herself — "and exhale for four counts. Again . . ." Soon the trembling ceased. "Wow, it worked! I learned that on a self-help tape I bought off the Internet." She held up a fisted hand so I would knock knuckles with her.

I complied.

"Now, please say you'll come." She crossed to the tasting counter, nudged a ladder-back stool out of her way, and fetched a morsel of the specialty-of-the-day cheese, Boerenkass Gouda, which we imported from the Netherlands. She offered it to me.

"Are you trying to bribe me?" I plopped it into my mouth. Boerenkass was a delicious two-year cheese with rich notes of caramel and a hint of cashews.

"But of course. And I'm throwing in this, too." She hurried behind the cheese counter and raced back with a decorative bag in hand. She thrust it at me.

Inside was a clear plastic box filled with sliced cheeses, jam, crackers, a plastic knife, and a bottle of spring water.

"Something to tide you over during auditions. The cheese is Rogue Creamery TouVelle."

"Mmm. TouVelle." The semihard cow's milk cheese tasted like chocolate and nuts with a teensy tang.

"Your favorite."

"My current favorite." I had many more

depending on the season and the setting. I've tasted over five thousand cheeses in my lifetime. I have certain favorites for dinner, others for appetizers, and others that are best eaten as a dessert, perhaps with a glass of port.

"Say you'll come. Ple-e-ease!"

She was as giddy as a kid on Christmas. How could I deny her?

Whenever I entered the Providence Playhouse, I felt a grand sense of purpose. My tireless grandmother loved putting on plays. According to her, viewing plays ennobled the spectator. It didn't matter whether the work was a musical or a straight play, a farce or a tragedy; the opportunity to get immersed in the moment of what she called *la vie imaginaire* — imaginary life — was a gift one should not refuse.

In the foyer, a bunch of volunteers were putting up decorations in honor of the upcoming Lovers Trail fest, including typical hearts and cupids. A string of hearts was draped from one end of the plate glass window to the other. One huge sign read: *Welcome to the* Love Letter *auditions!* In addition, smaller signs were posted on the walls with sayings like: *All you need is* Love Letters; *When you invest in* Love Letters, *you invest in life;* Love Letters *is where the heart is.* A table covered in a red checked cloth held sweet treats like heart-shaped cake pops, red-sprinkled cookies, and cherry-chocolate truffles that my grandmother must have made. She enjoyed keeping her actors, whether cast in the play or auditioning, fed and inspired. A pianist at an upright piano was playing very recognizable love songs — my grandmother's attempt to get the actors in the mood.

"Follow me," I said to Rebecca, nabbing a cake pop before going into the theater.

With Rags in my arms, I sauntered toward the stage, where my grandfather was pounding a nail into what was the most minimal set I'd ever seen at the theater. Black drapes hung on the sides of the stage. One wide black drape hung at the rear. Two platforms stood in the center of the stage, one platform with a window suspended over the rear edge, the other platform with a painting of a town suspended at its rear edge. On each platform stood two chairs and two writing desks with lamps.

Pépère rose to his feet and finger-combed his thinning white hair. "Ah, *c'est très agréable de tu voir, petite-fille.*"

I smiled. "It's lovely to see you, too, Pépère."

"Where is everybody?" Rebecca asked. Her voice sounded thin with tension. "Aren't the auditions tonight? Do I have the wrong day? The wrong time?"

I gawped at her. Had she missed all the fanfare in the foyer?

Rebecca spun in a circle. "Where are the auditions going to be held?"

"Droit ici," Pépère said. "Right here. Rebecca, sweet girl, do not worry. Bernadette —" He waved his hammer.

My grandmother's name was Bernadette; my grandfather's was Etienne. I, of course, had referred to them as Grandmère and Pépère all my life.

"She has taken all those who wish to read into the black-box theater for a brief —" Pépère whirled the hammer again, this time searching for a word.

"Chat," I suggested.

"Oui. Chat. To prepare them with the background of the characters and the play."

"You mean I'm late?" Rebecca cried.

"No. They just left. Go, Rebecca. That way." He pointed. The black-box theater, an intimate ninety-nine seat auditorium, was located at the rear of the theater complex.

"Break a leg," I said. No one was entirely sure where the expression *break a leg* came from. Some thought it meant if an actor performed well, the actor would take a bow, which, back in Shakespeare's time when all actors were male, required the pose of bending or *breaking* one leg accompanied by the genteel swoop of a hand. Others believed that if an actor performed well, he would break through the *leg* — or the side curtain — of the theater to return to the stage for applause. No matter what, saying *good luck* was bad luck.

Rebecca thanked us both and sprinted away.

"*Chérie,* come sit with me." Pépère slotted his hammer into his tool belt and descended the stairs into the theater. He sat down in a loge seat in the front row and eyed my package. "You have brought dinner?"

"Sugar treats aren't enough for you?" I teased.

"A man needs sustenance."

"It's only a snack, but I'll share." I set Rags on the floor. He wouldn't roam. He liked to stay close to my feet. I opened the bag, removed the goodies, and handed my grandfather a slice of the TouVelle.

He hummed his appreciation as he did whenever he ate cheese. He adored all types, ergo the reason he and my grandmother had opened Fromagerie Bessette so many years ago. I think he missed running the shop, but Grandmère didn't want him standing all day. It was much better for him to keep active by taking walks, working in the garden, and helping out at the theater. She also didn't want him adding to his expanding girth. A morsel of cheese here and there was fine; hanging around temptation for eight or more hours a day was frowned upon. No one would get fat eating an ounce of cheese a day. Moderation, she instructed, was the proper way to live life.

Minutes later, Grandmère led the actors back into the main theater. I recognized many as regular participants in the Playhouse's works. Rebecca, graced with a Mylar balloon, walked beside Deputy O'Shea. Both looked vibrant and in love, yet both appeared nervous, too. Rebecca's mouth looked tight. O'Shea seemed to have an itchy ear. He was rubbing it repeatedly. A friend back in high school did that whenever he was telling a tall tale. Did O'Shea feel he couldn't be truthful with the material, or was it a nervous tic?

Over the course of the next two hours, I watched the auditions. Though I was no critic, I couldn't help but assess the performances. I'd sat in on many auditions in the past at the behest of my grandmother.

When auditions concluded, she would ask for my opinion, as if I knew what made one casting decision better than another. Sometimes it was all about honesty. Did I believe the actor?

For all auditions, Grandmère wanted variety, so, as in the past, she asked the actors to read different scenes from the play. In *Love Letters,* the initial correspondence between the two childhood friends is teasing and mocking. They do not acknowledge that they love each other until after two failed marriages. However, when they finally hook up, their eternal love, which is so obvious through their written correspondence, cannot survive the woes that life has thrown at them. Every bit of the play's dialogue is read from their lifelong letters. Yes, the actors have to instill the reading of the letters with emotion, but there is no impetus to prance around the stage or to use one's arms grandiosely.

In between auditions, Grandmère continued to remind the actors to take his or her time with the material. She urged them to *feel* it. She had paired Rebecca with Deputy O'Shea. Rebecca did a nice job; she didn't overact. O'Shea seemed natural, too. He didn't read overly loud; he didn't force the lines; his itchy-ear syndrome vanished.

By the end of the night, because my grandmother had asked the actors to read nearly every piece of the material, I was weeping with regret. When Grandmère collected the last set of scripts, an overwhelming sense of doom enfolded me. I rested my head against the seatback and drew my arms across my chest.

Grandmère approached. "*Chérie,* are you unwell?"

I blinked back tears.

"Ah, you are crying," she said. "It is the play. It is *marvellieux, non*? So rich with expression. It stirs the emotions."

"*Oui,*" I lied. What was really coursing through my mind was my own personal drama. Watching the auditions had made me wonder again whether Jordan and I were destined to fail.

Oh, poor me. *Buck up,* I urged.

Pretending to be strong — I was in a theater, after all, so playacting was to be expected — I planted my feet on the ground and stood up.

"Ah, much better," Grandmère said. "There is your smile." She tweaked my cheek and returned to the stage.

Rags nudged my ankles.

I scooped him up. "Don't worry, fella. I wouldn't forget you."

"Charlotte." Rebecca ran toward Rags and me and threw her arms around us. "Wasn't it wonderful?" she shouted over the hubbub of the other excited actors. "Oh, the thrill of acting. I love it. I get these goose bumps right in the pit of my stomach and I feel all heady. That's good, right? Did you have a wonderful time? Wasn't everyone fabulous?" She lowered her voice. "Well, everyone except that bleached blonde. She sort of overacted, don't you think? And that guy with the comb-over. He's so full of himself."

Her enthusiasm was infectious. My woes melted away. "Yes, I had a great time. And you did a super job."

"Devon did, too, right?"

"Yes, the deputy is a natural."

"Sheesh! I almost forgot." Rebecca fished in the pocket of her coat and pulled out a folded piece of paper. "I meant to give this to you earlier. I found it taped to the back door of The Cheese Shop as I was coming in from gathering herbs from the hothouse." The town had a communal garden in the alley behind the store. "But I was so nervous about auditions, I forgot all about it." She thrust the paper into my hands.

I whipped it open; it was another love note from Jordan. He missed me. He wondered if I'd found his earlier note. He couldn't wait to see my beautiful face. He ended it by writing: *With love, ~J.*

All the dread I'd felt earlier disappeared. I stowed the note in my purse and pulled out my cell phone to call Jordan. As I did, the phone rang.

CHAPTER 13

I recognized the cell phone number: *Jordan.* Talk about timing. I hurried to the foyer, the conversation in the theater making it too loud to hear, and I answered.

"Charlotte." Jordan's voice was brimming with concern. "Are you okay?"

"I'm fine. I'm sorry I didn't call you earlier. Today has been, in a word, hectic."

"Where are you? There's a lot of static."

"I'm at the theater. Grandmère was holding auditions for her new play. By the way, thank you for the notes. I didn't get your latest until right now. Rebecca found it and forgot to give it to me before dragging me here."

"How did she do?"

"Pretty well, I think. She had a catch in her throat and love in her eyes. There were a couple of actresses who gave wooden performances. Hers was honest and heartfelt. I don't know which direction my grandmother will go, but Rebecca has nothing to be ashamed of."

"That's great. So" — he cleared his throat — "are you up for a date?"

"Absolutely." It was past ten P.M., but I could find the energy to see the love of my life.

"Have you got your cross-country skis ready?"

"You want to go skiing now?" I glanced out the windows of the theater's foyer. Most of the actors were heading for the parking lot. Lights illuminated their path. "Um, it's dark, if you hadn't noticed."

"Very funny." Jordan chuckled, which tickled me to my toes. I could listen to his robust laugh all day long. "I meant let's go tomorrow. With all that's been going on, you need a day off. You were going to take it anyway."

I was. To prep for the wedding: get my hair done; hem the wedding dress; maybe have a massage.

"I'll pick you up at your house at eight A.M."

"That's early."

"You wake up with the rooster. C'mon, I'll pack a picnic. In the afternoon, we'll take in the Loveland Singers. They're performing at the Bozzuto Winery tasting."

"It sounds wonderful." Maybe getting away from the center of town, I could refresh my critical thinking abilities so I could help out Urso. Perhaps Jordan and I could pin down another date to get married, too.

"I'll see you in the morning." He blew me a kiss and hung up. No *I love you,* but I tried not to read anything into that. We were going on a daylong date. Life was looking up.

At eight sharp, Jordan arrived on my doorstep with a bouquet of daisies and a cellophane bag filled with Hershey's Kisses, my one silly passion — silly, because customers often teased me that, given my palate for exquisite cheeses, I should crave a fine dark chocolate from, say, Brazil. But I don't. My mother had loved Hershey's Kisses; so do I.

After setting the flowers in water and the Kisses on the counter, I checked Rags's food and water, and we set off. Bundled in my ski gear and secure in the passenger seat of Jordan's Explorer, I hummed along with the jazzy CD Jordan had inserted, and I drank in the view of the countryside. The rolling hills shimmered with crystalline snow. None were scarred by snowmobile tracks. The towering oaks, cloaked beneath blankets of icy white powder, didn't look nearly as fearsome as they usually did. I avoided glancing at the mud-splattered snow alongside the road that had been scraped aside by snowplows. Who needed to ruin the dreamy mood?

Over the course of the drive, Jordan and I only spoke a few words. How pretty it all was. Idyllic. Peaceful. No talk of Tim or his murder. We caught sight of a pair of deer sprinting across an open space and, at the same time, pointed, but that didn't make us strike up more conversation. I felt tentative and shy and wondered what Jordan was feeling.

When we arrived a short while later at Nature's Preserve, dozens of SUV-type vehicles were already parked in the parking lot. The hiking trails frequented in the summer and fall were now the cross-country skiing routes. As we were donning our skis along with others who were chattering about their hopes for a clear day with no new snowfall, I paused to scan the area. There were remnants of wet tire marks and boot prints everywhere, which reminded me of the few prints found near the crime scene on Jordan's farm. Urso had complained that the prints were too generic; he would get no clues from them. If only one could reveal the killer's identity. The murder would be solved. Life — ours, not Tim's — could move ahead. But *if only* was not an option.

A half hour into our trek along paths lined with hickory, maple, and chokecherry trees, a chill gripped me. My teeth must have chattered, because Jordan said, "Want to take a coffee break?"

"You brought coffee?"

"And a midmorning snack."

We veered off the path to one of the many picnic areas, this one empty of other trekkers, and removed our skis. Jordan brushed snow off a wooden table and dug into his backpack. He withdrew not only a thermos of coffee but a pair of scrumptious-looking galettes, as well. Each of the flat round pastries was filled with a decorative wheel of pears.

"Did you make these?" I settled onto the bench next to Jordan and dove into my galette with cheerful abandon.

"Yep."

"When did you have time?"

"Okay, I'll fess up. I got them at the pastry shop. Dottie's a wizard, isn't she?"

Unable to help myself, I polished off the pastry in less than six bites. Dottie had used Pace Hill's Gouda. The combination, with a hint of nutmeg, was perfect. I took a sip of rich coffee — Jordan preferred using the French-press method — and said, "Wow, that was good. Almost as good as s-e-x."

"Never." Jordan pushed our coffee mugs aside and drew me into his arms. He pressed his lips against mine. We spent the next few minutes devouring each other. Lips only. If we'd brought along a winter tent —

A rustle in the woods startled us. We pulled apart.

A family of raccoons was huddling beneath a stand of bushes, watching us.

Jordan hustled to his feet. "Go away!"

The raccoons stared at him brazenly.

"Go!" He clapped loudly and lunged at them. That did it. They scampered off, but we knew if we left our meal out, they would return.

We packed up, put on our skis, and retreated to the trail.

A few minutes back into our trek, Jordan said, "By the way, I called Luigi. He's on the fence."

"About selling La Bella Ristorante?"

"About the whole move to California."

"Don't tell me he's sticking around because he thinks he has a chance with Delilah."

Jordan grinned. "I asked the same question. He said she's dating someone else."

"Who?"

"He doesn't know."

"Humph. News to me." How could she not tell me, her best friend? Bad Delilah. Maybe she hadn't told me who the new man in her life was because she hadn't wanted to take the limelight away from me before the wedding. Would she have shown up with him as a plus-one?

"I think Luigi has his eye on one of Tyanne's sisters," Jordan said. "The hair salon owner."

"No kidding." Shortly after Tyanne's husband ran off with a younger woman, her sisters came to town to give her moral support. They had settled in as if they were natives. "So where does that leave you about selling the farm?" I asked.

"In a quandary."

"Do you want to talk about it?"

"Not really."

A companionable silence fell between us. Though my insides were reeling with conflicting emotions, I focused on each plant of my pole, each stride of a ski, my heels rising and falling with ease. I paid attention to the sound of snow slipping off branches, the breeze whistling between trees, the skittering of hidden animals.

Rounding a bend, I said, "Everything is so fresh."

"Yes, it is."

"No, I'm not referring to the day . . . the forest . . . our trek. I mean, everything as in the drama in our lives. We're both so raw. I don't think you . . . *we* . . . should make any more decisions until Tim's murder is solved."

"But —"

"Let me finish. Yes, it was right to cancel the wedding," I went on, "but I don't think you should be making a determination about selling your farm or buying a restaurant yet. Wait a week or so. Give it time. Does it have to be decided this minute?"

"No."

At the edge of a clearing, Jordan pulled to a stop. I did, too. We both drew in a breath as we took in the sweeping vista. Snow glistened on the trees and hills.

"By the way," I said, interrupting the moment of calm, "did you talk with Tyanne about compensating her for any loss?"

"I did. As luck would have it, another couple decided to tie the knot tomorrow."

"Just like that? Spur of the moment?"

"Love is in the air. There's no waiting period in Ohio as long as both parties are over the age of eighteen and have valid proof of identification."

"Do you know the couple?"

Jordan shook his head. "Tyanne implied they were visitors with an open checkbook. She said she could use nearly everything from our wedding, other than the venue, for theirs."

"Let's hear it for Cupid."

Jordan mushed ahead. I hurried to catch up, eager to get the answer to my next question.

"Jordan," I said. My heart hammered my chest. Broaching tough topics wasn't easy for me. "What are we going to do about setting our new date?"

Jordan offered a sly grin. "Didn't you just say we weren't supposed to be making any important decisions?"

I batted his arm and nearly lost my balance. He reached over to steady me.

"Don't take me so literally," I said.

"What do you think about May? It'll be spring; the weather will be warm. Is that too far away?"

It felt like eons, but I could be patient. "May it is."

"As for our honeymoon . . ." he went on.

My heart wrenched with regret. We were supposed to leave Tuesday for Europe for two weeks. Jordan had hoped to woo me away for two months, but I simply couldn't commit to that length of time. Suitcases were packed in my bedroom. I hadn't had the energy to unpack them yet. The mere sight of them brought tears to my eyes.

"I've spoken to the travel agent," Jordan said. "Because the circumstances that made us change our minds were due to a grievous loss, we're allowed to postpone for up to three months without penalty, so May is perfect."

I smiled, but anxiety coursed through me. I worried that somehow, some way, another dire situation would crop up and keep us from taking that trip.

CHAPTER 14

Jordan put a hand on my shoulder. "Charlotte, are you okay?"

The chilly air cut through me. "Fine," I said cheerily. I was becoming quite adept at lying.

The rest of the morning came and went in a flash. Sufficiently exercised, we stowed our ski gear in the SUV and headed to the Bozzuto Winery.

Trailing a caravan of large vehicles, we drove along the road leading to the top of the hill. The winery abutted the extensive property that now served as the Providence Liberal Arts College campus. On both sides of us, fenced stands of leafless vines crisscrossed the grounds. The winery itself, which consisted of more than a dozen buildings and resembled a small town in Tuscany, smacked of old-world charm.

By the time we exited the SUV, the weather had warmed. The temperature was hovering in the low thirties. People crowded the many picnic tables set in the center of the winery's square.

At one table, Belinda Bell sat bundled up in a shocking blue parka and pants, her hair squished beneath a matching beanie. She reminded me of an aged version of the aggressively competitive girl in the movie *Willy Wonka & the Chocolate Factory,* the one that blew up into a giant blueberry. Beside her was a weathered, bearded man named Eddie Townsend who, when he wasn't in his cups, did pretty well selling and leasing commercial property. His motto: *If you're ready, call Eddie.* He was a regular at Fromagerie Bessette, preferring robust cheeses made with port and beer.

Beyond them I caught sight of Paige Alpaugh, who looked as horsey as ever in a furry caramel-colored parka, her matching mane of hair cinched into a ponytail. She was meeting with a handful of women that I could only describe as the most attentive moms in town. One of them was my friend Freckles. All the women were sipping from glasses of wine while hanging on a tale that Paige was telling. A few were scribbling in notebooks, too. Paige often gave seminars on how to run a successful Internet blog.

"Hear that?" Jordan said. An instrumental

version of "Stand By Your Man" spilled out of the barnlike building to our left.

I grinned. It wasn't your typical Valentine's Day music, but it would do.

Upon entering, I was surprised to see that the Bozzutos had transformed the structure into a winter wonderland. Artificial trees lit with white lights surrounded the outer rim. Twinkling tapestries of a variety of winter scenes decorated the walls. Burgundy-draped booths stood around the interior, each offering a different white wine for tasting: gewürztraminer, pinot gris, Riesling, and more. Vendors selling sausages and hot pretzels with mustard were drawing huge crowds. A cheese maker from Emerald Pastures Farm was offering tastings of a zesty new goat Gouda. Aged for longer than a year, the toffee-colored cheese's interior was smattered with crystals that gave the cheese a gritty, fun texture.

"This way." Jordan steered me toward the far end of the barn as the four-piece band — two guitars, a drummer, and an electric fiddle player — started in on their next song, "Hey, Good Lookin.' "

Couples moved onto the temporary dance floor. Dressed in their winter clothes and heavy boots, they looked pretty graceless as they did a Texas two-step. Clomping abounded.

We set our coats and Jordan's backpack at a small bistro table.

"Care to dance?" he asked.

"Not a chance. A glass of wine sounds like more than enough excitement."

We joined a line for grüner veltliner, one of my favorite wines. It had tons of complexity and a luscious dose of pepper in the aroma. When I spotted Jawbone Jones in line ahead of us, I nipped Jordan's elbow and pointed.

"So?" he said.

"He's a suspect in Tim's murder."

"That doesn't mean he's guilty. He's allowed to live his life while Urso is investigating."

In this ambiance, Jawbone didn't look very intimidating. Light gleamed off his shaved head. Even his goatee seemed to sparkle. He stood with his arm draped over the shoulders of a woman with fringed brown hair and what stylists called a rattail. It trailed over the collar of her biker-style jacket. They were chatting it up with a couple that reminded me of a hippie Mr. and Mrs. Santa Claus. Both were thickset and dressed in camouflage jackets and pants, their snow-white hair scraggly and unkempt.

"What do you think?" I asked Jordan.

"About?"

"Jawbone."

He threw me a troubled look.

"I'm allowed to theorize," I said. "Violet Walden said Jawbone threatened Tim."

"Why were you questioning Violet Walden?"

"I wasn't —" I pressed my lips together. "Okay, maybe I was. I want to help. Violet was at the pub the night Tim died. Yesterday, I went to the inn to check on her."

"Uh-huh." Jordan smirked, obviously not believing the innocence of my visit. "Go on. Jawbone threatened Tim how?"

"Jawbone wanted to buy the pub." I told him the rest of what Violet had said.

" 'Get him' is sort of vague, and Violet isn't the most reliable witness. Remember when she tried to oust your neighbor Lois from the bed-and-breakfast association?"

He was right. The B&B group met annually to establish guidelines for the inns in the area. Violet asserted that Lois, who ran a quaint place, had badmouthed Violet with the express intent of damaging her business. The claim, per the association president, could not be proven.

On the other hand, whether Violet was reliable or not, I was still getting a vibe about Jawbone. I eyed him and his date again. "Violet intimated that Jawbone was drunk at the time, so he might not remember the incident."

"The threat was hollow, and it was over a year ago."

"That's what Urso said."

"Aha! Our chief of police is investigating?" I poked him. "Don't tease."

"Charlotte." Jordan rubbed my shoulder. "Please leave the investigation to him."

"The woman Jawbone is with," I said, ignoring his plea. "I wonder if she's the one who gave him his alibi. Urso said Jawbone's band partner was the person that came forward. She looks like a rocker, doesn't she? The jacket she's wearing is covered with the names of bands."

"Don't judge a book by its cover. For all you know, she could be a teacher, a librarian, or a pastor."

"Yeah, right."

Jordan grinned. "Okay, fine, you've made me curious. What was Jawbone's alibi for the night Tim died?"

I told him. "Talking on a cell phone for the duration of a drive sounds feeble, especially since Tim couldn't get through with any clarity to either his nephew or Urso."

Even after we received our tasting of wine and returned to our table to eat the sandwiches Jordan had brought — a delicious torpedo laden with salami, baby Swiss, and pesto aioli — I was intrigued by Jawbone and his date. She started stroking his face. A brilliant diamond glistened on her left hand.

"Look at the rock on her finger," I said. "It must have cost a pretty penny. Do you think they're engaged? Do you think she's in love with him? Love can make people do all sorts of stupid things. Like lie."

When Jordan didn't respond, I pressed on. "Can a gun dealer in a small town make enough money to purchase something like a one-carat diamond? What if Jawbone stole the ring? What if" — I clasped his wrist — "Tim saw him take it?"

Jordan heaved a sigh. "Do you hear yourself?"

"What if the woman was with Jawbone at the time? Maybe she egged Jawbone on. Maybe she's the one that told Jawbone to kill Tim."

"Charlotte, please stop theorizing. Let Urso —"

"Charlotte, there you are!" Meredith raced toward me with the twins, Clair and Amy, in tow.

I rose to my feet. The girls looked downright willowy with their tights-covered legs poking from below their puffy parkas. Had they each grown two inches in the last week? They wrapped their arms around me and squeezed me so hard I thought I'd been attacked by a pair of boa constrictors.

"I'm so glad I found you," Meredith said. She smiled at Jordan. "Sorry to intrude."

"No problem." He looked relieved that I wasn't able to continue theorizing.

"What's wrong?" I asked.

"We . . . *they*" — Meredith pointed at the twins — "were so worried about you. They've had me calling you all day."

"I never heard my cell phone ring."

"They thought . . . ah, heck, they didn't know what to think, and I didn't douse the flames." Meredith lowered her voice to a hushed whisper as she pointed at the two wiggle worms clutching me. "They are so upset about the wedding being canceled, and they were concerned that you . . ." Her voice drifted to a whisper.

"That I what?"

"That you were hiding beneath the bed-covers. Moping."

"Me? C'mon." I wriggled free and tapped each of the girls' noses. Far be it from me to admit the fears that had cycled through my mind last night prior to my conversation with Jordan.

"You know how they can be," Meredith went on. "I told them to relax, but they couldn't. We went to your house. When you weren't there, we looked in the garage." She used her hands to describe the search. "Your car was still there, but Amy noticed your cross-country skis were gone. I suggested you had gone on an outing with Jordan, but the girls had to know for sure. Long story short, we called around. You were sighted up here."

"What sleuths," I said.

"Um . . ." Meredith hesitated. "They want to spend the night with you to make sure you're okay."

"We've got all week. It's the school holiday. Why tonight?"

"Because Matthew and I have decided to whisk them out of town tomorrow to get their minds off, you know . . ." *The canceled wedding.* Meredith tilted her head. "Can they stay the night?"

I reached for Jordan's hand. He winked and gave my hand a squeeze, his peeve with me a minute earlier dispelled. He mouthed: *Go ahead.* Family always came first.

I said, "Girls, would you like to have a sleepover at Aunt Charlotte's tonight?"

"Yes!" Amy yelled.

"Can we bring Rocket?" Clair asked.

A dog, a cat, two girls, and me. What could be better on the night before I was supposed to have gotten married?

"The more the merrier," I chimed.

The girls ran out of the building, with Meredith yelling, "Race you home!"

As we were leaving the barn, Jordan excused himself to go to the restroom. While I waited for him by the exit, something made me turn back. A feeling? Stirred by the music? The band had launched into a rousing rendition of "Your Cheatin' Heart."

Across the large hall, Jawbone, who had separated from what I assumed was his fiancée, was jabbing his finger into the paunch of hippie Santa. Santa looked so mad that if he'd had a reindeer whip handy, he would have used it to tame Jawbone.

In a flash Jawbone grabbed hippie Santa's finger and twisted. He said something that made his assailant writhe. He released the finger, made one more crack, and stomped outside.

An urge to learn more about Jawbone gnawed at me. I searched for Jordan but didn't see him. I couldn't hold off. I hurried after Jawbone.

CHAPTER 15

The parking lot was crowded with people. Jawbone was planting a knit cap on his head while walking toward a gray truck. I trailed him, wondering how I could get him to talk to me. What would I ask? I certainly wasn't going to point-blank demand to know whether he had killed Tim.

"Nice truck," I said. *Lame, but nonetheless, an opening.*

Jawbone swung around. Until now, I'd never really studied him other than from a distance. His skin looked polished to a shine. Did he use men's beauty products? Rebecca, bless her skeptical soul, would speculate that he scrubbed his skin to wash away his sins. Or maybe she wouldn't. She liked Jawbone.

"You and your friend were having quite a discussion," I said.

"We disagreed about the music. What do you want?"

He had a languid way of speaking. Words hung in the air longer for him than for most people. And a stench clung to his clothes. Had he been drinking something harder, like scotch, at the winery? Where had he gotten it? From hippie Santa? Did they really argue about the music, or had his Santa pal refused to give him another swig from a hidden flask? Did it matter? If I didn't hurry, I'd lose him.

"Do you like this truck model?" I blurted. "My —" *My* what? *Quick. My . . .* "My cousin Matthew is interested in buying a truck. For deliveries. His SUV isn't large enough." I ran a hand along the rim of the truck's bed while looking at him innocently.

Jawbone leveled me with his piercing blue eyes. Did he see through my ploy? A slow grin formed on his face. "It's reliable," he said. "Never breaks down."

"Four-on-the-floor?" I asked, like I knew how to drive one. I'd always used automatic transmission. My former fiancé had driven a car with manual transmission. He had begged to teach me how to use the stick shift. He said it was sexy.

"Yup. It's not a race car," Jawbone replied, "but a stick shift gives me that feeling of power."

"How does it take steep hills?" *Really,*

165

Charlotte? The hill to Jordan's farm wasn't any steeper than other hills in the area.

"Fine. Never stalls out." He shifted feet. "The fun thing about the stick is you can even slip it into neutral and coast downhill. Makes you feel like a kid on a sled."

We shared a smile.

"How are the tires holding up?" I said.

"Recently switched them out. Fifty thousand miles is about the limit."

I glimpsed his boots: *also new.* Had he gotten rid of his old tires and boots in the past few days to remove evidence?

He opened his truck to climb in. A denim tote bag sat on the seat, unzipped. I spied what had to be over a dozen guns inside the bag. Quickly Jawbone reached for the bag.

I instinctively stepped backward.

Jawbone zipped the bag and shoved it on the floor with a *thud.* The contents within clattered. He slued around and smiled at me again, exposing his wolf-sized incisors. "Did I scare you?"

Indeed he had, but I refused to let on. "You sell guns. Of course you'd travel with guns."

He leaned in. His breath was warm and rancid. "Was it you that sicced Chief Urso on me, Charlotte?"

"What? No. I . . . We're having a cheese

tasting on Thursday. Reservations are filling up. I wanted to make sure you knew about it. I'll be having that special Cheddar you like."

He assessed me with stern eyes. "I've already picked up tickets. Is that all?"

"Ye-e-es," I stammered. "That's it. Well, bye." I raced away, my cheeks red-hot with embarrassment. Luckily, Jordan hadn't seen me make a fool of myself.

An hour later, Jordan pulled into the driveway beside my house and parked. I gave him a hug and whispered in his ear, "Come by the shop tomorrow afternoon for coffee and a snack."

"Meaning you?" he whispered back.

"Yes." A tingle of delight zinged through me. "And I won't do any theorizing. Promise."

"Deal."

I entered the house first, via the kitchen. Amy entered next, ahead of her sister. She clapped her hands to beckon Rags. My adorable Ragdoll bounded to the twins and nuzzled their ankles. He didn't care that they were wearing winter clothes or that he couldn't make nose-to-skin contact. He simply wanted to be close. When Rags caught sight of Rocket, the French Briard that was a gift from the twins' mother and used to live with us until the twins and their father moved in with Meredith, he went airborne with joy.

Quickly I removed the leash from the dog's neck. The two animals tumbled together as if they were gymnastic teammates. I know, cats and dogs don't usually mix as playmates, but Rags wasn't convinced he was a cat, and Rocket didn't care what the heck Rags was. He wanted to play; that was enough for the energetic dog. They took off toward the foyer. Happy barks and meows and a clattering of claws on wood floors ensued.

I kept only one rule at my house on Saturday nights: no television. The twins were more than happy to comply.

"I'm starved." Clair headed straight for the refrigerator. "What shall we bake?" Honestly, she had grown the most in the past few weeks. She looked downright lean. "Gluten-free, of course."

I cocked a hip. "Do you think you need to remind me? How long has it been since you moved out?"

"October," Amy chimed. When Matthew married Meredith.

"That's three measly months," I said.

Clair giggled. "How about risotto?" The

twins had quite an educated palate. Their father couldn't do a lick of work in a workshop or garden, but he was a good cook; Meredith was even better.

"Oh, yum," Amy said. "Do you have any of that Alpha Tolman cheese?" Jasper Hill Farm's Alpha Tolman cheese was named for a philanthropic dairy farmer from Greensboro, Vermont. An alpine-style cheese, it had a savory, meaty flavor, and melted well. "And we'll need some fresh Parmesan." Amy was our cheese expert. When she decided she no longer wanted to be a race car driver — previously she'd dreamed of becoming a singer, a pet whisperer, or a world explorer — I figured she would settle down and realize she was born to be a cheesemonger. She had a gifted palate and a nose that could detect the intricate aromas of cheese ninety percent of the time in a blind test.

"How about green onions or shallots?" Clair said. "Do you have those?"

"Slow down. I'm sure we'll find something. Take off your coats and hang them up." I set out a bowl of water for Rocket and put the bag of food Meredith had brought for him on the counter. "I'll be right back." I sprinted upstairs. I needed to shed some layers of clothing or I would swelter.

When I returned downstairs, I heard whispering in the kitchen. Stealthily I pressed my ear to the door. I couldn't hear what the twins were saying. I nudged the door open an inch. They stood huddled in the corner of the kitchen by the sink. Clair was shaking her head *no,* but Amy was insisting upon something. The tableau made me think of Tim's last moments on earth. He told his nephew that he had *heard* something, then he revised that to he had *seen* something. Had he seen people whispering? Did he know, without hearing, what they were saying? I revisited my theory that Tim had seen Jawbone and his fiancée plotting to steal that sizeable diamond ring.

Stop it, Charlotte. It was wrong of me to presume the ring was stolen. I flashed on Jordan's worry about me investigating. What if he was getting cold feet about marrying me because I, more often than I liked to admit, was finding myself in hot water situations or facing off with killers? Could I help it if I was curious by nature? Could I help it if, like Rebecca suggested to Urso, I had a gift for figuring out what happened? I believed part of my ability was due to the fact that I'd lost my parents in a tragic accident. An event that had heightened my senses. An event that made me want — no, *need* — to right the world's wrongs.

I glanced at the phone, pondering whether I should touch base with Jordan, but thought better of it. His kisses — *our* kisses — while on our cross-country skiing trek had been filled with passion. Our parting kiss was nearly as good. No, he wasn't cooling to me. He was concerned. He didn't want me rushing headlong into danger. Though I felt confident that I could handle most instances, I liked that he cared so much.

On the other side of the door, Amy and Clair started sniping at each other.

"Are too."

"Am not."

I pushed through the door and cheerily said, "What are you two plotting?"

They spun around and stared at me innocently.

I bit back a snort. "Yeah, right. That works. Pretend you're not guilty."

They blushed.

"We're —" Clair started.

"Worried about you," Amy finished.

"She's more worried than I am," Clair said.

"Am not."

They playfully punched each other, then asked in unison: "Are you okay?"

"Did you go upstairs to cry?" Clair asked.

"You don't look like you've been crying," Amy said.

I held up both hands, palms forward. "Relax. I'm not crying. I didn't cry. I'm a big girl —" Lyrics from the song "Big Girls Don't Cry" flitted through my head. I mentally fanned them away and took a breath. "I'm fine."

"Are you going to marry Jordan?"

"Yes. In May."

"Yay!" Amy cheered. "On Mother's Day?"

"Or on Memorial Day?" Clair said.

"To be determined." I pointed at the refrigerator. "Now, let's get supper on the stove and quickly into our hungry stomachs."

In no time at all, we made a creamy onion risotto, extra heavy on the onions. We threw in diced shallots, too. A week ago I had grilled some extra chicken breasts and had stowed them in the freezer. I thawed three in the microwave, tossed a salad, and we sat down to dinner.

The twins were decidedly boy crazy. Amy still liked Tyanne's son Tommy. Clair had her eye on a new boy who was tall, dark, and handsome like Jordan, and he loved reading as much as she did. In fact, he was reading at a high school level, she bragged — mainly mysteries and adventures. Amy added that Clair had stolen him away from Paige Alpaugh's youngest daughter.

"Did not."

"Did too."

"Not."

"Girls."

"I would never steal. It's not nice."

Amy sputtered out a laugh. "Fine. You lured him away with those sexy eyes of yours."

"Sexy? Why you —" Clair knuckled her sister in the arm.

Amy whelped in mock pain. "You did. I saw you. Like this." She batted her eyelashes and offered a wink. "And you twirled your hair around your pinky."

Clair said, "I would never —"

"Girls do it all the time." Amy demonstrated, coiling her chin-length hair as best she could. "It's a mating ritual. Aren't you paying attention whenever we watch Animal Planet?"

Clair looked to me for help.

"Dishes," I commanded.

Later, after the twins and I ate cookies and read out loud in the attic, where they vowed that no matter how old they got, they were always going to love the custom we'd started the day they had moved into my house, I tucked them into bed and retreated to the office off the foyer on the first floor.

Thanks to the office's fresh new look — newly painted walls, refurbished desk, and spanking clean carpet — I never tired of snuggling into one of the Queen Anne chairs and finishing off the day with a chapter of a good book.

However, tonight I craved the opportunity to reread my parents' love letters. Maybe my desire was piqued by the fact that I'd found another love note from Jordan tucked into my pocket as I'd removed my parka. Maybe it was driven by the twins' squabble at the dinner table, and I needed grounding. No matter what the reason, I wanted to immerse myself in the past. My parents' past. I hadn't had the opportunity to get to know my parents. I wanted to understand them. This was one of the routes.

When I'd found the letters inside a hidden compartment of the antique office desk last November, I'd stowed them in a pair of airtight Tupperware containers. I had read the letters three times since then. One caught me up each time.

It was so simple, so informal:

Dear Megan, You take my breath away.
~Joe

Joe, not Joseph. It was the oldest letter, dated when they were in high school. It had been love at first sight, my father wrote in another letter, just as it had been for Jordan and me, although I didn't learn Jordan loved me until well into our relationship. I thought that I was the only one who had fallen head over heels in love. When Jordan confided that he had been smitten the instant we met, too, I'd melted into his arms.

Wanting to preserve our love in written form, I hurried up the stairs and fetched Jordan's latest note. Grouped with the one he had tucked into my apron pocket the other day and the one posted on the rear door of The Cheese Shop, I realized that three notes established the beginning of a collection.

Deciding Jordan should have one, as well, I returned to the office and sat down at the desk. I withdrew a fine piece of ragged-edge parchment stationary and a pen given to me at my college graduation, and I prepared to write him a letter. Before I began, I wanted to hear his voice. I dialed him at home. He answered drowsily. I apologized if I'd awakened him. I pinned down a time for our date for coffee tomorrow afternoon, and then we echoed each other's "I love you," and I ended the call.

Flush with amorous feelings, I picked up the pen and stared at the blank piece of paper. Where to begin?

Dear Jordan —

Someone pounded on my front door.

CHAPTER 16

The antique quartz clock on the desk read 9:45 P.M. Who could be stopping by at this hour? Rebecca? My grandparents? Definitely not Jordan. A neighbor in distress? I dashed into the foyer and looked through the sidelight window on the right.

Tyanne, teary-eyed and looking extremely vulnerable buried beneath a knee-length parka, stood on the porch. She was worrying the strap of her shoulder bag with both hands. I flung the door open.

"Hi, sugar." She was breathless. "Why doesn't your doorbell work?"

"It does."

"No, it doesn't." She stabbed it repeatedly.

No *ding-dong.* Rats. One more thing to add to my ever-growing to-do list.

I ushered her into the foyer and closed the door. "What's wrong?"

"I'm sorry to intrude. I've been having"

— she drew in a sharp breath and let her purse tumble from her shoulder to the hardwood floor — "thoughts about Tim."

"Do you mean visions?"

"Heavens, no." She wiped her tears with her knuckle. "I'm not seeing things. I'm completely sane. I've simply been thinking — all right, *obsessing* — about who might have killed him. He was so sweet. And kind. Perhaps the kindest man I ever did meet. Anyway, I got to thinking, and I remembered an encounter the other day that I'd witnessed at the pub. You see, I'd gone in to ask Tim about one of the appetizers he served. The stuffed potato skins. I wanted the recipe for an upcoming wedding shower. The bride-to-be wants everything understated. She's a real peach. No muss, no fuss." Tyanne twirled a hand to urge herself to continue the story. "As I was saying, Councilwoman Bell came into the pub. I used to like her. Back when her actress daughter was living here, Bell was sort of nice, but now that her daughter has moved on, the councilwoman has changed."

"Maybe she's lonely," I suggested.

"She sure can be crabby. That day, she lit into Tim something awful about the noise level at the pub."

I sighed. "Again with the noise level?"

178

"What do you mean?"

I explained.

Tyanne pointed a finger. "That's it. Exactly. She said the raucous music had to stop. Paige Alpaugh was there. She took the councilwoman's side. Can you believe it? Irish music isn't raucous. It's filled with life and fun. Tim asked politely if Bell had her hearing checked lately." Tyanne clucked her tongue. "Honestly the pub's music was no louder than it had been in the past, and Tim had never had complaints. Not one. The councilwoman huffed and puffed. I thought she might blow the place down with those mighty lungs of hers."

All puff and no air, Violet had said. An image of the Three Little Pigs flashed before my eyes.

"Do you think she could have overpowered Tim?" Tyanne asked. "Could she have heaved him into the cheese vat by herself?"

Another image of Councilwoman Bell facing off with the clerk at the police precinct the other day whizzed through my mind. What if Bell wasn't a little piggy, all puff and no air? What if she was a tigress with teeth?

"She is sizeable," I said, "albeit out of shape."

"Yes," Tyanne conceded. "You're right. She doesn't appear to have any upper arm strength." Her eyes lit up with a new idea. "What if she drugged Tim?"

"How?"

"I don't know." Tyanne sounded so mournful. "Maybe she slipped drugs into his coffee. He was always drinking coffee. Too much for his own good, all that caffeine. And, on occasion, I've seen Bell leaving the pharmacy with a veritable drugstore in hand."

I shook my head. "Tim drove to Jordan's. If he'd been drugged, he would have swerved off the road."

"Maybe Bell tailed him to the farm, and she sneaked up on him with a hypodermic needle." Tyanne mimed jabbing the needle into an imaginary person. "*Bam!* A shot to the neck."

"I doubt she could have stolen up behind Tim without him hearing her."

Tyanne's shoulders sagged.

"Have you told Urso what you remembered?" I asked.

"I have. Like a gentleman, he didn't dispute what I said. He simply wrote down my statement and thanked me." She sniffed. "Honestly, that man can make me seethe sometimes, he's so . . . placid."

Placid wasn't quite the word I would use for Urso. *Stoic* might be a more appropriate choice. Contemplative. Perceptive. Unwilling to jump to conclusions. Despite the fact that he'd asked me on more than one occasion to butt out of his business, he was one of my all-time favorite people.

"I'm telling you, sugar, the chief stares at me with those piercing eyes of his, and I feel like the stupidest woman in the world."

"I'm sure he doesn't mean to. He likes women. He values their opinions."

"Well, I wouldn't know it."

I rested a hand on Tyanne's arm. "Tim's murder has hit Urso very hard. He and Tim were good friends. I would bet that he's doing everything he can to maintain his composure while he investigates."

"Even so, you'd think he would hanker to have new ideas. Why, if I were him, I would confront Belinda Bell, and —"

"Don't." I never thought I would be the one to utter the next few words, but out of my mouth came: "Don't. Do. Anything. No going off half-cocked and possibly putting yourself in harm's way. Urso has it handled."

"All right, sugar. No need to yell."

Had I yelled? Perhaps I had because I was trying to convince not only Tyanne, but also myself, that doing nothing was the best course of action.

"How about some tea?" I said.

"I'd love some."

I steered her into the kitchen and switched on a light. The dog and cat lifted their heads from their resting places. "Go back to sleep," I ordered. Neither pet needed a second reminder.

Tyanne perched on a stool by the counter while I put on a pot of water to boil. In the glaring light, she looked pale and drawn. Her mouth was turned down. She pulled the sugar bowl toward her and repeatedly lifted and dumped sugar off the serving spoon. "So, how are you, Charlotte?"

"What do you mean?"

"It's nearly Sunday. By this time tomorrow, you were supposed to be, you know . . ."

"Mrs. Jordan Pace. I know. And I will be. We're setting a new date. In May."

"Wouldn't you prefer it to be sooner?"

"Of course, but in good conscience, seeing as Tim was murdered at the farm —"

"Like I said before, let's change the venue. There are all sorts of places that would be happy to host a wedding tomorrow. We can keep it simple. I know I promised all your goodies to another couple, but I'm sure I can whip up a fresh set of flowers. Dottie would be thrilled to make another cake. And who needs a sit-down dinner, right? Cheese and crackers will do. Let's see . . . I don't have anything scheduled at Harvest Moon Ranch or The Ice Castle." She ticked off the sites on her fingertips. "Or that darling chapel in the ravine. You know the one, with the stained glass behind the altar." She steepled her fingers. "If you want that one, you've got to snatch it up right now, though. My eager out-of-towners have mentioned that's one of their top three. They were enamored with it. They're even talking about having the pastor's wife do her celebratory modern dance."

I gaped. Nobody ever wanted the pastor's wife to do her dance. She was a darling, but the dance was sort of, um, *out there.* It involved a garment made of scarves and lots of harem-style dance moves.

"C'mon, sugar, what do you say? I'd be glad to —"

I held up a hand. "No. We've made our decision. Jordan and I will not get married until the pall of Tim's murder is behind us."

Which, of course, made my indecision of a few minutes ago vanish. I wouldn't rest until his murderer was captured and brought to justice.

CHAPTER 17

Meredith and Matthew arrived early Sunday morning to pick up the girls. Add a fresh snowfall to the mix and the hubbub in the house was cacophonous. Girls screaming: "Did you bring our mittens, our hats, our boots?" "Where are we going?" "When will we get there?" Surprises could be chaotic. Rags and Rocket weren't nearly as happy as the girls. They knew something was going down. When the house emptied, and it was the three of us — two pets and me — I donned a parka, hood up, and we headed outside for a quick playtime before our walk to work.

The moment I pushed open the back door, a piece of paper — no, an envelope with Jordan's handwriting — flapped in the breeze. He had taped it to the jamb. When had he left it? At midnight, after I'd gone to sleep? The sneaky devil. I peeled it off and opened it.

Good morning, my love. I know this is the day we had planned to become man and wife. It was with a heavy heart that I asked you to postpone the celebration. But, rest assured, we will be together. Forever. I adore you.

Love, Jordan

Feeling lighter than air, I raced inside, tucked the envelope into my purse, and returned outside to play with the pets. I tossed a ball across the backyard. "Fetch!"

Rocket tore off, leaving skid streaks in the inch of snow. Rags glowered at me as if demanding to know what his treat was to be.

I scooped him up and nuzzled him. "Relax, you big baby. He doesn't get to be picked up. He's not a lap cat."

Rocket returned, eager for another go. We played throw and fetch for ten minutes, Rocket making tracks across the snow. When he slid at the far end of the yard and nearly took out a boxwood bush, he barked loudly enough to wake the neighbors — it was the bush's fault, of course.

At the same time, the first round of church bells pealed in the air. Services all over town would soon begin.

A few minutes later, I settled in for a quick

morning coffee, apple wedges, and a slice of Aged Leicestershire Red, a flaky orange cheese with a caramel flavor. Soon after, I dressed and headed for the shop.

As the pets and I neared the Village Green, I caught sight of a number of women convening around the kiosk beside the historic clock. Paige and Violet were among them. Unlike Councilwoman Bell and her cohorts at the precinct the other day, these women looked rapturous to be together. All were bundled up; each wore a smile. Violet split from the group to peer around the kiosk, as if expecting someone else. Paige thumped her arm, gestured that Violet should forget about whoever was late, and handed her a fistful of flyers. Paige caught sight of me and hurried over. She shoved a flyer into my hand, which read: *Sugar kills.* I had to give her credit. The flyer was direct and to the point. No one would mistake her message.

"Join us," she begged.

I started to respond, but Rocket had other plans. He yanked me to the left.

"No," I said to him. "Stop. We're not going to the pet shop now. It's not open yet. Later." But Rocket didn't like my *later* idea; he wouldn't be dissuaded. He knew Tailwaggers encouraged owners to bring in their pets and let them browse. He tugged again. I thought my arm socket would give way. "Sorry, Paige," I yelled over my shoulder. "Another time." To the dog, I snarled, "Heel." He didn't. "When did you become so willful?" I had been diligent about training him. *Come. Sit. Stay.* He played when I wanted him to play; he did his business when I said. He obeyed the word: *Heel.* Had a few months without hearing my voice commands stripped me of power?

"Matthew," I muttered. He hated to discipline the dog. "Fine." I gave in. "We'll walk your direction, but we're not going into the store. I repeat, it's too early. It's not open. We can window-shop. We'll go inside when I take you for your bath later in the week." Rocket peeked at me with soulful eyes. "That's right. Bath. B-a-t-h. Water. Soap. You'll smell so good."

Rocket licked the Tailwaggers window trying to get to the display, which was made up of bones, pillows, leashes, and, of all things, a cardboard statue of a full-sized French Briard wearing a heart-shaped necklace around her neck and bows beside each ear. Had Rocket known this image of a girl dog was there? Maybe Meredith and the twins had roamed this way in the past few days.

"Keep moving, pal," I said. "True love will have to wait."

Rags yowled his agreement and pulled ahead as if demanding he be the leader. He was one of the few cats I knew that had taken to the leash. Reluctantly, Rocket did as commanded.

We rounded the corner and easily bypassed the theater and Memory Lane Collectibles, which was Belinda Bell's shop. Rocket made no sudden stops. However, outside Providence Pâtisserie, I drew up short. My stomach rumbled. Cheese paired with apples wasn't enough of a meal. Under the pretense of picking up sweets for my afternoon coffee with Jordan — how much would I hate myself if I ate two sweet rolls in one day? — I secured the animals on the hitching post outside the front door, and headed inside. I wasn't surprised that the shop was open for business; Dottie once told me, while giggling, that Sunday garnered huge sales. Churchgoers, she claimed, no matter how devoted to their faith, needed sustenance to endure the occasional boring sermon.

The buzzer above the door *ping*ed as I entered. No one was standing behind the counter.

"Hello?" I called.

Dottie didn't appear. Per usual, music was blasting somewhere in the rear of the shop. The Rolling Stones song "Brown Sugar" was playing. Dottie claimed music inspired her hands to make a better, fluffier pastry.

I dinged the counter call bell and waited. Still no one emerged from the back of the shop. "Dottie!" I yelled.

No answer.

I listened for the sound of running water or oven doors slamming. Nothing. Maybe Dottie was outside emptying garbage. Maybe she was in the restroom. I knew from personal experience that without an assistant to take up the slack, finding time to attend to personal matters while on the job could be challenging.

Daring to move past the counter, I pushed open the door with the porthole window and peered into the kitchen. "Dottie?"

I drew up short. Dottie was lying on the floor. Faceup. Her legs were askew, her pant legs scrunched up. Her arms were extended. The collar of her cowl-neck sweater lay loose and unruly.

Heart thrumming my ribcage, I pushed back the kitchen door and darted to her. I knelt down, but there was no need to check her pulse. She was dead. Her eyes were wide open and blank. Her skin was a faint blue.

A pastry jutted from her mouth.

I gagged. My breakfast tried to make its way north. I forced myself to swallow. What had happened? Had she fallen backward and, with the pastry in her mouth, choked? I rose to my feet and surveyed the area. Other than the way her body was sprawled, there didn't appear to have been a fight. In fact, the kitchen looked prepped to make lots of pastries. Kitchen tools, measuring cups, and sifters as well as ingredients like flour, butter, vanilla, cheese, and eggs rested on the huge marble-topped island. Three trays of unbaked pastries appeared ready to be popped into the oven. Unwashed mixing bowls and some trash had been set in the industrial-sized sink.

And yet, something didn't feel right about the scene. I gazed at Dottie again. The pastry. It wasn't simply jutting from her mouth. It looked jammed in tight. Had someone done that on purpose? Was she murdered? Why?

"Oh, Dottie, I'm so sorry." Grief coursed through me. Two lives snuffed out in the same week. Both people I knew and cared about.

I pulled my cell phone from my purse and dialed 911.

I was explaining the situation to the

respondent when a man shouted from the front of the store, "Dottie!"

Ray Pfeiffer burst into the kitchen. The mere sight of him in black shorts and black T-shirt, though not his typical outfit, gave me the shivers. "Dot. What's going on? Why isn't there —" He spotted me and halted. He glanced from me to Dottie and back to me. "What have you done?" Ray dashed to his wife and knelt beside her.

"What? No. N-n-not me," I sputtered. "I came in and found her lying there." I waggled my phone. "I've called the police. They're on their way. We should probably —"

Ray wasn't listening to me. Without pulling off his woolen gloves, he dug his fingers into Dottie's mouth. He scooped out whatever had been stuffed inside. It looked like a cheese Danish. "Breathe, hon," Ray commanded. He caressed her face, her hair, her shoulders. "Breathe."

I knew there was no possibility he could revive her, but what could I say? *Step away from the body.* Like I had the right. He was her husband. "Ray," I said softly. "She's dead."

"Breathe, hon," he repeated, not hearing me or not wishing to hear me. Following a long silence, Ray whispered, "All I did was

191

leave you to go to sunrise service at the chapel."

Dressed like that? Were black shorts the formal version of his jean shorts?

"One hour." He petted Dottie again. "I was gone one hour. Darn it, hon, how did this happen?"

"Ray, maybe you ought to leave the crime scene alone. The police will be here any minute."

Tears dripped from his eyes onto Dottie's face. He gathered her hands in his, yet again disturbing the scene by moving her outstretched arms. The muscles in his forearms flexed as he tried to will life into her. "No, no, no," he muttered. "Come back. I told her not to work alone. I told her it was dangerous. I told her to hire a new assistant. But when did she ever listen to me?"

Seeing him so emotionally undone yanked me back to Tyanne's grief-stricken visit to my house last night.

Ray's head jerked up. He must have heard the refrigerator and heater kick on, as I had. Like an animal on high alert, he glanced right and left. Silently he tucked Dottie's hands against her chest and bolted to his feet. Then he crept to the door leading to the front of the shop. He pushed it open a crack and peeked out. Seconds later, he let the door swing shut. He stared at me. I expected him to say something like "All clear," but he didn't. He strode to the far side of the room and flattened himself against the wall. He poked his head around the corner and returned to his pressed-against-the-wall position. Did he think someone other than us was in the building? Was he thinking what I was thinking, that Dottie had been murdered? She never would have eaten an entire pastry like that. She wasn't a gorger; she didn't scarf down food. She may have been plump, but I'd seen her eat on many occasions — a nibble here, a bite there, what some might call a sneaky eater.

Ray put his finger to his lips, signaling me that he heard something. He slinked around the corner and disappeared from sight.

I whispered, "Wait," but he didn't. Had he gone in search of an intruder? Had he fled? A chill cut through me. I was alone. With the body. I eyed the kitchen door. When would the police arrive? I moved toward the door but paused when I spied a wooden spoon and a crumpled towel on the floor just beyond the marble island. Beyond them was a smear of flour, as if someone had tried to hastily wipe up a mess. Had there been a scuffle? Was a murderer close at hand?

My chest tightened with fear. I heard footsteps. I crouched behind the island, ready to leap out if Dottie's killer returned.

"Charlotte?" Ray called. "You still here?"

I bolted upright.

"I knew it!" he cried. For a fit man, he was certainly breathing heavily. Fear could kick up all sorts of adrenaline. "He did it."

"He *who*?"

"Zach Mueller."

"Dottie's assistant?"

"Ex-assistant."

Right. Ex. He quit. I thought of my conversation with Violet at her inn. She'd said she didn't trust Zach as far as she could throw him. I sort of liked Zach, even though he was a speed-demon in that souped-up car of his. He knew his pastry and he liked every kind of cheese.

"Zach robbed Dottie and killed her," Ray said.

"Are you sure? I didn't see the cash register open, and the children's fund donation box seemed intact."

"He didn't take money. He broke into the safe in the office." Ray jerked a thumb over his shoulder. "The door is hanging wide open. He took Dottie's ruby brooch."

"Why would he take a piece of jewelry?"

"It was a family heirloom. All diamonds and rubies. A cluster is what Dottie called it. Shaped like a flower. About yea big." He formed a mini-donut-sized O with his fingers. "Ugly as sin, but it was worth over twenty-five thousand dollars."

"Wow! That's a lot of money. Why would Dottie keep something that precious at the store?"

"We didn't have a safe at home. She felt it was more secure here. She never wore it. She said it was gauche. But she couldn't part with it. She must have caught him —"

"Caught Zach?"

"Yes." Ray sounded exasperated with me. "Dottie must have caught him in the act. He knocked her down and shoved that" — he pointed at the wad of pastry — "into her mouth to keep her from screaming. She ran out of air."

"Zach would've had to hold it there and pinch her nose closed to suffocate her. Was he strong enough to do that? He's so slim."

"He wrestled in high school."

I thought of my lanky college-aged Internet guru. Wrestling had developed his muscles, too. Now he could lug seventy-five-pound wheels of cheese with ease. Zach Mueller had the same physique. I glanced back at Dottie. The collar of her cowl-neck sweater lay loose. Her neck was exposed. I couldn't see any ligature marks or bruises. Suffocation had to be the method.

Stop, Charlotte! Listen to you. You sound like Rebecca, theorizing à la a television detective.

Ray headed for the wall telephone. "I'm going to call the police."

"I already did." Hadn't he heard me before? Was his hearing impaired by grief? "They're on their way."

He looked at me as if he were surprised by my presence. "Charlotte?"

"Yes."

"Why are you here?"

"My dog steered me in this direction on our morning walk." Had Rocket sensed Dottie's death? Had he heard something going down? No. He wasn't an Asta or Lassie. He had wanted to stroll past the pet shop and get a gander of his ladylove cutout. And yet, here I was. Inside the pastry shop, faced with yet another death — murder. "I decided to come in and buy some pastries. Dottie's Sunday morning specials are" — ugh, she was dead; I had to use the past tense — "*were* always her best."

"That's because she spent all Saturday night preparing them," Ray acknowledged.

He started to pace by Dottie's feet. I caught him glancing at her. His face torqued into a mask of pain. He swung his gaze away. He wore a path in the linoleum until he finally stopped and looked at his watch. "Why aren't the police here yet? They're just around the corner."

"The precinct is," I conceded, "but the deputies might be on patrol." Or at church, I supposed.

Ray grumbled. "I never trusted that Zach kid."

"You don't know it was him."

"Who else could have done this? Dottie fired him."

"I thought he quit."

"No, she was being polite when she told you that. She fired him."

"Why?"

"Sloth," he said. "Proverbs 18:9. 'Whoever is slack in his work becomes brother to one who destroys.' That's Satan."

"I thought Zach was a good worker."

Ray shook his head forcefully. "He wanted it easy. He was always asking for time off. When Dottie fired him, he was angrier than a hibernating bear awakened in winter. He threw trays of pastries and sped off in that car of his. He's got itchy fingers, that kid. He knew about the safe." Ray gestured toward the rear of the store. "He was always into trouble growing up. Whenever he'd come to the ice-skating rink, he'd start something. An argument. A fight."

"Why did Dottie hire him in the first place?"

"She said he had a sensitivity toward baked goods, whatever the heck that meant."

I understood. Baking was an art. Not everyone was good at it. If Zach had a talent for it, then Dottie must have wanted to cultivate that gift. So why would Zach kill his mentor?

CHAPTER 18

I stared at Ray standing on the opposite side of the island, his finger raised in fury, his dead wife at his feet, and suddenly I went cold. What if his rage was bogus? What if he'd killed Dottie? What would his motive have been? Maybe The Ice Castle was suffering financially. Maybe he needed money. If he pawned the brooch, he wouldn't get its full twenty-five thousand dollar value, but perhaps half was enough to solve the problem. Was the brooch even missing? What if Ray had taken out a life insurance policy on Dottie? She had a business to run. Both Matthew and I had invested in what was called *key man* life insurance policies so that, if one of us were to die, the business would be the beneficiary, and the proceeds would go into Fromagerie Bessette to help with the transition.

Wrestling with the theory made me shiver. Honestly, I couldn't believe Ray had killed his wife. From all I'd seen, he had adored Dottie. They had grown up in Providence. They had built a solid life here, with the ice rink and the pastry shop. They had been tireless at raising money for the Providence Children's Fund. And Ray was wearing what I assumed was his Sunday best. He didn't look like he'd killed anyone. There was no evidence of a struggle on his clothing. Wouldn't pastry dough or flour have splattered him somehow? Dottie, though petite in height, had been on the heavy side, and she had spunk; certainly she would have tried to fight off her attacker, unless, of course, the attack came from someone she treasured. A loving hug. A warm embrace. And then *wham!*

Could Ray have forced the breath out of her? Was he that evil? I'd seen him on numerous occasions at The Ice Castle. He had a smile for everyone. He was especially helpful to the kids. One time, I saw him pick up a child who had fallen on the ice. The girl looked like a baby giraffe with her long legs splayed. Ray had dusted her off and had personally escorted her to her folks.

Ray muttered, "Zach Mueller. Yeah, it makes sense."

I didn't have time to discuss his theory, because right then Urso blazed through the kitchen door.

"Zach Mueller did it," Ray blurted as if he were set on auto-repeat mode.

Urso didn't address either of us. He took in the scene quickly and crouched beside Dottie. He checked her pulse and her exposed neck, all while whispering notes into the recording device on his cell phone.

When he stood, I said, "Where's Deputy Rodham?"

"Hospital."

"Still?"

"There were complications. Baby's fine. He'll be out of commission for a few more days."

It dawned on me that Urso was now two deputies short. Should I offer my services? "Chief —"

"Hush!"

I didn't bristle at the harsh tone. I understood.

Urso circled Dottie, then scoped out the kitchen. He squatted beside the spatula and the flour on the floor but didn't touch anything. He strode to the door leading to the main shop and peered out. He looked back at Dottie. He wasn't trying to figure out a bullet entry angle, so what was he looking for?

After what seemed like an eternity of

silence, Urso addressed Ray. "Mr. Pfeiffer, I'm sorry for your loss." During investigations, Urso liked to show respect and call people by their formal names. "Can I get you anything? A cup of coffee?"

The aroma of coffee made it to my senses. I hadn't noticed it when I'd first entered the pastry shop. Dottie always made a fresh pot. She didn't sell it, but she offered complimentary four-ounce cups to anyone who made a purchase.

"No," Ray muttered. "No coffee. I never drink coffee."

"Water?"

"No." Ray shifted feet and continued to steal glances at his wife. "Zach Mueller killed Dottie. Aren't you going to arrest him?"

"Sir, one thing at a time. I assume you found the body."

"No, she did." Ray jutted a finger in my direction.

"You, Charlotte?" Urso said.

I was one of the few Urso never addressed formally; we had known each other for so many years. His gaze was penetrating and unwavering. I winced. "Yes." What was it with me finding dead bodies? I wasn't psychic. I wasn't drawn to the macabre. "I came in for some pastries. Dottie opens early." *Opened,* I mentally revised. "I was on my way to work."

"Why in this direction?"

"I've got Rocket and Rags with me." I thumbed toward the front of the shop. "Rocket often likes to take the scenic route." Why in the heck was I being so glib? Was it a defense mechanism? Maybe I was on edge because Urso was staring at me. Hard. I rushed to add, "The dog likes to pass by the pet store to window-shop. There's a girl dog cardboard statue, and —" *Shut up, Charlotte. You sound like an imbecile. Urso doesn't care about the dog's habits or his love life.* "That route forced me to head south on Honeysuckle. When I saw the shop was open, I came in. The place was empty. I called for Dottie. She didn't answer, so I slipped back here and found her lying there." I pointed. "Her arms were outstretched. A pastry was crammed into her mouth. Ray —"

He moaned, then crossed his arms across his lean body and tucked his hands beneath his armpits. I suspected, as emotional as he was, the gloves weren't enough to keep him warm.

"Ray what?" Urso said.

"Ray hurried in after me. When he saw her, he couldn't help himself." I explained

203

how he tried to remove the blockage. I indicated the wad of old Danish. "Chief, I think she suffocated."

"The medical examiner will be here shortly," Urso said. "He'll make that determination. Go on."

Ray cleared his throat. "Zach knew about my wife's brooch." He explained that it was a family heirloom and why he thought Zach had stolen it. "I'd seen him admire it. I'll bet he sneaked up on her and pinned her with an arm to her windpipe." He demonstrated in the air. "He was a wrestler in high school. He could have grabbed her, pushed her to the ground, and shoved the pastry inside her mouth."

Earlier, Ray had said Dottie must have caught Zach in the act of stealing. Was changing up his theory enough reason to believe Ray had killed his wife? No. Everything he'd said before was said in the heat of the moment. I refused to jump to conclusions.

"He must have held the pastry there and pinched her nose closed," Ray went on, repeating what I'd suggested, "until she was out of air."

"Like suffocating her with a pillow." Urso nodded, seemingly agreeing with Ray's assessment. "How do you think he entered?"

"The front door was unlocked," I said.

"He could have entered through the back, too," Ray said. An alley flanked the building in the rear.

"Other than the flour and spatula on the floor," I said, "the scene looks cleaned up. I don't think you'll find fingerprints."

"All right. No more speculating." Urso held up a hand. "Let's hold all theories for now. I'm going to secure the area. Mr. Pfeiffer, if you and Charlotte wouldn't mind exiting the building. But please stay nearby. On the sidewalk. I'll need to ask more questions."

Ray and I moved into the main portion of the shop. The medical examiner, a shaggy-haired man, his eyes partially hidden behind a mane of bangs, jogged in. I pointed toward the back. He expressed his thanks, hoisted the shoulder strap of his kit higher on his shoulder, and mushed ahead.

I retreated to the sidewalk and nuzzled my pets. "Sorry, fellas, we've stumbled onto something." *Something? A murder, for Pete's sake.* Another *murder.* "We're going to be here for a while." I pulled my cell phone from my purse and dialed Fromagerie Bessette.

Rebecca started to cry when she heard about Dottie. "She always had a joke to share or a tale to tell," she murmured. "Is Ray distraught?"

Ray stood a few feet from me, shifting from foot to foot. He looked aimless and dejected.

I whispered, "Yes."

"How are you doing?" Rebecca asked.

"I'm fine."

"No, I mean, really? You've seen two bodies in less than a week."

I shuddered. "I'm alive."

Urso appeared. I ended the call to Rebecca, pocketed my cell phone, and faced him. He asked Ray and me a litany of questions. A crowd amassed while we responded. When Urso was content to let us go, I hugged Ray and promised him I would do everything I could to find Dottie's murderer. He mumbled one last time that Zach did it, and we parted.

Throughout the remainder of the morning, I roamed The Cheese Shop as if I were lost in a fog. I could rearrange shelves and serve slices of quiche and sandwiches, but I was awful at answering questions about a particular cheese. My mind felt stuck in second gear while trying hard to climb a steep hill. Rebecca, as usual, interrogated me about the crime scene, but I didn't have any answers. I had walked in and found

Dottie dead. Ray had entered and had tried to revive his wife. That was all I could remember. I was numb from my feet up.

Around three in the afternoon, when the fog started to lift in my brain and I could communicate with customers again, I roused myself to organize the wine tasting in the annex. We always offered a Sunday wine trio, often of the same type of wine. With Matthew gone, either Rebecca or I had to arrange it, and I was infinitely more wine-savvy than Rebecca, which wasn't saying much. Today's tasting included three Rieslings. Matthew said a common misperception about Riesling was that the grape only produced sweet wine. Not so. A Riesling grape could produce a dry, complex wine. The three we'd chosen to share came from the Alsace region in France, the Mosel region in Germany, and the Columbia Valley in Washington State.

Beside the array of wines, I set a tray of bite-sized cubes of Appenzeller, a firm cow's-milk cheese cured with an herbal brine. Afterward, I perched on a stool beside the antique bar and observed as customers came and went. Some had heard about Dottie and wanted me to tell them about the murder scene, but I refused. Urso would have my head if I revealed an iota of what I knew to anyone other than Rebecca. *Her* he would understand. He knew she would grill me doggedly and I would cave, but he also knew that whatever she gleaned, she would keep to herself — not that I'd told her anything.

At three-thirty, when Jordan entered, I was itching to talk to someone I could trust about new thoughts — evidentiary in nature — that were forming in my mind.

One look at my face and he hurried to me and enfolded me in his arms. "Why didn't you call?"

"I knew you'd be stopping by for coffee."

"I would've come sooner, but gossip didn't make it north of town. I only now heard about Dottie while getting out of my car. You were there?"

I nodded and led him into the kitchen and seated him at the preparation counter. Rather than make coffee, I pulled a quiche from the refrigerator, cut a slice, and heated it in the microwave. As I did, I told him my initial impression of the crime scene. "Jordan, there was cheese on the counter. Your cheese. Pace Hill Farm Double-cream Gouda. I only realized it moments ago. The stamped gold wrapper had been removed, but there were remnants of it in the sink with the unwashed mixing bowls."

I set the warm quiche in front of Jordan and provided a fork. "I remember Dottie bragging about how she liked to use local ingredients to make her pastries." An icy shiver shimmied down my back. I thought of something else. Something I'd told Rebecca. Other than the dusting of flour and the spatula on the floor, the place had looked clean. Had the murderer cleaned up? "You don't think —" I hesitated. The theory was way off base.

"Think what?"

I waved a hand. "You don't want me to speculate."

He smiled sadly. "That was yesterday. Today you've had another encounter. You have the right to come up with whatever hypotheses you can think of."

"Okay." I took the theory out for a test drive. "Could Tim and Dottie's murders be related?"

"How?"

"Because of the Gouda cheese. *Your* cheese. And the fact that the murderer cleaned up after himself."

"Herself."

"Himself, herself. Whatever."

"Don't get snippy." He took a bite of quiche and downed it, and then set his fork on the plate and pushed the quiche aside.

"Go on. I'm not following how the murders could be related. Explain."

"The murderer scrubbed the floor in your cheese-making facility. I think he — or she — wiped up a mess of flour on the floor at the pâtisserie. It was a rush job."

"To remove evidence."

"Exactly."

"How else could the two crimes be connected?"

"Remember Tim's call to his nephew? He said he *saw* something. Ray Pfeiffer believes Zach Mueller robbed Dottie and killed her. What if Tim saw Zach robbing someone at the pub? Maybe Zach realized Tim was watching. Zach tailed Tim to your farm. They fought. Zach knocked out Tim, dumped his body in the cheese vat, and unleashed the milk." I explained how Deputy O'Shea and I had seen Zach speeding in the opposite direction as we'd driven to the farm the night of the murder. "Ray thinks that Dottie caught Zach while he was filching from her safe. Zach forced her to the floor and suffocated her. What if Zach, feeling like he wanted to put one over on the police, chose a pastry with your Gouda in it and shoved it into Dottie's mouth? Ray said Zach was a pretty talented baker; he would have known the difference between the pastries."

"That's a stretch. Not to mention, I've seen Zach. He's slim, almost slight. He might have been able to overpower Dottie, but not Tim."

"Zach used to wrestle in high school. He's got to be as strong as Bozz." My young Internet guru who was currently keeping his nose to the grindstone at junior college.

Jordan rubbed the back of his neck. "I thought Jawbone Jones topped your suspect list for Tim's murder."

I flashed on the diamond ring that Jawbone's fiancée — or whatever her significance might be to him — was wearing the day I'd seen them at the winery. What if Jawbone was a jewelry thief? What if he'd known about the brooch in Dottie's safe? I said as much to Jordan.

He didn't agree. "Jawbone makes a good living. Have you seen what guns go for nowadays? A decent shotgun starts at upward of a thousand dollars."

I wriggled my nose. "I hate guns."

"So do I, but that doesn't mean Jawbone is a bad guy."

Tim *saw* something the night he died. I said, "What if Jawbone was doing something illegal outside the pub, you know, like buying stolen guns?" The deputy had floated that theory the other day in the shop. "If Jawbone would buy stolen guns, he might steal jewelry. His girlfriend looks like she could be a seller or go-between."

"Right out of central casting," Jordan joked. "Charlotte, c'mon."

"You're right. I shouldn't stereotype."

He drew me into his arms. "Sweetheart, it's possible the two murders aren't related, but to be safe, tell your concerns to Urso."

Tears flooded the corners of my eyes. "I still see Dottie lying on the floor, and I see Tim, and . . ." I blotted the tears with my fingertips. "I can't rest until these murders are solved. For both of them and their loved ones."

Jordan kissed my forehead. "For you, too."

CHAPTER 19

Needless to say, I didn't sleep well Sunday night. Even with Rags and Rocket at the foot of my bed, I heard creaks and sounds. My dreams were filled with clanging church bells and people choking. I awoke coughing and feeling like a head cold was ready to attack.

In the kitchen, I downed a lot of zinc and vitamin C, drank a strong cup of Earl Gray tea laced with honey, and ate a breakfast heavy on fats because that was what my grandmother would have recommended — she swore fats kept a person's energy up so the body had enough oomph to beat a bug. And then I called Urso. He wasn't in yet. I left a message with my suspicions, as flimsy as my proof was, about how both murders were related.

By the time I arrived at The Cheese Shop, Rebecca was in the kitchen kneading dough vigorously. Despite the chilly weather, she was wearing a short skirt and short-sleeved blouse. The makings for chicken-pecan quiche sat on the counter, as well as the ingredients for biscuits using Gorgonzola Dolce from Lombardy, a blue-veined cheese with a nice bite.

"Are we selling biscuits now?" I asked.

"Those are for me. I have a craving."

"Why are you so pumped up?"

She spun around, a huge grin on her face. "I got it. I got the role in the play."

"You did? Congratulations!"

"I heard last night at ten. Your grandmother called me. But I didn't want to telephone you and wake you. You'd had such a tough day."

Dottie Pfeiffer had a tougher day, I thought, and bit my lip to keep fresh tears from falling. Poor Dottie. Who had killed her? Why? How could I help Urso solve the crime other than by providing the information I'd already given him?

"Guess what?" Rebecca continued, with no awareness of my inner turmoil. Her excitement was too lively to contain. "Deputy O'Shea is going to play the role opposite me. We're going to act together. We perform this Friday."

"Friday? That's so soon," I said. Grand-mère usually rehearses her actors for a minimum of three weeks. She likes the material to sweep them up and take them to a new world of emotion.

"There's nothing to memorize and no blocking to speak of," Rebecca said. "We read directly from the letters. Grandmère has cast another set of actors in the roles for the following two weeks. Isn't that shrewd? That means there will be six different actors. The whole town should come out to see the play, don't you think? People will have their favorite actors, of course. I hope they'll come to see me."

"I'm sure you'll have a packed house. Jordan and I will be there, and Matthew and Meredith will be back in town by then. And Deputy O'Shea has lots of friends."

"I'm so excited." Rebecca divided the dough into twelve portions, one for each of twelve quiches, then dusted a rolling pin and started to roll out one crust. "I hope I don't get nervous. I mean, with all those people watching, I'm bound to get a little nervous, but I hope I can contain it. The play is so intimate. Did you know I have to cry at one point? I think I can do it. We're rehearsing every night this week." She stopped mid-roll. "Is that okay?"

"Sure. We don't have any evening obligations at the shop other than the Lovers Trail event. I can cover that." I had set limited hours for the shop this coming week because of Jordan's and my wedding and because of our honeymoon plans. I thought limited hours would help Rebecca and my part-timers manage on their own. The wine-and-cheese-pairing event at the shop on Thursday evening was the one exception. Now, with me in town and Matthew due back by then, I didn't need Rebecca to shoulder the burden.

Rebecca sighed. "Do you think acting in a play will pull Deputy O'Shea out of his funk? He's miserable. I think he wants to cry, but he won't."

"I'm sure the play will give him something else to focus on."

"Did you know he's investigating his uncle's death on his own?"

As I'd guessed. "He shouldn't."

Rebecca scoffed. "Do you think I can stop him? Not on a bet." She peeled the crust off the cutting board, placed it into an aluminum pie pan, and crimped the edges. "And, honestly, he ought to investigate. Tim was his favorite uncle. They were very close. Devon is dead set on Jawbone being the culprit. He said he's had run-ins with Jawbone before. Jawbone drinks, and when he drinks, he gets feisty."

But did he get violent was the question. Had Tim seen him doing something illegal? Had Jawbone chased Tim down? Had he attacked Tim and, after a struggle, dumped him into the cheese vat to keep the secret?

Rebecca rolled out another crust. "I overheard you talking to Jordan yesterday."

I cocked my head. "How? We were in the kitchen, far away from you."

"I tiptoed close so I could listen in." She spun the cutting board to roll the dough in the opposite direction. "Do you really think Tim and Dottie's murders could be related?"

"It's only a theory. I've called U-ey, but he hasn't returned my call." I would wager Urso had been too busy this morning to breathe, let alone call me. He had no deputies, no backup. How I wished he would turn to me for help.

"Why would Jawbone Jones want to kill Dottie?" Rebecca asked.

"I have no idea, unless Dottie caught him stealing the brooch." Had Urso followed up on that angle? Was the brooch really missing?

"Jawbone walked by the store earlier with Zach Mueller's mom."

"I don't think I've ever met her."

"She has fringed hair and —" Rebecca

waggled her finger down the nape of her neck to demonstrate.

"A rattail?" I asked. Rebecca was describing the woman I thought was Jawbone's fiancée. "She's Zach's mother?"

"Yep."

"How did I not realize that?"

"Do you know everyone in town?"

"Everyone who is a local and comes into the shop."

"I don't think she's ever come in here," Rebecca said. "Maybe she's lactose intolerant."

"We sell wine."

Rebecca smirked. "She looks like hard liquor might be her beverage of choice."

I had to agree. "How did you find out she was Zach's mom?"

"Tyanne was in the store at the time. She told me that Ilona — that's the woman's name — ended the marriage when Zach was two. I only mention it because Jawbone gave me the willies. He looked sort of alien-creepy, all bundled in a peacoat and scarf, with only that bald head of his poking out. Doesn't he need a hat or something?"

Recalling how scared I'd felt when I'd questioned him in the parking lot at the Bozzuto Winery and suddenly feeling queasy from all the stress and sorrow, I held up a hand and said, "Let's not discuss the murders right now."

"But —"

"No. We have so much to do to prepare for this week's event. I'd like to concentrate on the positive."

Rebecca bristled. "I wasn't going to discuss the murders. I simply mentioned seeing Jawbone because then I waved and they waved back and smiled, and the willies went away."

I fetched a pad and pencil and started writing a list of the cheeses needed for our Lovers Trail event on Thursday. All of the neighboring shops on Hope Street were participating in Thursday's festivities, too. La Chic Boutique was having a fashion show. The Country Kitchen was offering a *Savor the Love* food tasting, which would include ten mouthwatering desserts. Delilah had told me about the triple-chocolate pudding she was whipping up. It was laced with espresso coffee. Yum. I couldn't wait to try it. At Sew Inspired, Freckles intended to teach customers how to stitch a heart-shaped pillow. And we at Fromagerie Bessette were offering tastings throughout the store. I planned to set out more than a dozen platters of cheeses. For the wine —

I tapped the end of my pencil on the

paper. "Rebecca, can you remember the name of the California champagne Matthew selected for Thursday's event?"

"Oh no, no, no. Don't call it champagne," she cautioned me. "You know better."

I did. Matthew had been adamant that I learn. Back in 1919, during the signing of the Treaty of Versailles, the French ordained that the word *Champagne* could only refer to bubbly wines made using age-old methods and grapes grown in the Champagne region of France. Except somehow the United States found a loophole. So, in 2006, the United States, as a show of good faith, signed a wine trade agreement with the European Union, not to use terms that were semi-generic, like Champagne, Burgundy, Chianti, et cetera. Of course, if a vineyard had an approved label, that vineyard could be grandfathered in. But Champagne in the U.S. was now called sparkling wine. On the upside, many considered American sparkling wines to be sunnier and less earthy than Champagnes and exceedingly more affordable. *C'est la vie!*

"Fine," I conceded. "What was the name of the sparkling wine?"

"Roederer Estate Brut Anderson Valley L'Ermitage 2003," she said, the name tripping off her tongue. Maybe she did know more about wine than I gave her credit for. She was an eager student. "It's the same wine we were serving at your —" She halted and cut me a regretful look. "Sorry."

"My bachelorette party."

She jammed her lips together and nodded.

"You don't need to pussyfoot around that," I said. "It was fun while it lasted." I still couldn't forget how quickly the fun had fizzled, and I couldn't erase from my mind the string of events that had occurred after Deputy O'Shea listened to Tim's message: the panic on his face; the race to the pub; the sprint to the deputy's car; the mad dash to Jordan's farm. Finding Tim.

Suddenly, everything started to move in slow motion.

"Charlotte, are you all right? You look pookie."

"I'm fine." I wasn't dizzy, but in my mind, I had zoomed back to yesterday morning when I'd entered the pastry shop and found Dottie. I pictured the body, the Danish, Jordan's cheese, the spatula, the flour. Was my gut instinct right? Were the two crimes related? Who would want to kill both Dottie and Tim? Jawbone Jones had a slim motive to kill Tim, but I couldn't imagine, other than robbery, that he had one for Dottie. Belinda Bell wanted both Tim and Dottie to stop with the noise. Zach Mueller, if Ray Pfeiffer's assertion was right, had stolen Dottie's brooch. Tim had *seen* something. Had he seen Zach stealing something at the pub? And what about Ray Pfeiffer? He might have had a motive to kill his wife. Did he have a motive to kill Tim?

I considered Jawbone's girlfriend — Zach's mother, Ilona. What light might she be able to shed on Jawbone's activities? Had she abetted him? Would she confess if a non-threat like me approached her?

"Yoo-hoo, Charlotte love, are you there?" Sylvie Bessette, my cousin's British ex-wife, appeared in the doorway. She had abandoned Matthew and the twins years ago, but had moved to Providence to rebuild the fractured relationships. Sylvie never failed to amaze me with her offbeat style choices. Today, she wore a snow-white fake fur over black stockings and black boots. If she'd dared to dye half of her ice-white hair back to its original black, she would have been the spitting image of Cruella de Vil, an evil character from Disney's *101 Dalmatians*.

"Oh, there you are." Sylvie wiggled her high-gloss fingernails. "I saw the shop was empty, and I started to worry, what with

Dottie Pfeiffer meeting an untimely death. I'm so glad to see you're alive."

"Me too," Rebecca whispered.

I swatted her.

"I have a quick order, if you don't mind," Sylvie continued. "I want to offer a cheese platter at today's event." She owned an upscale dress boutique and spa around the corner. She and her neighboring businesses were part of today's Lovers Trail festivities. "We don't want the people coming in for the lingerie show to go away hungry, do we?"

My grandmother had protested Sylvie's lingerie show decision, but Sylvie wouldn't budge. She swore that locals and tourists alike would be thrilled to have a sexy soiree to attend, not like those boring *do*'s that the other shops were offering. According to Sylvie, love required passion to light the flame.

"Come." Sylvie beckoned me with her forefinger.

Far be it from me to keep her waiting. I set aside my paperwork, threw on an apron, and met her by the cheese counter.

"Hard cheeses only. None of those gooey messes." She pointed to the Colston Bassett Stilton, imported from the UK.

"Good choice," I said. "It's smooth and

creamy with a mellow flavor. No acid bite."

"Of course it's delicious. It's from the area in England where I was born. What's this?" She pointed to the Cypress Grove Chevre Bermuda Triangle, and read the cheese flag out loud: " 'If you're feeling vulnerable, then definitely don't taste a morsel of this deliciousness. Truly, you will become a slave to its allure.' Are you saying it's divine?"

No one could put anything over on Sylvie. "Want a taste?" I asked. "It's tart and tangy with notes of pepper."

"No. Just wrap up a portion. And this?" She leaned closer to the glass case and wiggled a finger. "Read that one in the back to me. The one with the specks of red spice." Was her eyesight getting weak? She was pushing forty.

The door to the shop opened and Tyanne entered.

"C'mon, love, read," Sylvie ordered.

I obliged. " 'No Woman cheese: The perfect cheese if you need to spice up your life.' "

"Ooh. I like the sound of that one. What fun."

"Perhaps it's too spicy for you," Tyanne quipped.

Sylvie offered a sour look, but when she realized it was Tyanne speaking, the look vanished and she smiled. She actually liked Tyanne. I'd never heard her say a rude thing about her. As for me? She'd said plenty. But I was inured to her caustic charm. "Good morning, love. How are you holding up?"

Tyanne shrugged. "I'm keeping it together. I almost lost it at the weddings for the two non-local couples I put together at the last minute yesterday and today, but I didn't. I am woman; hear me *meow.*"

"I have just the thing at my shop if you do become a puffy-eyed mess," Sylvie said. "It's a detox cream. Icy cold when applied. You should try it. Complimentary."

"Perhaps I will."

"Come by the shop today. You too, Charlotte, if you can break free. Your love life could use a lingerie pick-me-up, if you know what I mean."

"No, Sylvie, I don't." Of course, I did. She was being insulting, inferring that Jordan and I weren't getting married because our relationship suffered in the sex department. It didn't. We were a great match. I'd never met a more attentive, loving, romantic man.

"But you called off the wedding, love."

Tyanne jumped in. "She didn't call it off. She's postponing."

I added, "We didn't think it was appropriate to get married at Jordan's farm within days of Timothy O'Shea's death. And now with Dottie —"

"About that." Sylvie ran a tongue along her lips. She peeked over her shoulder, as if looking for someone to be listening in. No one was. She swiveled back to us. "Councilwoman Bell was in my shop yesterday afternoon. That woman. She has no decorum."

This coming from the woman whose picture might accompany the definition of *no decorum* in a dictionary. Sylvie barged in wherever she wanted. She had crashed the taste-testing at the venue for Matthew and Meredith's wedding. She had arrived uninvited at Matthew and Meredith's rehearsal dinner. She invariably tried to horn in on an outing with the twins when it was clearly Matthew's, Meredith's, or my turn to have them. She was a good mother, frequently gushing over her *girlie girls,* but she defied logic when it came to social correctness.

"What did Belinda Bell do?" I said, knowing Sylvie wouldn't leave until she had imparted her bit of gossip.

Sylvie lowered her voice and said, "Gather around."

CHAPTER 20

Rebecca slipped up beside me at the cheese counter, eager to glean whatever gossip Sylvie might share.

"Belinda Bell was whispering with a few of her cronies," Sylvie said. "But I sidled close to listen in."

I would have expected no less. Listening in on another conversation had helped Sylvie discover a long lost treasure buried in the bowels of an old winery cellar in Providence.

"Bell was wearing a horrid perfume," Sylvie went on. "Cloying and cheap, like what teenagers douse themselves with. How ever does she hope to woo a man smelling like that?"

Did Councilwoman Bell want a man? Her husband had died ten years ago — heart attack. She'd raised her daughter on her own. Maybe, as Tyanne had suggested the other night, Belinda Bell was lonely now that her daughter had moved to Los Angeles and become a star. Perhaps she visited her daughter's room and sampled her fragrances. There was nothing wrong with that; it showed how much she loved her daughter.

"And don't get me started about the outfit Bell was wearing," Sylvie continued. "She certainly didn't purchase it at my store. Ruffles and more ruffles. Way too many for her pear-shaped frame. I could teach her a thing or two about taste. Her daughter, too. Did you see the photo spread of Aurora in the latest *People*? The girl looked positively deranged, dressed as she was in Goth black with a double-dose of black eye makeup. Whatever happened to the girl who looked like the morning goddess, her strawberry-blonde hair lustrous, her eyes wide with innocence? Talk about a disaster." Sylvie lowered her voice. "I think she might be doing —" She tapped her nose and sniffed to make her point.

I spanked the cheese counter. "Sylvie, what did the councilwoman say?"

"Oh, right-o. Bell said she wasn't in the least sorry that Dottie died."

Rebecca gasped. So did Tyanne.

"Well, perhaps she wasn't that blunt," Sylvie revised. "But she did say that she and all of Dottie's neighbors wouldn't miss the pastry shop."

I said, "Surrounding business owners didn't like Dottie?"

"She played that blasted rock-and-roll music at all hours of the night."

I remembered hearing a Rolling Stones song when I'd entered the shop. Had Dottie's penchant for loud music made someone — like Bell — snap? On the other hand, would a killer utter that kind of hateful statement so openly?

"By the way," Sylvie went on, "Bell sounded excited that she would be able to find a new tenant for the pastry shop."

I gaped. "She's the landlord?"

"Yes, and you remember, from personal experience, how mean landlords can be, don't you, Charlotte?"

I did my best to ignore the taunt, but it still stung. Our previous landlord, a bitter miserable man, was murdered nearly two years ago during the re-opening party for Fromagerie Bessette. Grandmère had become the leading suspect in his murder because she was found clutching the cheese knife that the killer had used to stab him. Our new landlord was Jordan, or rather Providence Arts and Creative Enterprises, the specially constructed acronym, or *back-*

229

ronym, using the letters of Jordan's last name: Pace.

I said, "That's a blast from my past that I'd soon enough forget."

"I'll bet you would." Sylvie snorted.

"What else did you learn from Councilwoman Bell?"

"This should really infuriate you. I heard that she and others are planning to oust your grandmother as mayor if she can't get the noise pollution under control."

"Not again," I said. The spiteful wife of our former landlord had tried to force my grandmother out of politics with lies and innuendoes. I thought back to my visit to the precinct the other day. Bell and her pals had been filing a complaint about noise. Were she and her posse going to ride roughshod over our fair town, demanding their way or the highway? Was murder an option if someone didn't comply?

Sylvie continued. "Maybe Belinda Bell is making a stink about noise simply because she wants to empty all her buildings of tenants so she can free up the rental space and raise the rent. I'd do that if I could get away with it, but all my tenants and neighbors are as quiet as church mice."

The door to the shop opened and Urso entered, hat tucked under his arm. "Good morning, ladies."

"Chief," I said. "Is it lunchtime already?" The wall clock read ten to noon. Time was speeding by.

He regarded the group. "What are you conspiring about?"

"Nothing," Sylvie said a trifle too quickly. She wasn't nearly as skilled at keeping secrets as Rebecca, Tyanne, and I, who a few months ago, at Rebecca's insistence, had formed The Snoop Club. Silly nonsense, and yet by sleuthing together, we had come up with clues that helped figure out who had killed a charming sommelier.

While I prepared a platter of cheeses for Sylvie's order, Rebecca tended to Urso's sandwich. None were made yet. She needed to concoct a fresh one: salami, mozzarella, and pepperoncinis. He'd asked to include the last item.

Rebecca teased him. "Hoping to score points with Delilah, chief? She's the only one in town who likes those pepper thingies."

Urso shot her a wry look. Like he would tell her anything about his personal life.

As Rebecca wrapped the sandwich, she informed Urso that Deputy O'Shea was cast in the play. "Don't worry. It's only a week's commitment."

"It'll do him good," Urso said.

"He —" Rebecca stopped herself. I could see in her eyes that she'd almost blabbed that her beau was investigating on his own. Had O'Shea learned anything? Was he tailing Jawbone? Might he get himself in trouble? Would he tell Urso if he discovered anything pertinent to the case?

Rebecca cleared her throat and beamed. "You'll come to the play, won't you, chief?"

"Wouldn't miss it. By the way, have you seen Devon this morning?"

"No, why?" Rebecca gulped — hard.

"He hasn't checked in at the precinct."

Sylvie waved her hand. "I saw him." She flounced toward the register to pay for her platter. "He was wandering outside Providence Pâtisserie. He seemed to be inspecting the crime scene tape. When he saw me eyeing him, he pretended like he was headed to All Booked Up down the street, but I think he was trying to decide whether to enter the pastry shop."

"Did you ban him from that investigation, too?" I asked Urso.

"I don't think he's ready for anything other than precinct work. He's emotionally raw."

"Maybe he would heal faster if he could

focus on another case. Did you get my messages?"

He nodded curtly.

"Do you think the two murders are related?"

"Not based on the theories you've offered. Cheese and a cleanup job? Thin."

I bobbed my head. He was right.

Rebecca handed Urso a bag with his sandwich tucked inside. "Do you want anything to drink? How about a bottle of wine for your dinner tonight?"

That made me think about the wine tasting I'd gone to with Jordan. "Chief, I meant to mention that I had a suspicion about Jawbone Jones again. I —"

Urso held up a hand to stop me. "I spoke to him about the altercation with Tim. He said he was arguing about a bill. He said Tim overcharged him for a beer."

"A beer?" I raised an eyebrow. "According to Violet Walden, Jawbone drinks rye. Too much rye."

Urso sighed and turned toward the door. I asked Rebecca to finish up with Sylvie and hurried around the register to Urso.

I tapped his forearm. "Hey, U-ey. Are you okay? You look pale and wrung out."

"Charlotte, there have been two —"

"Murders inside of a week. I know. What

is our town coming to?"

He didn't answer. He moved toward the door. How I ached for him. I'd never seen him so defeated. If he couldn't get these murders solved in a timely manner, would he give up on Providence? Would he change his mind and take the job his brother had offered on his campaign, after all?

Something on the street caught Urso's attention, and his whole demeanor changed. He drew tall, shoulders back; his eyes lit up with good humor. He sped out the door and headed across the street toward The Country Kitchen.

I peered out the window looking for what had fascinated him. Delilah stood on a ladder, changing out the letters on the sign above the diner. So far, it said: *Delicious food, made with . . .* I suspected *love* would finish the slogan. Paige Alpaugh and a pair of thirtysomething women that owned one of the children's stores in town scooted behind the ladder and entered the restaurant. Had one of them sparked Urso's interest? He was strutting like a man in love, which made me much less fearful that he would split town. Not yet, anyway.

CHAPTER 21

Monday evening was typically girls' night out. Occasionally my friends and I would attend a yoga class or a self-defense class. Most often, however, we wound up at Timothy O'Shea's Irish Pub and sipped beer and snacked on tasty appetizers while catching up, which was what we'd decided to do tonight. After I dropped Rags and Rocket back at the house, I headed to the pub. The moment I entered, I sensed the gloom. Whereas usually a trio performed boisterous Irish music, tonight a solo pianist — the same from the theater the other night — was playing a mournful "As Time Goes By." There were no sports programs airing on the TVs. No Cleveland Cavaliers basketball, no Columbus Blue Jackets hockey. The bar was only half full. The pair of Tim's brothers, who had come to town to run the pub to keep it afloat until the family decided what to do with it, stood behind the bar pouring drinks, but they didn't seem to have their hearts in their work. They didn't smile and chat with the customers like Tim had. They merely poured and moved on. It was hard to be charming when grieving.

Delilah had arrived at the pub early to make sure our table was secured. She was sitting on the far side of the booth, texting on her cell phone. Tyanne was there, as well. She looked blue. It didn't help that she was dressed in a drab blue shirt and matching scarf — a hip color in a magazine; not so good on a person in mourning.

I arrived at the booth, and Tyanne said, "Delilah ordered the mini-macaroni and cheese appetizer and some veggies with blue cheese dip."

I loved the mini-macs. The recipe included wine and a savory complement of spices.

"Oh, and she has some news." Tyanne's tone was flat and uninvolved.

"Are you okay?" I asked.

Tyanne looked at me blankly, then tears sprang to her eyes. "You know what? No. I'm not feeling so hot. I'm going to go home and crawl in bed." She scrambled off the bench.

I reached for her, but she pulled free.

"I'll be fine," she said. "Don't worry."

I did and I would continue to do so. I didn't have sisters. My girlfriends were my extended family. I hated that Tyanne was in pain. I wanted her to feel better. Fast. But what could I do? I slid in beside Delilah.

At the same time, a waitress appeared with a couple of beers. She placed them in front of Delilah and me, said she'd run a tab, and sauntered away.

Delilah set aside her cell phone and said, "How are *you* doing?"

"Better than Tyanne." I fingered the moisture on my glass of beer. "The love of my life is still alive."

Delilah offered a consoling smile. "Have you reset the wedding date?"

"Not yet."

"Why not?"

"He's deliberating a career change."

"He'll sell the farm?"

"Maybe."

Delilah took a sip of her beer. She licked the foam off her lip. "Where's Rebecca?"

"At rehearsal. She got the part in *Love Letters.* She performs it this Friday."

"I'd heard your grandmother was planning to do that. Daring. And where are Jacky and Freckles?"

"Freckles had another blogger moms meeting. I'm not sure about Jacky" — Jordan's sister — "but it looks like it's just you and me. So, spill. What's your news?"

She pushed her glass aside and leaned forward on both elbows. "I'm in love."

I grasped her forearms and squeezed. "About time you told me."

"You knew?"

"Jordan mentioned it. He heard from —" I waved a hand. "Never mind. Who's the lucky guy?"

"I can't say."

"What?" I squeaked and spanked her arms. "I'm your best friend. You'd better blab."

"I don't want to jinx it."

"Telling me won't —" I paused. "Aha! I get it. You're afraid I'm going to run to him and ask him how he feels about you. Do you know the answer?" I felt like we were back in high school talking about the boys in our English class. She'd had such a crush on a couple of them. She had liked Jerry because he was a real cutup in a Robin Williams way. She'd adored U-ey because he had a quick, incisive mind, and he could hold his own on the dance floor. She had swooned over Vic because of his Nordic good looks and his beautiful bold baritone. "C'mon, tell me. I promise I won't tell a soul, cross my heart" — I made the gesture

— "hope to die."

Delilah shook her head vehemently, but her eyes twinkled with delight. "We're taking it slowly."

Was everyone doing that nowadays? Violet had said the same thing. A fertility clock started to *ticktock* loudly in my mind.

"But I know it's forever this time," Delilah added.

"At least tell me this, is he someone I know?"

"Yes."

"Have you known him for a long time?"

"Yes."

"Is he tall, dark, and handsome, or short, light, and clever?"

"Yes."

"You!" I reached for her cell phone. "Who were you texting? Him?"

She nabbed it and clasped it with both hands.

"No fair," I said.

"Soon. Let me make sure we're working."

"You said it's for forever."

"For me. One day at a time. We reconnected in a magical way."

"Reconnected. Aha! That means you were a couple before."

"Not necessarily. We might have dated once." She grinned.

"Uh-uh." I wagged a finger. "You can't put one over on me. I'm an ace sleuth, or so my sweet assistant tells me. Do you know she actually tried to pitch me to U-ey to be a temporary deputy?"

"She didn't."

"Yep. He's shorthanded because Rodham's wife gave birth and Devon O'Shea is not functioning on all emotional cylinders. O'Shea is going to be acting in the play this week, too."

"I heard. Rebecca must be agog about that."

"She is. She's hoping the play will give Devon something to concentrate on other than his uncle's death."

"Hard to do, but one can hope." Delilah took a sip of beer. "Did Urso jump at the idea of you and him working together?"

"Hardly."

"Do you want to help?"

"That's a given." I couldn't stop reworking theories in my mind.

"I'll talk to him."

"Don't antagonize him."

"Don't worry. He's become quite partial to the diner's chicken potpie, packed with crisp veggies, a luscious sauce, and a butter-laden crust." She sniggered. "I'm not averse to withholding satisfaction. Pinky swear."

She held out her baby finger; I latched on. We squeezed then released. "Now, what do you know about Dottie's murder? I heard you found her." She shook her head. "You certainly have bad timing."

"Tell me about it."

"Or Fate is keeping you in the loop regarding murders around here because you're good at solving them."

I moaned. "Now you sound like your mother." Delilah's quixotic mother had shown up a few months ago, out of the blue. They'd been estranged for quite a long time. A believer in the mystical, her mother would have been all over the coincidence of me finding victims. *It's your karma,* she would have cried. She wouldn't have been able to tell me *why,* just that it *was.* I pressed the thought from my mind and recapped the scene at Providence Pâtisserie. "I can only come up with a few suspects at this time. Zach Mueller." I explained his possible motives. "And Belinda Bell, who clearly didn't like the noise that Dottie created at the pastry shop." I repeated Sylvie's account as well as the incident with Bell that I'd witnessed at the precinct.

"Why were you at the precinct?" Delilah asked.

"To speak to our illustrious chief of police."

"You see?" Delilah grinned. "You're already helping him."

"He told me to butt out."

"Forget him. Back to Belinda Bell. Is it possible, as the owner of the building, that she intends to clear out all the neighboring businesses so she can renew the leases at higher prices or even sell the building?"

"Sylvie suggested the same."

"Great minds. *Not.*" Delilah snorted. She didn't like Sylvie in the least.

Our appetizers arrived. I gobbled down the mini-macaroni and craved another. When had I last eaten? I took a sip of beer then said, "I've got this nagging suspicion that Dottie and Tim's murders are related." I explained the coincidence of Pace Hill Farm Double-cream Gouda being present at both scenes. "I mean, why choke Dottie with a pastry? A rag or towel would have done the same thing. And faster. I truly believe the pastry is significant."

"Not necessarily. What if Bell slipped down the alleyway behind that row of buildings? She stole into the kitchen. Dottie wouldn't have heard her with that music playing. Bell wasn't quite sure what she was going to do. She might have come in to rant at Dottie. But then she saw Dottie dancing around, like she did, probably lip-synching to some song while holding a spatula to her mouth — I've seen her do that."

"Me too."

"And Bell lost it. The first thing Bell spotted was the cheese Danish. She snatched it and ran at Dottie. Bell is nearly twice Dottie's size. She knocked her flat and crammed the pastry into her mouth. Dottie fought, but she wasn't strong enough."

I held up both hands. "Okay, I'll concede that the Gouda cheese might be coincidental."

Delilah took a sip of her beer. "You know, come to think of it, Bell has a lot of noise issues. She's complained to me about the music here. She loathes when the waitstaff sings and dances. Do you think she might have a hearing problem? Maybe it's painful when she hears loud noises."

"I wonder if Tim said he 'heard, no saw' something because he was trying to clue in Deputy O'Shea that Bell, who has a problem with noise, was the killer."

Delilah squinched her mouth and nose. "Then why not come right out and say it was Bell?"

"Because he was afraid that whoever he'd overheard would hear him."

"Ha! Not Bell, if our theory is correct. And why would Tim be so cryptic?"

Tim hadn't been cryptic; the cell phone reception had cut out. Even still, why hadn't he blurted out a name? Dang! One name could have solved everything.

Delilah said, "What would Bell have had against Tim?"

"Not only was she upset with the noise from the pub, but according to Dottie, Bell was also upset with the people wandering the streets drunk. A pub owner is responsible for the inebriated state of its clientele."

"Is Bell a teetotaler? Because if she is, why would she hang out with that Realtor that's a sot? You know the one I mean, with the beard" — she drew her fingers along her chin then waggled them above her head — "and the scruffy hair." She was describing Eddie Townsend, Bell's companion at the Bozzuto Winery. "They were in the diner the other night chowing down on turkey and vegetables, deep in conversation. Bell was stabbing the table with her fork to make each point."

"They're both members of the city council. Maybe —" I balked. "Maybe Townsend is one of the people who is going to join Bell's quest to oust my grandmother as mayor."

"Bell wouldn't dare."

"Yes, she would. Sylvie told me. Hey!" I jutted a finger in the air. "Maybe Tim heard Bell and Townsend plotting the uprising."

"And Bell went after him to silence him? Nah, I don't buy it. Would you kill someone to keep that kind of secret? I wouldn't. I mean, it's local politics. Big deal. And let's face it, Bell might be big and rather hippy, but I don't think she could have overpowered Tim. He was a scrapper." Delilah eyed her cell phone.

"What if Bell drugged Tim?" I said, reiterating Tyanne's theory. She'd seen Bell leaving the pharmacy with a veritable drugstore in hand. I paused. *A veritable drugstore.* "What if the drugs Bell was buying contained pseudoephedrine, used to make crystal meth?"

"Ew."

"Providence isn't immune."

Delilah frowned. "Do you hear yourself? You're constructing conspiracy theories out of thin air."

I laughed. "I'm being out-of-my-mind ridiculous, aren't I? The next thing you know —"

Someone rapped on the wooden back of our booth.

245

CHAPTER 22

"I thought it was you two." Violet poked her head around the pub's banquette and wiggled her fingers at Delilah and me. She looked almost pretty in tailored trousers and a snug sweater, her hair hanging loosely around her shoulders. "Hi, ladies." She left her booth, wineglass in hand, and slid into ours. "Mind if I join you?"

"Who are you with?" I thumbed toward the booth she'd been occupying.

"Me, myself, and I. Paige and the others left a while ago. We were having an Internet buzz class. I figure anything I can glean will help the B&B."

Hmm. I hadn't seen Paige or Violet's other friends exiting. Was Violet lying about having a meeting so she could tail me and find out what I was investigating? Okay, now I wasn't simply out-of-my-mind ridiculous; I was officially paranoid.

Violet hoisted her glass of bubbly-looking

wine. "I thought I'd finish my spritzer while writing down notes from the meeting." She brandished a spiral-bound booklet. If she was tailing me, she had gone to some length to establish a cover. "I couldn't help overhearing you talk about Belinda Bell."

Sure she could have. We were whispering. She had to have craned her ears to listen in.

"You know," Violet went on while running her finger along the collar of her sweater, "I saw Belinda when I left the pub the night Tim died. She was getting into that tank of a Chevy she drives. It looked like she was saying good-bye to some guy in a big, dark truck. I probably shouldn't make more of it than it was. I mean, Belinda's allowed to date, being a widow and all. Her husband, rest his soul, used to stay at my inn whenever they were separated." She tilted her head and *tsk*ed. "Don't look so shocked, Charlotte. People —"

"Was the truck gray?" I asked.

"Yeah. I think it was Jawbone Jones."

"It couldn't have been him. You saw him drive off."

"What if he came back?" Violet said.

"He didn't. He was at a jam session."

"Says who?"

"His band partner, Ilona Mueller."

Violet raised a skeptical eyebrow, not

believing a word.

"How do you know that, Charlotte?" Delilah cut in. I was surprised she was able to keep up with the conversation, seeing as she was repeatedly checking her text messages.

I said, "Urso mentioned it."

Delilah set her cell phone aside, facedown, and wagged a gleeful finger. "So he *is* consulting you."

"No, he's not."

Violet said, "Did you tell him Jawbone threatened Tim if he didn't sell the pub to him?"

"I did, but Urso said since a year or more had passed —"

"I still put my money on Jawbone having killed Tim." Violet shifted in her seat. "Here's why. If it was Jawbone in that truck — I'm just saying it could have been — and if there wasn't anything romantic going down between him and Belinda Bell, then why else would they meet? Zow! It came to me." She tapped her head. "What if Jawbone was bribing someone on the city council — okay, Bell — to ensure easier gun regulations? The county has been setting all sorts of restrictions. A gun shop owner must hate that." Violet glimpsed her watch and leaped to her feet. "Oh, sorry, I've gotta run. I have another appointment."

"What kind of appointment could you have at this time of night?" Delilah teased.

"It's with a client at the hotel," Violet said defensively. "He sells gym equipment."

"Uh-huh." Delilah smirked. "Hope you get a good, um, *workout.*"

Violet laughed; she sounded like an air conditioner on the fritz, with all the hissing coming through her nose. "Get your mind out of the gutter. See you."

She headed for the exit, and the front door opened. Ray Pfeiffer entered. He shuffled to the bar and perched on a stool. Violet swung by and patted him on the back, offering her condolences, I was pretty sure. Ray nodded his thanks, and Violet left.

Delilah leaned closer. "You know, seeing Violet and how trim she's gotten made me think of another angle regarding Belinda Bell. What if the scent of the food coming from Dottie's shop was driving Bell to distraction?"

"I'm not following."

"Bell is forever trying to lose weight. At the diner, she either orders the diet special or the protein platter. No sugar or fats for her. I couldn't even get her to try the grilled cheese competition's winning sandwich, even though everyone in town is ordering it. Pears, blue cheese, and bacon. The flavors melt together in a sassy way with just the right amount of bite." For years, Delilah had been vying to hold a Midwest grilled cheese competition at the diner. In January, her dream had become a reality. Over five hundred people had shown up to watch or participate.

"No sugar, no fats," I said more to myself than to Delilah while wondering whether Paige Alpaugh had a hand in the councilwoman's new health kick. Was Paige trying to convert everyone in town to her way of thinking? Could she have had anything to do with Dottie's death? A pastry had been crammed into Dottie's mouth. Was that symbolic? Paige's flyer read: *Sugar kills.* No subtlety there. And she was in the vicinity when Dottie was killed. Would she have had any reason to want Timothy O'Shea dead, too?

Heedless of my train of thought, Delilah continued. "Why does Belinda Bell even try to diet? Some people are born with a shape" — she outlined Bell's bottom-heavy figure — "that no diet can change."

Ray coughed . . . or was he crying? He sat hunched over his drink, the beer untouched. A serving of carrot sticks with dip also looked untouched.

I whispered, "Poor Ray."

"Yeah, poor guy. He looks pretty miserable." Delilah's cell phone beeped. She flipped it over again to look at the message.

My curiosity couldn't be curbed. I reached for the phone. She tucked it into her chest.

"C'mon, spill," I said. "Who's the lucky guy? Give me a peek."

"No. Talk to me about Ray. Has he lost weight?"

"He does look leaner."

"Should I make him a meal and have it delivered? Maybe he could do with a brioche or two."

The word *brioche* made me think of Dottie's brooch. I drummed the table. "Ray thinks Zach Mueller, the kid that worked at the pastry shop, might have killed Dottie to get his hands on an expensive heirloom. A brooch."

"Zach has an alibi."

"How do you know that?"

She grinned. "I have my sources."

"Did you ply Urso for answers?"

"Yes."

"What did you have to bribe him with, donuts?"

"Pie." She leaned forward. "He said Zach was talking on the phone to his girlfriend at the time of the murder."

I couldn't believe it. Had Zach taken his

cue right out of Jawbone Jones's weak-alibi playbook? "What is the girlfriend's name?" I asked.

"I'm not sure. I assume it's Belinda Bell's daughter."

"Aurora?"

"Bell only has one. Rumor is that Zach and Aurora were going to get married. However, out of the blue, Aurora went to Hollywood, got cast in that series — which didn't please her mother — and, well, the rest is history." Delilah's gaze turned inward. She had always wanted to be a star. She'd failed on Broadway. Was she regretting not having given Hollywood a chance? Her cell phone *ping*ed. She scanned the readout and her eyes lit up, and I realized I needn't worry about her wanderlust. Her current love would trump her ambition, for now. She typed a message into her phone, hit Send, and eyed me. "Something is bothering you. Talk to me."

"Doesn't Aurora live in Los Angeles?"

"Yes. Well, actually, in Studio City. That's an area in the valley."

I did the math regarding time differences. "That would mean Zach and she were talking around four A.M. her time, or earlier."

"Maybe she was awake because she had to be on the set."

"On Sunday? Wouldn't that be a day of rest for her, and if so, wouldn't she have wanted to sleep until noon? I've heard working on a television drama can be exhausting. Fourteen-plus hours a day." I shook my head. "Talking on the phone is a weak alibi."

"But if it holds up, then we're back to Councilwoman Bell and Jawbone being the best suspects, right?"

CHAPTER 23

First thing Tuesday morning, I popped the pets into my Escort and headed to the twenty-four-hour grocery store. I needed chard for the quiche I intended to make.

"I'm making a quick in-and-out stop," I assured Rocket and Rags as I rolled down the window an inch, despite the brisk temps, to let in fresh air. "Be good. No barking or hissing."

The grocery store was nearly empty, as I'd expected. There were only a few other early birds wandering the aisles. While perusing the vegetables, I spied Ray Pfeiffer on the other side of the display. He had a cart loaded with miniature apples and California clementine oranges, the little ones that resembled tangerines.

I swung my cart around next to his. "Hi, Ray."

He looked up and blinked hard, as if he didn't recognize me. Finally dawning recognition struck. "Charlotte. I'm sorry. I'm in another world."

"How are you?"

"Hanging on by a thread." He offered a weak smile.

"I'm so sorry that I —" That I *what*? Didn't get to the pastry shop in time to save Dottie? Didn't see the killer? Didn't do *something*? Could I have? I gestured toward his haul. "Having a party?"

"The memorial service is tomorrow. Family only. Dottie's sisters and my folks. Urso hasn't released the body yet, but —" He reddened. "That wasn't what you were asking me, was it?"

I shook my head.

"This stuff . . ." Ray patted the shopping cart handle. "I'm stocking up on good snacks for the kids that are coming to The Ice Castle this week. We've been so busy with all the events. I know it doesn't seem appropriate that I'm keeping the rink open, but it's not only Lovers Trail week, it's also President's Day and winter break week. A triple-whammy. We are busy beyond our dreams. Dottie . . ." He sighed. "She was so excited about how my business was building. Thanks to the publicity, families from all over are flocking to the arena. We even have a few Olympic hopefuls in the mix.

Did you hear that a coach from Chicago moved here recently? Dottie said Providence — the ice rink, her pastry shop, our town — owed it to families to keep kids happy."

I reached over to Ray and squeezed his arm. "She was a wonderful woman. She will be greatly missed."

His eyes grew hazy with tears.

By the time I'd settled the pets in the office, set the quiches in the oven, and was ready to open the shop, people had lined up outside. I glanced at Rebecca and asked if we had some special promotion going that I didn't know about.

"Yes." An impish look brightened her face. "It might have something to do with the window display I put together while you were baking."

"You rearranged what we had?"

"Busy hands."

I hurried to the window and peered in. Rebecca had expanded the display she'd created the other day. Now there were three baskets filled with fruit, jams, and crackers. To the arms of each basket, she'd attached more heart-shaped balloons. Beside the baskets, she had placed crystal flutes, bottles of sparkling wine, and a copy of the play *Love Letters* as well as other romantically themed books — most with bare-chested men. On the window, she had written in foam, "Now is the winter of our *content*," which was a play on Shakespeare's words. She'd added: *Come inside and enter to win the Cheese Shop Lovers Trail Basket, which includes two free tickets to* Love Letters. *Winner announced on Friday.*

First to enter the shop was Paige Alpaugh and three of her girlfriends, all of whom were foodie bloggers. Another dozen customers followed. I'd seen Paige earlier on the street chatting with Belinda Bell, and I'd wondered whether she was planning to join Bell in trying to oust my grandmother as mayor.

"I adore what you've done to the place, Charlotte." Paige strolled leisurely between the displays. "All the little cupids and arrows and the Mylar hearts over the archway leading to the wine annex." She sniggered. Was she being flippant?

Paige crossed to the register and took an entry form. She started filling out her name and address and encouraged her friends to do the same. When they finished and inserted their forms into the satin box Rebecca had created for entries, the foursome resumed roaming the shop. Two picked up containers and read the labels. One *tsk*ed.

Were they checking out the sugar content in each container? Would my shop make it into one of their blog posts, favorably or unfavorably? Did I care? Yes, ultimately, I did. Reputation mattered.

I crossed to Paige. "Is there anything I can help you with?"

"Oh, Charlotte. I feel so horrible for you."

"For me?"

"Finding Dottie like you did." She shook her head. "Such a tragedy. And to think I'd seen you only minutes before. If I'd detained you in the Village Green, perhaps you could have been spared the heartache. On the other hand . . ." Her voice trailed off.

"On the other hand, what?" I asked.

"Now, please understand" — Paige pursed her lips — "I'm not saying Dottie deserved to die, but she could be such a stickler. I'll bet she ticked off someone something fierce."

Her words caught me off guard. Was everyone in town talking about the motive for Dottie's murder? Wouldn't promoting Providence by chatting up the Lovers Trail events be a better way to spend one's time? *Heed your advice, Charlotte.*

"Did you know Dottie well?" I asked.

"We went to school together. Same graduating class."

Paige looked years younger than Dottie had. Perhaps her healthy glow was due to the paleo diet she was touting — otherwise known as the caveman diet. It consisted mainly of fish and grass-fed meats, vegetables, and grains. Nothing artificial. Not an ounce of sugar.

"We were at odds so often," Paige went on. "There I was, campaigning for better food in the cafeteria, while Dottie was touting more comfort food. She swore that comfort food made students study better. Can you imagine? Whenever I eat meatloaf or mashed potatoes, I feel like I'll sleep for days. Mind you, on occasion, I crave a good macaroni and cheese dish, like that five-cheese recipe you gave me. It was sinful. Truly sinful." She fanned her well-manicured hand to keep herself from swooning then giggled. "I'm prattling. I hate that. Don't you?" She wasn't asking me. She was asking her friends. Each nodded in agreement.

"About Dottie," I said, trying to propel the conversation forward. Paige must have had a reason to visit the shop, other than commiserating with me or inserting a form into the prize box.

"Yes, back to Dottie," Paige went on. "She said comfort food made people feel good, and when a person felt good, well, they could be successful. I emphatically disagreed. Denial of body is good for the soul and can lead to inner purity."

I shifted feet, not understanding why Paige was, as she'd put it, prattling. Did she want me to know the gossip? Was she feeding me information so I could help or hinder the investigation? Frustrated and ready to move on, I cocked a hip. "Paige, get real."

She widened her eyes, the epitome of innocence. "Whatever do you mean?"

"Why are you telling me all about Dottie? You obviously didn't like her."

"No, no, no. That's not true." Paige wagged a finger. "I did like Dottie. She had pluck. Right, girls?"

Her friends bobbed their heads in agreement.

"Dottie danced to the beat of her own drummer. That's something I tell my daughters to do all the time: *March to a different drummer.* I think sometimes Dottie was so willful because she didn't have kids. You know, without kids, you can become quite selfish of your time and your efforts. No sacrifices required. Motherhood is a challenge. Mind you, Dottie wanted kids, but when she miscarried —"

"She lost a baby?" I said. Dottie had never mentioned that. Why would she? I hadn't known her intimately, only professionally.

"Yes. It was tragic. Obviously you didn't know." Paige shook her head. "Ray and Dottie were *the* couple during high school. So perfect for each other. They married two years after they graduated. First, however, Ray went off to get a business degree. He had to have some smarts to run that skating rink of his. Now it's a cash cow. Runs year-round. It's a good place for kids to hang out. All the moms know. Missy, here" — she thumbed toward a beaming friend — "writes about all the terrific places in Providence and Holmes County where families can frolic. Isn't The Ice Castle one of the in places?"

Missy, if that was really her name and not meant to be a put-down, nodded.

I said, "Back to Dottie losing the baby."

Paige's mouth thinned; her eyes glistened with tears. "It was so sad. Two years into their marriage, Dottie got pregnant, but she couldn't carry the baby past the first trimester. She never got pregnant again. At least, not that I know of. For a while, Ray blamed her because she had too much fat in her diet, but he backed off riding her about what she ate. He loved her and I think he realized some people weren't meant to have children. Dottie learned to live with it. She basically *adopted* all the kids in town. That's why she gave free treats at the shop. That's why she started that fund. And that's why she hired people like that ne'er-do-well Zach Mueller."

Apparently Paige didn't like Zach any more than Violet did.

"Dottie believed in giving people second chances. That Zach." She spit out his name. "He had a couple of run-ins with the law. Petty thefts."

So Ray hadn't lied about Zach being a thief.

"If Dottie was so good to Zach," I said, "then why would he kill her?"

"That does beg the question, doesn't it?"

Paige looked at her friends triumphantly, as if her mission for coming into the shop — to tell me about Dottie's failed pregnancy and Zach Mueller's thieving life — was complete. Was I reading more into her visit than I should?

"Ray believes Zach killed Dottie to steal a piece of jewelry," I said, not revealing anything that wasn't public knowledge. Ray had freely shared his opinion with a local reporter.

"I heard that, too," Paige said. "Do you

happen to know Zach's alibi?"

"Why would I —"

"Because, Charlotte" — Paige snorted — "you know everything."

My cheeks warmed with embarrassment. "He claims he was talking to his girlfriend."

"At seven A.M.? *Pfft,*" Paige said dismissively. "Oh my, the time." She didn't look at her watch or the clock behind the cheese counter. She was done sharing her tips and theories. She strode to the cheese counter and peered into the case. "I'd like to buy some of those Bijou cheeses."

"Good choice." In French, *bijou* means jewel. The cheeses she wanted were little rounds of tangy goat's milk. Lovely to look at on a platter, easily downed in a few bites.

"And a pound of your best Cheddar."

At least she wasn't rude enough to enter the shop, gossip about Dottie — who could no longer defend herself — and split without making a purchase. Her girlfriends also made purchases. And then they left.

While Rebecca and I tended to the other customers — we put together multiple orders of Gouda and Cheddar — I thought about Paige's response minutes ago, which was pretty much what I'd said to Delilah. Zach Mueller's alibi — talking to his girlfriend at seven A.M. — seemed mighty

263

early for a chitchat. Was Zach lying? Had he really talked to Aurora Bell? Would Urso fill me in?

The door to the shop swung open. Jordan entered carrying a fistful of daisies. My spirit lifted at the sight of him. I don't think I will ever get tired of seeing his face. The easy grin, the twinkle in his eye.

He met me by the register and said, "Boy, are you busy." He looked at the crowd. "Is there a sale that I don't know about?"

"You must not have seen Rebecca's window display." I explained the giveaway. "Put your name in to win."

He slung an arm around my waist. "I've already won. How about you take off from work?"

"Now?"

"We could use some one-on-one time, don't you think?"

"We had some Sunday."

"And now it's Tuesday. We're supposed to be on our honeymoon." He clandestinely ran a finger along my arm. "I was thinking, since we're still in town, that we should make your grandmother happy by enjoying some of the special events. The Ice Castle is having a twofer today. Two people skate for the price of one."

"I can't." I gestured to the customers.

"And later I'm attending the event at All Booked Up. Octavia is sponsoring the Lovers Lane readings. I don't suppose you'd like to join me."

He wrinkled his nose.

I smiled. "I know. Not your cuppa. But I promised Octavia I'd be there. I can't renege."

Rebecca sidled up to me. "Who's coming in to help me out?"

"I arranged for Pépère to assist. He's feeling useless. Grandmère doesn't need him at the theater because of the minimalist sets."

Jordan ran his hand down my back. "How about going skating tomorrow, then?"

"Not tomorrow," I said. "There's too much to do for the Lovers Trail event."

Jordan pecked me on the cheek. "You work too hard." He beckoned Rebecca. "Do you think you could hold down the fort during the day on Thursday?"

"Thursday?" I squeaked. "But that's the event day."

"Not until evening. If you're not ready by that morning, you're not going to be ready." He whispered to me, "Until then." He dropped something into my apron pocket and left.

I couldn't wait to see what he'd written. It wouldn't be poetry, but it would be sincere.

265

However, I would have to wait, because Delilah raced right past Jordan into the shop and made a beeline for me. She was only wearing her diner uniform, no coat or sweater. Her face was flushed. "You won't believe what happened."

CHAPTER 24

Delilah clasped my hand and pulled me toward the exit at the rear of the shop.

"Are you crazy running out without a jacket?" I lifted my parka off the coatrack and thrust it into her hands.

"I'll survive." She draped it over her shoulders. "I couldn't wait to tell you. You won't believe it. Belinda Bell's daughter called me."

"Aurora? Called *you*?"

"Me." Delilah swooped a hand through her wild curls.

"How did she get your number?"

"She phoned the diner."

"What did she want to talk about?"

"She asked if Zach Mueller was all right and whether his alibi held up. She swears Zach is innocent, which I assume means she was talking to him at the time."

"Why did she contact you?"

Delilah grinned. "She said we were

kindred spirits, both of us being actresses."

"Did she specifically say that he called her that morning?"

"Not in so many words."

"Either she did or didn't."

Delilah shrugged.

"I'll take that as a *no,* she didn't." I cocked my head. "Calling you is weird. Why would she do that?"

Delilah twirled a curl around her finger. "Because I'm cute?"

I frowned. "What if Zach put her up to this? Maybe he counted on you coming to me, and he's betting that I'll go to Urso to establish his alibi."

"Does that mean Zach is guilty?"

"It sure doesn't make him look innocent."

I dialed Urso and left him a message, but I didn't go to the precinct. There was too much to do at the shop. A few hours later, I went to All Booked Up, one of my favorite stores. Octavia hadn't simply lodged books on shelves and that was that. She had given each aisle a theme. Cutouts of Harry Potter and fairies hovered above the YA section. Magnifying glasses and Sherlock-style hats adorned the mystery area. Octavia wanted to stir one's senses. Reading, to her, was the lifeblood of imagination.

"Yoo-hoo, girlfriend, over here." Octavia waved. Her light brown skin glistened with health. Her eyes twinkled with vibrancy.

"Nice outfit," I said.

Octavia often dressed up in clothing that complemented whatever theme she had going on at the bookstore. This afternoon, she wore a saucy outfit that hugged her voluptuous frame. She had asked all who attended the tea to wear a sexy, sensual costume, as well. She assessed me with a frown. "Ahem. Who hasn't dressed for the occasion?"

"Guilty as charged." My wardrobe consisted of a pair of slimming trousers and snug sweater. That was my limit when it came to dressing sexily during the daytime. "Sorry, but I'm still on the clock."

Pop!

Startled, I whipped around to see what had happened. One of the waiters had opened a bottle of sparkling wine. A group of women *ooh*ed as he poured flutes for each of them. So much for a sober tea.

"What a ton of people," I said.

"Everyone likes to have fun." Octavia pushed her corn-rowed braids over her shoulder. "Lots of people have volunteered to read poems. Do you want to?"

I faltered. "No thanks."

"I'm sorry. I'm not being sensitive to your plight."

"No, I'm not bowing out because Jordan and I aren't getting married. I'm just not up to it."

"Of course." Octavia petted my shoulder. "You've had quite a week, haven't you? First Tim and then Dottie." She clucked her tongue. "I don't think I will ever understand why evil exists. I don't think others will, either. I've had such a run on spiritual books this week. I would imagine folks in our fair town are praying more than they used to. It's hard to make sense of one murder, let alone two. My last memory of Dottie . . . rest her soul. Last week, she —" Octavia pressed her lips together. "No, I shouldn't speak ill of the dead."

"What happened?"

Octavia curled her hand around my elbow and led me to the bay window. We looked north toward Providence Pâtisserie. "I remember seeing her outside the doorway. She was with her assistant."

"Zach Mueller."

"Nice boy. Quite a reader. He loves Donald Westlake's Dortmunder series. Odd, I know. It's way too mature a series for him, but readers come in all sizes. He loves biographies, too, especially the ones about

Hollywood stars."

Poring over biographies about stars made sense, especially if Zach hoped to understand why Aurora had left him to pursue her career, but his interest in the Westlake books intrigued me. The Dortmunder books were humorous tales that revolved around an offbeat gang of thieves. Did reading those capers inspire Zach to steal things like, say, an expensive brooch? Did that minor clue connect Zach to the murder?

"Dottie was lighting into the boy." Octavia mimed the event. "Her arms were flailing. At one point, Dottie aimed a finger at Zach. He defended himself by batting her hand away."

"Did you hear what she was saying?"

"No, but my word, it wasn't a happy moment. He stormed off, feet stomping the pavement."

"Did you ask Dottie later?"

"How could I? I wouldn't want someone nosing into my business. If I have an argument, I have a reason. I don't lose my temper unprovoked. I would imagine Zach had done something wrong."

Like steal from her? I wondered. Did Dottie catch him taking money from the till?

Octavia released my arm and folded her hands in front of her. "I knew Dottie well. She adored her clientele. Just like you, she had a talent for knowing who preferred what. She was a magician when it came to luring people into the shop. She would stand on the sidewalk with a tray of goodies. Why, she even tried to cajole Paige Alpaugh into becoming a customer. Can you imagine? Miss No-Sugar-Ever-Touches-These-Lips!" Octavia chortled. "Fake lips, by the way. So much for au naturel."

I'd thought the same thing about Paige. I assumed her full lips were a result of injections. I wasn't sure why she had the work done. She'd had a pretty mouth before. My grandmother would say that some people never felt comfortable in their own skin.

I said, "Did you ever see Dottie and Belinda have an argument?"

"Never. Belinda wouldn't go near that place. She'd pass by, peering with longing into the window, holding her hands in check as if, were she to release them, she might be forced to go inside and buy something."

Delilah said Belinda Bell had passed on the opportunity to taste some of the most scrumptious, fattening foods at the diner — the grilled-cheese-competition-winning combination, for instance. Was the woman truly on a diet? Would she have killed Dottie because she was angry that Dottie's pastries were so tempting?

I said, "Dottie was Belinda's tenant, correct?"

"Indeed. I'm her tenant, too."

"Is she a fair landlord?"

"It depends on your definition of fair. Belinda doesn't make it easy. For example, we never meet at my store to talk business. That's not the proper way to conduct a transaction, according to her. One must meet on one's own turf."

"You meet at Memory Lane Collectibles?"

"Heavens no!" Octavia let loose with a belly laugh. "When it comes time to discuss the lease, each of us in the neighborhood are summoned to The Country Kitchen."

"Why there?"

"Belinda might avoid sweets, but she absolutely *must* have her caffeine. She threatens that if I'm a minute late, she'll raise the rent." Octavia shrugged. "She's a blowhard, but what can I do? I'm not about to give up this prime spot. Location, location, location. Your previous landlord was equally demanding, if I recall."

Yet again, I was forced to remember that horrible time. *Let the past remain in the past.*

I said, "I heard Belinda didn't like the

music Dottie played."

"Belinda can be a stuffed shirt at times. Dottie's music was fun. Sure, I prefer classical, but an occasional Stones tune lightens the heart. Say, why are you so curious about —" Octavia cut me a quick look. "Oh-oh-oh." She moved her head right and left like an Egyptian goddess, a move I could never master no matter how many times as a teen I'd tried in front of a mirror. "I see those tiny gray cells at work." Octavia and I had often discussed Agatha Christie works, particularly the Poirot series. "Talk to me, girlfriend."

"I've also heard that Belinda expressed her loathing for Dottie openly. Sylvie overheard her."

"Sylvie," Octavia scoffed. There weren't many fans of my cousin's ex-wife. "So what were you thinking?"

"If Belinda wouldn't enter Providence Pâtisserie — or perhaps she didn't deign to be seen entering — if she'd had a beef with Dottie, she might have stolen down the alley behind."

"Possibly."

"She would have had easy access, seeing as her collectibles shop is next door. Dottie wouldn't have heard Belinda enter over the music. Belinda was much larger than Dottie.

She could have overpowered her."

Octavia's mouth formed into an O. "No, you can't think Belinda killed Dottie. She wouldn't. I mean, she's acerbic, true, but she's a huge proponent of literacy and the arts —"

"But not music." Granted, my new theory wouldn't tie Dottie and Tim's murders together. Because Bell wasn't a sweets-eater, she most likely wouldn't have known that the pastry she'd stuffed into Dottie's mouth was filled with Jordan's specialty Gouda, so the cheese link would be a bust. But solving one murder would free up Urso to pursue the other. "Do you happen to know why Belinda is always complaining about noise in town?"

"I don't. She's never griped to me. Of course, the bookshop and the library are two of the quietest places in town." Octavia scanned the growing crowd of poetry attendees. "I'm sorry, Charlotte. I've got to get this party started. I know you'll figure it out. I have faith in that overactive brain of yours." She pecked me on the cheek and left me staring up the street.

"I have an opinion," a woman said.

CHAPTER 25

Prudence Hart joined me by the bookshop window. She was dressed in a rose-colored sweater dress, the prettiest I'd ever seen her wear. It fit her ultra-thin form nicely. She had draped a softer rose-colored infinity scarf around her neck, and she had donned makeup, including a glossy dress-matching lipstick. Her cheeks looked flushed with what I could only call happiness. I checked out the nearby men, searching for someone that might have stirred this kind of contentment in grumpy old Prudence. The silver-haired owner of the jewelry shop that was located next to her boutique looked quite dashing in a gray suit. And he was a bachelor.

"Did you hear me, Charlotte?" Prudence said.

The snippy way she addressed me zinged me back to reality. *A zebra can't change its stripes,* I mused. "An opinion on what?" I asked, bracing myself for another attack on my grandmother's performance as mayor or a critique of some aspect of The Cheese Shop. Perhaps the window display was too garish or the giveaway basket too crude. Prudence always had an opinion — rarely kind.

"I believe Belinda Bell *should* be on your suspect list." Prudence strolled to the buffet table, which was laden with cookies, mini-scones, and homemade candies, beautifully set on tiered china. I followed. Prudence took one of the goat cheese sugar cookies and wiggled a finger, bidding me to do the same. The cookie tasted like one I make using my grandmother's recipe. Tangy with a nice kick.

"Don't deny it," Prudence said. "I know you have a suspect list. You always do."

I nearly fell backward I was so stunned by her assertion. When I found my voice, I said, "Aren't you and Belinda Bell friends?"

"Just because we're friends doesn't mean I don't feel the truth is important. By the way, Belinda has a problem with her hearing. She suffers from tinnitus. Loud noises can disturb someone with an ear condition."

Apparently, Prudence didn't suffer from any hearing loss. How much of my conversation with Octavia had she overheard?

I said, "I knew a boy back in college, a tuba player in the marching band, who developed tinnitus. Poor guy had to hang up his horn."

"That's exactly what happened to Belinda, though she's loath to admit it. Back in college — we both went to OSU —"

"So did I. Go Buckeyes!" I grinned. "Look at that, Prudence. We have something in common."

"Of course we do," she said, oblivious to the fact that we'd never had anything in common before. She didn't like cheese; I didn't like to purchase overly expensive, froufrou dresses. "We're both savvy businesswomen."

Ah, yes, there was that.

" 'Blest as the immortal gods is he,' " a woman began, reading from a blue bound book. " 'The youth who fondly sits by thee.' " She had a booming voice with no hint of nuance for the material.

Prudence nudged me away from the buffet toward the reading corner, which was packed with a collection of overstuffed chairs. "Belinda played trumpet in the college band. About two years ago, her hearing started to go haywire. Constant ringing and hissing, she told me. She tried treatments; nothing worked. Needless to say, she gets

278

very irritated by the way people turn up the volume on everything. It makes her wild with fury."

"Wild enough to suffocate Dottie Pfeiffer?"

Prudence peeked over her shoulder at the debonair owner of the jewelry store. "On that, I do not have an opinion." She started to move away.

I gripped her forearm. "Wait. Let me ask you one more thing. Is Belinda dating someone? She was seen meeting up with a man who owns a dark-colored truck the other night, outside the pub."

Prudence chortled. "She was probably conferring with Eddie Townsend."

"The Realtor who —" I mimed *drinks too much.*

"The same. He drives a truck. A rather large one. But they certainly aren't dating."

I thought back to when Violet horned in on my conversation with Delilah. Violet hinted that Jawbone Jones might have returned to the pub, that he might have lied about jamming with his band. Had Urso nailed down that alibi?

"Is Belinda seeing Jawbone Jones?" I asked.

"Lord, no! Why would you think that? He and she are entirely different. They have none of the same sensibilities. Not to mention, he has a girlfriend, who happens to be his blues partner. I doubt he'd step out on her. He —"

"Blues? I heard that Jawbone played heavy metal rock." Actually, that wasn't true. Rebecca assumed he played heavy metal, which fed into my theory, because the biker jacket that Ilona Mueller wore featured rock band names.

"No, he plays the blues, and rather well."

Okay, I was feeling like I'd been sucked into a tornado. Prudence's revelations were whipping me around with force. She had an opinion on blues, and it was favorable? I'd imagined she was solely a Stravinsky aficionado. I happened to love the blues: B.B. King, Muddy Waters.

Prudence continued. "His partner —"

"Ilona Mueller."

"Right. She has a side business."

"Selling illegal guns?"

Prudence gawped at me. "No. Wherever do you get these crazy notions? Why would you think that?"

Because I was atypically cynical at the moment.

"She makes soap," Prudence said. "With the yummiest smells. She sells them at the farmers' market."

Knock me silly. Prudence went to the farmers' market?

"I've encouraged her to open a real shop," Prudence went on, "but she's not interested. Music is her life. Oh, listen —" She wiggled a finger toward the current speaker. "It's one of Shakespeare's sonnets." She recited along with the speaker: " '. . . that in the autumn of my years has grown, a secret fern, a violet in the grass, a final leaf where all the rest are gone.' " Prudence pressed a hand to her chest. "I love that poem. I must go."

"Prudence, wait. One last thing. On a personal note. Is it true that Councilwoman Bell wants to oust my grandmother from her position as mayor?"

Prudence pursed her lips.

"Please tell me," I urged.

"Yes, it's true."

"Why? You know my grandmother has made the town safer and the economy stronger."

"Bell's cronies don't like how many events the town is holding this year. They think your grandmother has gone overboard. They want the town to be calmer. Less open to tourists."

"Less friendly."

"Less riffraff."

There it was; the word Prudence used that I hated, the word that bonded her to Bell and the others. *Riffraff. Commoners. Not good enough for us.* Well, Prudence — all of them — were wrong. It was too bad, because during our momentary encounter, I'd almost started to like Prudence.

She looked down her narrow nose, her beady eyes as judgmental as ever. "By the way, Charlotte, FYI, you can't save everyone. You're not Wonder Woman."

Maybe not, but I still had the cape from the time I'd worn it for Halloween at the age of seven. I'd stowed it in the hope chest with my parents' mementoes. Perhaps if I draped it over me tonight when I slept, I would be magically infused with her superpowers. Perhaps I would be able to divine whether Jawbone Jones or Belinda Bell or Zach Mueller . . .

I paused. Zach was the lone connection between all the suspects. His mother was dating Jawbone. His girlfriend was Belinda Bell's daughter. He'd worked for Dottie. I'd seen him racing in the opposite direction from Jordan's farm on the night Tim was murdered. Was he the killer?

CHAPTER 26

Upon leaving the bookstore, a cool breeze kicked up. I shuddered and buttoned my coat while glancing along the street at the pâtisserie, wishing it were open and wishing even more that Dottie was alive and I could slip inside and have a cup of coffee. We would chat about her latest pastry creation. A recent one that had surprised me was a muffin she'd made with winter squash and brown sugar. True to Dottie's claim, it had been delicious and savory.

Feeling the need to see inside the shop one more time, I hurried north and peered through the window. The display was a beautiful presentation of crystal plates filled with pastries, muffins, and cakes. Tulips that still looked fresh stood in crystal vases. All rested atop a luxurious drape of red satin. Light from spotlights attached to the rim of the window — the lighting system must have been on a timer — made the display glisten. I eyed the counter. Sweets still rested in the trays in the glass case. Loaves of bread jutted from wicker baskets behind the counter. I wondered whether Ray intended to clear out the food before it spoiled. It would be his responsibility, wouldn't it? Would he be open to the suggestion of giving the food to needy families in Providence?

I gazed toward the kitchen. Was it only two days ago that I had passed through that door and found Dottie dead? Had Zach killed her? A chill gripped my insides. If only —

The door to the shop next door opened. Councilwoman Bell was entering Memory Lane Collectibles. I hadn't heard her approach. She huddled forward as if to block the cold and closed the door with a snap. For a moment, I wondered whether Urso had questioned her in relation to Dottie's death. Did he know that Bell was Dottie's landlord? Did he know how much she complained about noise?

Courage welling within me — remembering my Wonder Woman cape had something to do with my pluck — I headed to Memory Lane. I didn't have to return to The Cheese Shop for another fifteen minutes. I had time to shop for a curio for my lover, right?

Shoulders squared and head held high, I strolled into the shop. "Good afternoon, Mrs. Bell."

She had removed her coat and scarf and had hung them on a handsome antique oak coatrack. She spun around, wielding a feather duster like a sword. "Charlotte, you startled me."

"You're open, aren't you?" I gestured toward the *Open* sign on the door. At that moment, a gentleman entered. I breathed easier knowing we had company.

"Yes, it's, well . . . with Dottie's murder, I'm somewhat breathless to be in the shop by myself."

Did her fear indicate she was innocent, or was she simply acting?

While the other customer browsed in the front of the store, I drew nearer to Bell. I detected an overly sweet, fruity scent. Was it the perfume that Sylvie had said was so horrific? "How's your daughter?" I asked.

"Thriving in Los Angeles."

"Do you miss her?"

"More than you know. The house is empty; the silence, unbearable."

Perhaps in addition to Bell's hearing condition, loneliness was the reason noise irritated her so much; she lived in a quiet home now, and noise of any sort reminded her of how much she missed her ebullient daughter.

I dragged my fingers over the various antique pieces. Every item was set out to make one feel at home: lamps atop desks, quilts on quilt racks, candelabras on top of dining sets. A baker's rack held kitchen items like saltshakers and peppermills, as well as copper pots, molds, and utensils. Tucked in a glass-topped case by the cash register were smaller treasures, such as tooled cigarette cases, letter openers, hunting knives, and hair combs.

A second glass-topped case, fully dedicated to jewelry, stood against the wall behind the register.

Bell moved between the two cases, dusting the glass. "If you see anything you like, let me know."

Before I knew it, I found myself eyeing the jewelry case to see if the brooch Ray had described to me was within. I didn't spy anything that resembled a cluster of jewels in the shape of a flower, but did I really expect to? If the councilwoman had killed Dottie and stolen the piece, she would have been a fool to set it out at this juncture, and Zach would have been equally reckless to have sold it to a local dealer.

However, something else caught my eye.

At the top of the trash bin behind the counter was a wadded-up, pale pink pastry bag out of which protruded half a pastry; it looked strikingly similar to the one the killer had stuffed into Dottie's mouth. Both Delilah and Octavia claimed that Bell would have nothing to do with eating pastries.

"What are you staring at?" Bell demanded.

I pivoted. When I saw that she had opened the glass top and had started to dust the knives and letter openers within the case, a clot of fear crept up my throat. I forced it back down. The gentleman customer was still in the shop. Bell wouldn't attack me with a witness nearby, would she? Besides, although I might be shorter and slighter than her, I am quick, and I would have no compunctions about using one of the items in the store to defend myself. A peppermill or an old-fashioned iron meat grinder would do the trick.

Bell gazed in the direction I had been looking . . . *staring.*

I cleared my throat. "Why do you have a pastry in the wastebasket?" I asked. "I heard you don't eat pastries."

"I don't."

"Then why is it there?"

Bell looked at me as if I was nuts. "Because a customer brought it into the store. She was finished and tossed it out. What's the big deal?"

"The pastry shop has been closed since Sunday."

"And I haven't opened this place since Saturday. I'm only open a few days a week. I've got too much on my plate otherwise. I guess I should have emptied the trash, for fear of ants, but it's cold and ants —" She tilted her head and regarded me with disdain. "Why are you really here, Charlotte?"

"I want a curio for Jordan. A money clip." I indicated an item in the treasure case. Beside the cigarette holder was a lovely gold-plated clip. A tag read twenty-five dollars.

Belinda fetched it and handed it to me. "Now, tell me the truth. Why are you here?"

I met her gaze. "I'm curious."

"So I've heard." Her tone was blatantly snide. Something like dawning recognition spread across her face. "You couldn't possibly think that I —" She gasped. "You do. You think I had something to do with Dottie's death."

"You didn't like the noise coming from her shop. You filed a formal complaint."

"I will complain, but I would never murder."

"You wanted to raise her rent."

"I repeat: I would never murder. Not for money. Not for any reason. We have the law to contend with such things."

"Why do you ask your renters to meet at The Country Kitchen?"

"Because the food is delicious and the coffee is excellent," Bell said. "I happen to like a strong brew. Caffeine is good for you. Did you know that it increases the neuronal firing in the brain and helps release other neurotransmitters?"

"Neurotransmitters?"

"Like dopamine."

"Are you ill?"

"Hardly. But I can always use something that benefits my reaction time, my memory, and my cognitive function. Can't you?"

I did like a cup of coffee or tea each morning.

"Not everyone gets the shakes from caffeine." Bell held out her hand. Steady as a rock. She smiled tightly. "Did you have any other questions for me?"

"Where were you Sunday morning?"

"Here."

"You said you've been closed since Saturday."

"I come in when it's quiet to repair things. I was fixing a teapot." She aimed a finger at a Haviland Rose teapot that my neighbor, who collected such items, would give her eyeteeth for.

"So you were alone."

Bell jammed her hands onto her ample hips. "Yes."

"Did you hear any screams? Any thuds?"

"How would I have, with that raucous Rolling Stones music playing?"

I again wondered whether Dottie and Tim's deaths were related. "Where were you the night Timothy O'Shea was murdered?"

"Tell me, Charlotte, when did you become an investigator? Oh, that's right, you're not. If you'd like to become one, I know a few who could give you tips to getting your license. But, honestly, don't you have enough to keep you occupied with your business?"

The sarcasm in her tone was meant to throw me off, but it didn't. I stretched my neck and pressed on. "Where were you?"

Bell's nostrils flared. "What day did Tim die?"

"Thursday night." The night of my party. The night my future with Jordan had changed. We would fix it; we would set a date; all would be right with the world. Soon. "Well?" I asked.

Bell looked upward, as if searching for an

answer. "I was meeting with my Realtor."

"Eddie Townsend."

"Yes. For almost two hours."

"In the parking lot outside the pub?"

"Who —" She hesitated. "Someone saw us, I imagine. Oh, how tongues wag. No, we didn't meet outside or inside the pub. I'll have you know that I never go into that place. We met elsewhere. I was dropping Eddie off at his truck."

Her testimony removed Jawbone Jones from the equation.

"Will Townsend corroborate that?" I asked.

"What business is it of yours? You can't possibly think . . ." Bell ground her teeth together. "Just because I was in the vicinity of the pub doesn't make me —" She hissed air out her nose. "I thought Zach Mueller was the main suspect in Dottie's murder."

"I don't think Chief Urso has made a definitive call yet. Your daughter Aurora —"

"What about my daughter?"

"She corroborated Zach's alibi." Okay, she hadn't really, but why else would she have called Delilah?

Bell lasered me with a glare. "What alibi?"

"Zach said he was chatting with his girlfriend on the phone at the time Dottie was killed."

291

"It certainly wasn't Aurora. They are no longer an item."

I shrugged. "You might want to talk to Chief Urso."

Bell drew taller. "If *he* would like to speak to me, he may do so himself. In the meantime, I'd like you to leave. You are no longer welcome in my shop." She held out her hand for the money clip and gestured toward the door. "When you contact the chief, which I know you will, tell him that I have nothing to hide."

CHAPTER 27

When I returned to Fromagerie Bessette, it was almost dusk. I loved the look of the shop in the glow of amber lights. Pépère was working behind the counter. Keeping busy agreed with him. His eyes were bright, his cheeks rosy. He was almost giddy with joy.

"Chérie." He welcomed me into a hug. "Rebecca is in the wine annex, setting up decorations for Thursday. She has many good ideas, this girl." He tapped his temple. "She's put signs on each of the bistro tables with cheese and wine pairings offering a deal: buy two bottles of wine and get a quarter-pound of cheese free. Brilliant. We should have many lovers taking advantage of that kind of offer, *non*? They will coo contentedly." He linked his arm with mine and nuzzled my cheek. "How are you, *ma petite-fille*? You have not asked your grand-mère or I for advice. You have not even

requested a shoulder to cry upon."

"No tears required, Pépère. Jordan and I are still getting married. We are setting a date in May." At this juncture, I figured we'd better pick a specific date so everyone would stop asking. I excused myself and said, "I need to call him."

I escaped to the office and dialed. I reached Jordan's voice mail and left a message. Then I called U-ey. He had yet to call me back about my previous message. If he answered, would he be teed off that I was contacting him again? Too bad. I needed to find out if he had an inkling about who had killed Dottie Pfeiffer. I also wanted to learn whether he was aware of Belinda Bell's loathing for Dottie. Alas, he too was unavailable.

The moment I rejoined my grandfather at the cheese counter to face a line of last-minute customers before the shop closed, Rebecca slipped in beside us.

"Hey, Charlotte." She gave me a teensy hug. Energy thrummed inside her.

I pulled apart. "Are you okay?"

"Yes, just pumped up. I love going to rehearsal!"

"To see Devon?"

"And to act. It's so stimulating. So exciting. So fascinating." She let out a giggle.

"Say, I saw Jawbone Jones and Zach's mom a few minutes ago. They were heading into The Country Kitchen. Boy, were they all over each other." She wrapped her arms around herself and pretended to be two people in a passionate embrace. " 'Get a room,' I wanted to yell, but I didn't." She tittered again. "This whole town is gooey with love, if you ask me."

Sure it was, I thought, if you didn't count the hate that went into committing two murders.

Pépère said, "Rebecca, my wife would say you have *Love Letters* on the brain."

Rebecca grinned. "I can't help it. I'm swept up in this play. The two people are so much in love, but they don't get to be together. Life keeps getting in the way. It's breaking my heart, but it's also making me realize how special it is that I'm in love with someone I want to spend the rest of my life with. Like you and Grandmère and Charlotte and Jordan." She pressed a hand to her chest. "I'm blessed."

A customer hailed me. Another signaled my grandfather.

"Go, go," Rebecca said.

My customer, a local artist, asked for suggestions, and I gave him a full accounting of what was good in the winter, suggesting the alpine cheeses, as they typically are the best in the cool months, which was why, historically, they were served warm in dishes like gratin, fondue, and raclette. He ordered a pound of Gruyère, and I rang him up.

When I was once again idle, Rebecca wedged between my grandfather and me and helped us reface or rewrap cheeses. "How was the poetry reading?" she asked.

"Fine."

"Was Octavia pleased with the turnout?" Pépère said.

"Yes." I told them about my conversation with Prudence, how she had all but accused Belinda Bell of having motive to kill Dottie, and my follow-up chat with Belinda Bell.

"You went inside her store?" Rebecca said. "Alone?"

"No. There was another customer. You know I wouldn't have taken the risk otherwise."

"Ha!" Rebecca smirked, as if she'd caught me in a lie, which she sort of had. I'd entered the shop when it was empty. It was only fortune that had brought another customer into the shop seconds behind me. "Tell me what happened?"

I filled them in about the pastry in the trash and Bell's flimsy alibi.

"You know," Rebecca said, "it still irks me

that she and her group plan to oust Grandmère from her position as mayor."

"*Sacre bleu,*" Pépère muttered. "Say it is
not so."

I sighed. "It is. Prudence confirmed it."

"Grandmère will be as mad as a hornet,"
Rebecca went on. "Which, come to think of
it, is how Mrs. Bell is all the time lately.
Mad about the noise. Mad about the
calories and fats in foods. I wonder if it irritated her that Dottie offered freebies to
children."

"Violet said something along the same line
the other day," I said.

"Hey!" Rebecca held up a finger. "I've got
another suspect for you. What if a band of
irate mothers led by Paige Alpaugh lashed
out at Dottie? Paige can rally the troops better than anyone."

I thought of the women that had huddled
around the kiosk Sunday morning. How
long had they been there? Would Paige have
been able to skip away unnoticed, slip into
the pastry shop, kill Dottie, and return as if
nothing had happened?

"If that's true," I said, "then Dottie and
Tim's murders aren't related, because Paige
was at the pub at the time Tim died. She
has a solid alibi. I saw her. Violet was with
her."

"Unless" — my grandfather held up his hand — "Paige was working with a partner."

I gaped. "I considered something like that earlier." I explained the possible matchups I'd concocted, between Bell and Townsend or Bell and Jawbone.

Pépère nodded. *"Oui, exactement."*

"Let's face it," Rebecca chirped. "The food at the pub isn't that good for people, either. Talk about fats. That makes me think of that movie called *Who Is Killing the Great Chefs of Europe?* Did you ever see that?" Within weeks of leaving her Amish community, in addition to becoming addicted to mysteries and thrillers, Rebecca had become a film hound. Over the course of the past few years, she had watched hundreds of award-winning films. Last fall, she had focused her attention on the films of three female stars. Currently, she was devouring comedies. "A gourmand is killing off the chefs because he absolutely has to lose weight or he'll die."

"But the pub food isn't targeting children," I said, "and Paige is all about protecting children."

Tyanne entered the shop and said, "That's an understatement." Apparently, she had caught the drift of our conversation. "Paige is like a mama bear protecting her cubs. She

298

has all sorts of suggestions for the moms at school. What the lunch menu should be. What we shouldn't include in lunches brought from home."

Pépère said, "I have heard the same from the twins."

Tyanne shook her forefinger. "Don't get me started about the school parties. We get printed lists of things not to include, like peanuts and gluten. Some moms really don't like Paige. On the other hand, some people benefit from her advice, like Violet, who looks much better thanks to Paige's dietary plan."

"Except Dottie wasn't a mother," I said, which Paige had pointed out to me.

"Are you talking about Paige having it in for Dottie? Oh, sugar, if anyone had it in for someone, it was Dottie wanting a piece of Paige."

"Why?" Entry forms were poking out of the slot of the satin box. I tried to nudge them inside.

"Dottie accused Paige of swiping a recipe."

I sputtered. "I can't imagine Paige wanting to make anything Dottie baked."

"It wasn't a pastry," Tyanne said. "It was a vegetarian Cheddar cheese dish. Ray had raved about it. One day, at a party at the

Pfeiffer house, Paige slipped into the kitchen and filched it."

Huh. I liked vegetables, but I couldn't imagine stealing a vegetarian recipe. If it was that good, I'd ask politely and hope the cook would share. Most would.

"A recipe, I might add," Tyanne drawled, "which became the most popular on Paige's blog. Dottie threatened Paige and told her to take it off the site. I still remember the way they were going at it. Paige went semi-ballistic. How dare Dottie challenge her integrity."

"When you say they were *going at it*" — I succeeded in pushing all the entry forms into the satin box and then squared the edge of the box on the counter — "do you mean they were exchanging blows?"

Tyanne wagged her head. "Heavens no. Words. All words. But Paige was cruel, as she can be sometimes. She said Dottie would have a better figure and longer life if she'd eat less fats and sugar."

Dottie would have had a longer life if someone hadn't killed her, I mused.

"Chérie," Pépère said. "Moments ago, on my break, I saw Paige heading into Sew Inspired Quilt Shoppe."

Rebecca nudged me. "Why not go over

300

there and ask for her alibi on Sunday morning?"

"In the meantime," Pépère said, "think about with whom she might have conspired to kill Tim." He also prodded me to move.

I hesitated. Was every one of my family and friends thinking like a detective nowadays? Was that my fault, or was it simply a matter of too many murders in one town in such a short time?

CHAPTER 28

In the end, I followed my friends' and grandfather's advice. I breezed into Sew Inspired Quilt Shoppe and paused inside the door. Paige stood at the rear, huddled with other mothers near the tartan plaids. Each mom was admiring the work her teenage daughter was doing on a sparkly T-shirt. The class was a regular occurrence and no part of the Lovers Trail events. Paige's eldest daughter, an angelic girl with a mane of gold hair and the lightest eyelashes I'd ever seen, held up her artwork for her mother's approval. Rings adorned every finger of both hands. Paige, rather than assessing her daughter's work, snatched her daughter's left hand. She said something. The girl wrenched away and fled to the restroom at the rear of the shop.

Freckles, who was dressed in her signature orange, approached me with a broad smile. "Charlotte, hi! What brings you in this evening? The twins aren't scheduled for a class."

"I'm not here for that." Matthew's girls took classes at Sew Inspired. Meredith, Grandmère, or I would pick them up. Their mother, Sylvie, was boycotting the shop — forever — because Freckles had made the twins' dresses for their father's wedding.

"Oh my. I know why." Freckles fluttered her fingers. "We never finished your dress. The hem. Come here." She grabbed my hand and tugged me toward the dressing room. For a bitty thing — she wasn't even five feet tall — she was strong. Daily workouts, as well as lifting huge bolts of fabric, contributed to her power. "Let's get it done."

"I don't have time."

"Uh-uh, no arguments." She pushed me into the storage room at the rear. It wasn't a dressing room, but it served the purpose.

She handed me my cocktail-length dress, which was ecru silk with lace cap sleeves and a lace overlay on the bodice. She'd added a dappling of gold beading. It was so pretty, I nearly cried.

Don't dwell, Charlotte. The month of May is right around the corner.

"Put it on. I won't take *no* for an answer." She started to tug on my sweater.

Knowing I couldn't dissuade her, I obeyed, slithering out of my clothes and into the dress.

"How are you doing?" she continued. "Are you depressed? Silly question. Of course you are. You didn't simply postpone the wedding, you also found two —" She stopped herself from saying more. "Listen to me. What a dolt. Happy thoughts. Happy-happy. Here, let me zip you." She whistled as she spun me around. "It fits like a glove. Perfect! Step on the platform in front of the three-way mirror. I'll get my pin cushion." She ran off and returned in seconds. "How do you feel about the hem being at the middle of the knee? Okay? It's a very classic, chic look. I can go longer or shorter —"

"Middle is fine."

"I'll have it ready by tomorrow. Do you have a new date set? Is Tyanne arranging a location?"

"Freckles, slow down. We haven't set a date. We'll get married in May."

"May? That's eons away."

"Only three months. And, yes, Tyanne will still be our wedding planner. But the dress isn't why I came in."

"Why, then?"

"I need to talk to Paige."

"About?"

I didn't want to blurt out the theory that my comrades and I had concocted seconds before. I needed a few facts first. I also intended to see Paige's eyes when she responded. Was she still in the shop, waiting for her daughter to reappear from the restroom, or had I lost my opportunity? "You know Paige pretty well, don't you?" I asked. "I mean, you hang out."

"Occasionally. Our oldest girls are the same age. They do gymnastics together, and they're both waiting to hear on their college applications."

"You also attend Paige's blogging seminars, right?"

"How did you know?"

"I saw you at the Bozzuto Winery the other day."

"That was such a fun day. Wine, women, and song." Freckles laughed. "That was Paige's description. Catchy, don't you think? She's a wizard with that kind of stuff. Logos and slogans. She has so many tips on how to grow a business it's mind-boggling. I have reams of notes. 'Go on a social networking site every day. Share something personal. Let your fans get to know you. Create a street team.' Do you know what that is? You give away things so that people following you online will help spread the word about your site. Teamwork, she says, is vital to any plan."

Teamwork, as in having a partner to commit murder?

Freckles continued. "Paige is the most organized person. Why, she's the only woman I know who wakes up every morning with a to-do list and accomplishes it. 'One foot in front of the other,' she says. If any of us balk at a suggestion, she tells us straight out that we're our own worst enemies. 'Doubt sabotages productivity.' "

"Maybe I need a class with Paige."

Freckles stood, brushed off her hands, and gestured for me to remove the dress. "But that's not what you want to know, is it?" She unzipped me. "You have something on your mind. I've seen that look before. Does it involve the murders? Do you think Paige can fill in some blanks, like maybe she saw something, but she doesn't realize she saw something?"

"Er, not exactly."

"She's got her finger on the pulse of Providence."

But is it a beating pulse? I wondered wryly.

I put back on my clothes and handed the wedding dress back to Freckles. "What I wanted to know was whether Paige might be involved somehow."

Freckles inhaled sharply. She hurried to the drapes that separated the storage room from the main shop and peeked out. Quickly, she stole back to me. With a finger to her lips, she whispered, "She's still here. Go on. Tell me how."

I explained my reasoning.

"But Paige couldn't have killed Dottie," Freckles said. "She had a foodie blogger meeting Sunday morning. I know because I attended."

"I didn't see you at the kiosk."

"The kiosk? I don't know about that. We met at Paige's house at six A.M."

"Why so early?"

"Because Paige likes to get a jump on the day. Why else?" Freckles laughed. "I had to scoot at the end of the meeting. It ran over by a half hour. I was going to be late for church, and my hubby hates if I'm late. Paige doesn't attend, so what does she care?"

"Paige was at the meeting the whole time?"

"Do you think she'd let anyone else run one of her meetings?" Freckles snorted. "Not likely."

If I put the timetable together right, there was no way Paige could have murdered Dottie. Ray said he had left her for one hour; that set the time of death between 6:30 and 7:30 A.M., when I'd arrived. And there was no reason to think Paige had a hand in Tim's death. I thanked Freckles for her input and left the shop without approaching Paige.

CHAPTER 29

When I arrived back at Fromagerie Bessette, the lights were off; my grandfather had left. I found Rebecca in the office changing into skinny jeans, a black turtleneck, and dance shoes. Someone must have told her that was what theater people wear; prior to now, I'd never seen her in a pair of jeans.

She said, "Pépère took Rags and Rocket. He wanted some cuddle time. Hope that was okay. He'll drop them off at your house later."

"Of course."

"So, how'd it go?" Rebecca asked. "Did you wheedle a confession from Paige?"

"No. I heard another impeccable alibi. Cross her off our list."

"Wait a second. Couldn't one of her acolytes have done both murders?"

"Acolytes?"

"New word for the day. It means —"

"I know what it means: admirer; hanger-on." I grinned. "I really don't see that as a possibility. Even Freckles said that Paige is too controlling. She wouldn't assign something as critical as murder to someone who might mess it up or leave evidence."

"Yeah, you're probably right."

"Go to rehearsal. I'm heading across the street to eat. We'll rethink this in the morning."

Clearly miffed — Rebecca wanted answers as badly as I did — she hoisted her tote onto her shoulder and left grumbling and mumbling.

In desperate need of a warm meal and small talk, I dashed across the street to The Country Kitchen. As I entered, Delilah and her waitstaff were sashaying down the middle of the restaurant singing a bluesy rendition of Elvis's "Are You Lonesome Tonight?" Whenever a patron made an Elvis selection on the jukebox, the waitstaff sang. It was part of the fun and flavor of the diner.

Delilah waved at me.

Slipping past her, I said, "Have you seen Urso lately?"

She shook her head and held up two fingers: *two minutes to go.*

I perched on one of the stools at the red Formica counter and perused the menu. Cheese-anything sounded good. The diner often bought cheese from us and used it that day in a recipe. When I read that the special was raclette potatoes with rosemary, I closed the menu. Perfect. My mouth started to water in anticipation.

"Let me eat in peace!" a woman said loudly enough to be heard over the music.

I spun on my stool and spied Octavia, sitting in a booth by herself.

"Did you hear me?" Octavia said to a frothy woman, with cheeks tinged the same pink as the ream of paper she was clutching to her chest. "Go!"

The woman scurried away and out of the restaurant. Octavia never lost her temper. What had happened?

I slid off my stool and hurried to her table. "Are you okay?"

Octavia frowned. "Bad me. I'm so mean. That poor woman didn't deserve my wrath. All she was doing was promoting a Lovers Trail event at her new candy shop, but honestly, I come in here so rarely. What are the odds that I would be accosted twice in the same night?"

"Did she accost you?"

"No. Not really. All she did was give me a flyer." Octavia tapped a piece of paper that was lying on her table.

"Then who did?"

"Belinda Bell. She claimed she didn't get my rent check."

"She dunned you for payment?" I said, shocked.

Octavia scowled. "I paid her. I always do, on the first of the month, like clockwork. I don't even risk the mail. I drop it through the slot of her shop door. I can only imagine she moved my envelope into a junk mail pile and tossed it out. I suggested that, but she —" Octavia clucked her tongue.

"Is she hard up for money?" It made me wonder again whether Bell had the wherewithal to have killed Dottie to get her hands on the cluster brooch.

"Ha! She's as rich as sourpuss Prudence with the same amount of bluster." Octavia fluttered a hand. "She wants what she wants, sooner rather than later. Don't we all?" She patted the tabletop. "Join me?"

The music stopped. Delilah tapped me on my shoulder. "I've got a few seconds," she said.

I thanked Octavia for the offer but begged off and returned to my seat at the counter.

Delilah took my order, put it on the spindle for the chef, and returned. "Like I said," she began, as if we were in the middle of a conversation, "I haven't seen Urso. He's been really busy. He must be interviewing ten people a day. He hit every shop owner on Honeysuckle Street."

Where Providence Pâtisserie was located.

"Not to mention, he's all over Ray about Dottie. He's also questioning Dottie's family, all of whom have arrived in town, and every supplier of goods to the pastry shop. The milk and butter deliveryman, the cheese and fruit guys. He's leaving no stone unturned." She sighed. "I've got to give him credit. He's diligent beyond words."

"If you haven't seen him, how did you learn all that?"

"The precinct clerk came in for a late afternoon snack. Boy, is she chatty." Delilah poured me a glass of water. "I did leave a message for Urso about Aurora's call to me, but he didn't ring me back." She pulled her cell phone from the pocket of her apron, scanned it for messages, and then eyed me with a sly smile as she dropped the phone back in the pocket. "I'll bet you'd like to get your hands on this baby."

How well she knew me. If I could review her call list, maybe I could see who her lover was — could it possibly be Urso? No. He wasn't returning her calls, either. Soon, when I had the energy to scrabble, I would make her confess. Urso, too.

"Get my raclette potatoes," I ordered.

313

Snickering, she strutted away.

Someone at the far end of the diner spanked a table. I swiveled on my stool and caught sight of Jawbone sitting with Zach's mom, Ilona. I recalled Rebecca saying she had seen them entering the diner earlier. Ilona appeared a bit frazzled. She was shaking a tablet as if trying to wring information from it.

Jawbone swatted the table a second time. "Dang!"

Mr. Nakamura, the hardware store owner who used to practice law in Cleveland and often did legal work for clients in Providence, sat with the couple. He appeared the epitome of calm, but when didn't he look like that? None of them had meals on the table, only beverages. And paperwork, strewn end-to-end.

Why had Jawbone spanked the table? What had upset him? Was he consulting Mr. Nakamura on a legal matter? A plea bargain, perhaps, although Nakamura didn't typically do criminal work; he specialized in divorces and real estate contracts. I remembered Violet telling me that Jawbone had wanted to purchase the pub. With Tim out of the way, was Jawbone moving ahead with that plan? According to Deputy O'Shea, he and his cousins weren't interested in keeping the place.

"Aiyee!" Ilona shouted, much to the surprise of everyone in the diner. "We got it. See?" She held up an iPad to her table-mates. "Here. Right here. Proof!" Like a display floor model, she spun in her seat to show the rest of the customers. "Jawbone is innocent. We have a copy of our Face It exchange." Face It was a face-to-face cell phone application. "No court will be able to disprove digital proof. You're free, babe. Free!"

Curious, I scrambled off my stool and moved closer.

Mr. Nakamura was peering at the iPad.

"I asked my geek friend," Ilona was explaining, "who got a copy of the exchange from the cloud." The cloud was computer-speak for an ethereal Internet data-collection space. "This" — she stabbed the screen — "proves Jawbone was talking to me the entire time that he said he was."

Mr. Nakamura uttered something I couldn't make out.

"Yes," Ilona continued. "I know he was stupid to drive that way." She leveled Jawbone with a withering stare. "Bluetooth, babe. Bluetooth."

Jawbone flicked her arm with a finger, but a grin spread across his face.

"Take this to Chief Urso. Show him." Ilona thrust the tablet at Jawbone. "I'll pay the tab."

Hurriedly Jawbone and Nakamura rose from the banquette and raced out of the diner.

Ilona raised a hand to get a waitress's attention.

I sidled to her table.

"Charlotte." She reached out as if we were old friends. "Isn't it wonderful?"

The two of us had never met. How did she know my name? Maybe she'd read the proprietor names on the window of Fromagerie Bessette.

"I'm so glad you get to hear this." Ilona pulled me into the booth and pushed aside the beverage glasses. "I know you found Timothy O'Shea, and I know he was your friend, and I'm so sorry — so sorry — that he died, but Jawbone is innocent." She drummed the table with her fingertips. "Ooh, I love that man, and I knew he didn't do it. Having proof is powerful, isn't it? So who else do you suspect?"

I couldn't believe she was being so open with me. "Ms. Mueller," I began.

"Call me Ilona."

"Ilona." How could I possibly say that I also suspected her son of murder? I'd been thinking about Zach, on and off, ever since I'd realized he was connected to all involved. I worked my lower lip with my teeth. "I think that's the police's business."

She waved her hand dismissively. "You've got a reputation. Don't deny it. I'm not saying you're meddlesome, but you are inquisitive and compassionate. Word gets around. I listen. Now, who else?" She drummed the tabletop again. Her fingernails looked raw from chewing.

"Ilona," I sputtered.

"I know. You're probably thinking, *Who is this woman?* We've never met. Never chatted. I'm not a cheese person. Never have been."

"Lactose intolerant?" I asked.

"Actually there's all sorts of food I can't eat. The doctor says it's because I'm such a *sensitive little girl,* the patronizing jerk." She hiccupped out a laugh. "Thankfully, I can eat chocolate. I'd perish without chocolate."

Close up, she had an appealing face: a few freckles, a simple nose, and a naturally turned-up mouth. The look didn't match with her messy-hair/rattail hairdo choice. I wasn't quite sure what to make of her.

"I'm sorry if I'm coming on too strong," she continued, "but I'm excited. So, what's the scoop?"

"Ilona, I'm sorry, I can't tell you a thing. I'm not privy to Chief Urso's investigation." I sighed. When would he get back to me? If ever. I wanted to help. I know, I know. As Belinda Bell had rudely pointed out, I had plenty on my plate, with The Cheese Shop and family, but I also cared about Tim and Dottie, whom I'd considered my friends. I wanted resolution for Tyanne and Tim's family. And my mind was whirling with theories.

"My son says he was questioned in regard to Dottie's murder." Ilona scrunched her cute nose. "Can you imagine? Both my men under scrutiny? Zach wouldn't hurt a fly. He's as gentle as a lamb."

As long as she'd brought up the subject . . .

I said, "I heard he gets into scrapes."

She waved her hand. "Past tense. Back when he was thirteen. Not now. He was so angry then. At his father. Zach felt he needed to defend me. His father was . . . *is* a player. He didn't hide the fact. Zach thought his father's bad choices reflected on me. It didn't matter that we'd been divorced over a decade." She sighed. "My son can be quite the romantic."

Was he a romantic right out of a Shakespeare play? Would he slay an enemy to preserve a secret?

"When Zach grasped that I really and truly was fine," Ilona added, "he stopped lashing out."

"I heard he was a wrestler in high school."

Ilona smiled. "He still wrestles in an amateur league."

Interesting.

"It's a small group, but it keeps his skills up and his aggression low." She tilted her head warily, like a wren waiting for a larger bird to attack. "You want to ask me something, don't you?"

I nodded. "Zach used to date Belinda Bell's daughter."

"Indeed he did. They were quite a sweet couple."

"Would he do anything to win her back?"

"Gack, no. He's *so* over Aurora. She dumped him when she left town. He's moved on."

"To whom?"

"To Paige Alpaugh's daughter, Pixie." Ilona leaned forward. "Shh, don't tell anyone, but they're engaged."

I flashed on the myriad rings Paige's daughter wore on her fingers. At Sew Inspired Quilt Shoppe, Paige had snatched her daughter's hand; the girl had fled. Had she been wearing a promise ring? Had that incensed Paige? And when Paige visited The Cheese Shop to fill out a contest form, she'd reacted oddly when I'd said Zach's alibi was talking to his girlfriend at seven A.M.

"For obvious reasons," Ilona went on, "the two-year age difference being one and Zach's bad reputation being the other, Paige does not want Zach to date her precious girl." Ilona chuffed like an irritated cat. "As if children listen. Zach and Pixie see each other on the sly."

"How did you find out?"

"My son never hides anything from me. I might be the only one who knows about their relationship."

I wondered about that. Paige had called Zach a ne'er-do-well, which implied that she knew about the relationship and didn't approve. I said, "You don't seem to mind that they're a couple."

"I believe in love," Ilona crooned, then snickered. "Pixie is a doll, and she understands Zach. He's a creative, like me. He wants to be a French chef."

Don't hold your breath, I mused. I'd dated a guy that my friends had dubbed Creep Chef. I'd been thrown for a loop when he left me in the lurch to pursue his lifelong dream.

Ilona said, "After Dottie fired Zach, he

320

got a job at La Bella Ristorante."

"As a chef?"

"I wish. No, as a waiter, but with the promise to graduate to the kitchen staff as soon as a position becomes available." She twisted the diamond ring on her finger. She caught me watching her and stopped abruptly. "Not all girls understand creatives like Zach. Aurora certainly didn't. Life was all about *her*."

"I heard Aurora and Zach were talking on the telephone the morning Dottie Pfeiffer was killed."

Ilona gaped. "That's impossible."

"Why?"

"Because he was talking to Pixie."

"How do you know?"

"I already told you. He tells me everything." Ilona grumbled. "How dare Aurora lie about something like that! Did her mother put her up to it? I wouldn't put it past Belinda to —"

"Hold on."

"If Chief Urso gets wind, who knows whether he'll believe Zach and Pixie were on the phone at the time?"

"Wait. I might have misspoken. You see, Aurora called Delilah to check up on Zach, and Delilah assumed they had talked that morning." Dang. I should have nailed down that lead. Heat suffused my cheeks. "It's great to know Zach has a solid alibi. I'm sure Chief Urso will believe him."

"Really?"

"Yes. Definitely."

"I'm calling the chief right now."

"Perfect." I couldn't slip away fast enough.

CHAPTER 30

After I finished my meal and exited the diner, I was thinking about Zach and his conversation with Pixie Alpaugh when whom did I spy? *Zach.* Not twenty feet from me. My grandmother has told me that thoughts can conjure up a telephone call from a person, but could thoughts summon a person in the flesh? No way. My mental powers were not honed to that degree.

Zach was walking past The Silver Trader jewelry store, acting as though he wasn't interested in the display window, but he was. He peeked in three times before moving on. Was there a piece of jewelry he was admiring, or was he casing the joint?

Bad, Charlotte! Cut the kid a break. But how could I? I was as curious as all get-out. Zach couldn't have enough money to buy something in the shop, not working as a waiter at La Bella Ristorante. Tips were good, but not that good. Was he a thief? Had he stolen Dottie's brooch? Had his mother lied about his alibi? Mothers could be fierce protectors.

With no particular place to be, I hung back and observed him. He jammed his hands in his pockets and strolled toward the corner. Before he reached it, Ilona Mueller appeared. Next to her, Zach looked tall and muscular and intimidating. Ilona threw her arms around him and ruffled his hair. She said something to him. He grinned from ear to ear.

At the same time, someone tapped me on the shoulder. I whipped around, so edgy that I threw my hands up to defend myself.

Jordan backed up, arms raised, a big smile on his face. "Whoa, don't punch me. Whatcha doin'?" He knew exactly what I'd been doing.

In spite of the dozens of people roaming the street, I hurled myself into his arms for a hug and a kiss. Nobody seemed to pay attention to us; we were one of many enjoying the pleasures of a fond embrace. It was, after all, the most romantic week of the year.

When we came up for air, I said, "How did you know I'd be here?"

"I ran into Rebecca on her way to the theater. She said you went to the diner for dinner. Without me."

"You didn't answer my phone call. I assumed you were busy."

"Never assume. When you tried to reach me earlier, I was tending to a sick cow." He lifted my chin and kissed me again, simply, deliciously.

We strolled the streets, drinking in the atmosphere. We didn't speak about what I'd gleaned at the restaurant from Ilona Mueller until we were back at my house, sitting at the kitchen table with warm mugs of fresh-brewed coffee and a plate of raspberry gem cookies. Rags and Rocket galloped around our feet, begging for love.

I obliged them with nuzzles and cooing and a treat for each, then said, "No more." Obediently, the pets settled down.

"Okay," Jordan said. "One more time. Why would it matter whether it was Aurora or Pixie talking with Zach at the time of the murder?"

"With conflicting alibis, Zach looks like he's hiding something."

"Unless they're not conflicting. Have you questioned him?"

"I don't —"

Jordan smirked.

"Fine," I conceded. "I inquire, occasionally, and people tell me things."

"But you haven't talked directly to Zach."

"No." I took a sip of coffee and let it warm me.

"Have you talked to Pixie?"

"Like Paige would let anyone get within ten feet of her precious girls."

Jordan winked. "Apparently Zach has gotten within ten feet."

A notion began to take form in my mind. "Do you think Paige would kill Dottie and set Zach up to take the fall so her daughter would be free of him?"

"That's a stretch."

I took a cookie and bit into it. "I've left messages for Urso."

"But he hasn't returned your calls?"

"No. I'm sure he thinks he's protecting me, Jordan, but who is helping him? Not his deputies. Not the county. He's on his own. Have you seen him lately? He looks tired and strained. His eyes —" I wiggled my fingers beside mine. "He's hurting, Jordan. He needs answers about Tim's murder as much as you and I do."

Jordan ran a finger along the back of my hand. "He might be hurting, but he has other things on his mind, too. Life things."

"Life things?"

"Okay, *love* things."

"Do you think?"

Jordan nodded. "He was in the park

earlier today, buying flowers and balloons. I doubt they're to decorate his office."

My heart filled with hope. "I was wondering about that when U-ey hurried off to lunch the other day. He said he had a date, and he nearly broke his neck to dash across the street when Paige and her girlfriends were at The Country Kitchen."

Jordan kissed my cheek. "Despite the curves life throws at us, we rally. He will, too."

Jordan left at eleven P.M. He wanted to check on the sick cow and oversee the first milking. I tossed and turned.

At dawn on Wednesday, I awoke with a start. There were no sounds, nothing alarming. I was just tense. Meredith, Matthew, and the twins were due back today, so I decided to take Rocket for his bath. I dressed quickly, ate a light breakfast of apple slices paired with Cheddar, and then leashed up Rags and the dog and we strolled to Tailwaggers. On weekdays, they accepted early risers at seven fifteen. At first, the Briard was more than delighted to get a glimpse of the cardboard statue of his ladylove in the window, but when I led him inside and he believed I was going to abandon him — forever — he howled like a trapped animal.

I did my best to reassure him that *forever* was less than eight hours, but he didn't believe me. Luckily the owners of Tailwaggers were gifted with animals and calmed him immediately.

At Fromagerie Bessette, while I booted up the computer in the office and checked email, Rags settled into his favorite spot. An hour later, I made a dozen pine nut and asparagus quiches and threw together some sandwiches using Bear Hill, a Grafton Village sheep's cheese that was fruity and nutty, and Creminelli's bacon salami, which was made with Duroc pork and all-natural cooked American bacon. The combination was superbly flavorful.

Midmorning Paige sauntered into the shop with two of her pals. She explored the store and poked her head into the annex. I flashed on how delighted Urso had acted the other day when he'd spied Paige and the same two women entering the diner. Was Paige the one Urso had his eye on, or was it one of the other two? Did Paige know? Maybe she had come into the shop hoping to catch sight of him.

"Help you, ladies?" I asked.

Paige pushed her friends toward the barrel set with wineglasses. "Be with you in a sec," she said to them and ambled toward me. She offered a big toothy grin. "Charlotte, how are you?" She dragged out each syllable.

"Fine."

"Curiouser and curiouser." Was she playing some kind of guess-the-book game? Did she want me to yell: *Alice in Wonderland*? She swatted the air. "What is it with you? Always asking questions."

I gulped. Had Freckles spilled that I'd suspected Paige of murder? "I don't know what you're talking about," I said, being as vague as possible.

"A birdie told me you want to join my blogging education group."

My shoulders eased instantly. I hadn't been found out. Freckles had kept the secret. "Yes," I said. "But I'll bet you have a long waiting list of applicants." Honestly, *applicants*? Had I regressed to being thirteen years old? Would she assume I was trying to butter up the most popular girl in school? How inane! Besides, hers wasn't the only club. There were others in town that knew their way around social networking.

The front door swung open and Ray Pfeiffer hurried in. A gust of cold wind trailed him inside. I shivered.

"Charlotte," he cried. "Help!" No one was pursuing him. He wasn't in trouble. He was wearing black shorts, black T-shirt — his churchgoing attire for Dottie's memorial service.

Paige swatted the air. "Take care of Ray. We'll talk. I might . . . *might* have an opening. Let's go, girls." She twirled a finger and her posse exited with her. As she passed Ray, I heard her say, "So sorry about Dottie. So sorry."

Ray accepted her condolences and rushed to the counter. His forehead was pinched with tension. His eyes looked red-rimmed from crying.

"Aren't you cold?" I simply had to ask. The tawny sweater and corduroy pants I'd worn were barely keeping me warm.

"Never. I've always had good circulation." He pulled off his gloves and pointed at a cheese in the cabinet. "I'd like a pound of that Taylor Farms Maple Smoked Farmstead Gouda, sliced thin." The cheese, slowly smoked using maple wood chips and therefore milder than cheeses that were smoked using hickory chips, had won numerous awards from the American Cheese Society. "My in-laws" — he heaved a sigh — "are hungry."

"Where did you hold the service?"

"In the ravine. At the ch-chapel." His voice broke; his eyes welled with tears. He must have remembered that he had been at the chapel the day Dottie had died instead of with her at the shop. He mashed his lips together before pressing on. "What will go with that cheese? Dottie would have wanted me to serve a tasty spread."

"Apricot or fig jam would be a lovely choice. And crackers, of course."

"A loaf of Dottie's bread would have been nice," he muttered. "But it will have gone bad by now."

"Not necessarily. If she had some bread refrigerated, it might still be good. Bread lasts longer than you think." I hesitated. "Um, Ray, when will you clear out the remainder of her baked goods?"

"I don't know. I haven't been given the okay." More mashing of lips. The muscles in his jaw ticked.

"Have you considered donating the food to the poor? Maybe if you asked Chief Urso with that caveat, he would consent."

His eyes brightened. "What a great idea."

I helped him pick out the crackers and jam and stowed them in a gold bag. While paying, he said, "Thank you. For all your help. And" — he cleared his throat — "for being there at the end with Dottie." On a mission to contact Urso, he exited with a jauntier gait.

On the sidewalk, he ran headlong into Violet.

Rebecca cut around them and blazed through the front door. "Sorry I'm late." She tore to the back of the shop, shrugged off her coat, strapped on an apron, and joined me at the counter. While slinging her hair into a ponytail, she said, "We went long at rehearsal and I overslept, and . . . well, I apologize."

"No worries. Only one paying customer so far." I jerked my chin in Ray's direction. He was still talking to Violet. She touched his elbow and mouthed what I could only imagine was sincere sorrow at his loss. Seconds later, he moved on, and Violet entered the shop.

"Hello, Charlotte." She flung back the furry hood of her parka and stamped her feet. "Good weather for jackrabbits."

The snow was drizzling down and turning wet and sloppy the moment it hit the ground.

"Do you have any Fromager d'Affinois on hand?" she asked.

"Plenty. How much?"

"Three pounds. It'll be my specialty on the cheese plate this afternoon."

While filling her order, a car whizzed past the shop. Not just any car. A souped-up Camaro. I flashed again on the night Tim died, when Deputy O'Shea and I saw Zach speeding in the opposite direction. Had he been coming from Jordan's farm? Had he followed Tim there? Had Tim caught him doing something wrong outside the pub? Zach was too young to have been inside.

I said, "Violet, at the pub on the night Tim died, do you remember seeing Zach Mueller when you went outside for a smoke?"

"Why would you care if —" Violet's eyes widened. "Oho! You think Zach killed Dottie, and now you're trying to link the two murders. You think Tim might have caught Zach doing something illegal." Her eyelids fluttered, as if she were turning her gaze inward to picture the evening. "Zach . . . hmm . . ." She tapped the knob of her chin. "Now that you mention it, I did see him. In that car of his. He was parked near the rear of the lot."

"Parked?" I said. Maybe he was scouting out someone to rob. "Did you see him —"

"Someone was in the car with him," Violet added. "A girl."

I perked up. "Pixie Alpaugh, Paige's daughter?"

Violet screwed up her mouth. "Wow! Do you think? I guess it could've been. I remember how the parking lot light glistened on the girl's golden hair."

Rebecca shot me a look. "I thought Zach had a thing for Mrs. Bell's daughter."

"We were wrong about that," I said. "He's in love with Pixie."

"Uh-oh," Violet mumbled. "Paige will not be pleased, if it's true."

Rebecca thrust a forefinger in the air. "What if Tim passed by Zach's parked car and overheard Zach and Pixie plotting to elope, you know, like Romeo and Juliet?"

"Elope?" Violet squeaked. "Double uh-oh."

"That's an interesting angle." I recalled Ilona Mueller saying her son was a romantic, and I'd wondered whether Zach, à la a character right out of a Shakespeare play, would kill to preserve a secret. "Zach realized Tim heard them and figured Tim would tell Pixie's mother."

Rebecca nodded. "So he tailed Tim. He and Tim argued —"

"And Zach attacked," Violet concluded.

"Wait a sec." I held up a hand. "He tore after Tim with Pixie in the car?"

Violet wagged a finger. "No way. The girl got out."

"You saw her exit the Camaro?"

"Of course not. Like I said, I wasn't out there that long, and I don't even know if it was Pixie, but would you have gone along for the ride?"

"Okay," I said. "Let's say we're right. We have star-crossed lovers, unwilling to bow to their parents' wishes. They plan to run off. They need money. With that, we've linked the two murders. Dottie had the jewelry they could steal and pawn —"

"And Tim found out about the elopement," Rebecca said.

"It sure paints a picture, doesn't it?" Violet said. "You wouldn't believe what I've seen at my inn. There have been so many hookups. I'm not one to kiss and blab, but love is in the air, and not only for the past week. Speaking of love, Charlotte, I almost forgot." She reached into her purse and pulled out a wad of stuff, all tangled up. A tissue, a couple of folded pieces of blue paper, and something small and red. She separated the red item from the rest, and while stuffing the mess back into her purse, handed it to me — an origami heart. "Earlier, I was having coffee across the street and saw Jordan tape this to the door. I'm not sure where you were. You're usually at work so early."

"I was at the dog groomer."

"Jordan tried the door, but it was locked. I was afraid his note might blow off or get damaged. I hope you don't mind. It looks intriguing. Remember, later, to tell me what it says. Oh my." She glanced at her watch. "I've got to run. Ticktock."

CHAPTER 31

I left Rebecca in charge of the shop and raced to the office. I unfolded the heart and read Jordan's note:

Dear Charlotte, I'm sorry I didn't attend the reading at the bookshop with you. I know how you love poetry. It was wrong of me. If it makes a difference, every moment with you is poetry.

He went on to include a poem I knew well: Elizabeth Barrett Browning's famous "How Do I Love Thee":

How do I love thee? Let me count the ways. . . .

By the final line, tears were streaming down my cheeks:

. . . and, if God choose, I shall but love thee better after death.

I wiped the tears off my face:

So, my love, how does May 1st sound? Will you? Marry me.

Love ~J.

Rags, knowing something was up because I was snuffling, butted my ankles with his head. I bent down and nuzzled his ears. "It's okay. These are happy tears."

"Aunt Charlotte!" Amy and Clair yelled from the main shop.

Meredith appeared alone at the door. When she realized I was crying, she closed the door and dashed to me. "You poor thing. I can't imagine what you're going through. We heard about Dottie." She crouched down and hugged me with all her might. "How are you holding up? Feeling despondent? Wishing you could kick all the bad guys' rear ends?"

Since grade school, Meredith had been my best-best friend, and although her marriage to my cousin had cut into our one-on-one girl time, she was still the person who could make me laugh . . . and yet gave me the space to cry.

I let loose. I'd been holding in tears for too long. She patted my back.

The door burst open. Amy and Clair ran

in and skidded to a stop. "What's wrong?" they exclaimed.

"Nothing," I said.

They didn't believe me. They bolted to Meredith and me and joined the group hug.

In seconds, I couldn't breathe. "Off!" I said. "Each of you, on your feet. I'm fine. Stand up. I'll live. Now, tell me about your adventure." No pity parties today. I usually gave myself a maximum of twenty minutes whenever an oh-poor-me moment cropped up, but rarely with the twins around. I pinched my cheeks to stimulate some color. "Where did you go? What did you do?"

"We went to Cleveland," Amy said. "We ice skated on an open-air rink." She was a natural athlete.

"I'm going ice skating with Jordan soon. Was it fun?"

"It was!"

Clair chimed, "We went sledding, too. On real wood sleds."

"And we went to the planetarium," Amy said.

Clair nodded. "It's called the Nathan and Fannye Shafran Planetarium."

It never failed to amaze me how the girls could keep a conversation going, one sentence at a time, each filling in what the other was thinking. Did all twins do that?

"It's one of the biggest in the nation," Clair continued. She was the more studious of the two girls. "Visitors at night can use the building's roof to locate the North Star. It's got fiber optics embedded in it, or something like that. Isn't that cool?"

I smiled. "Very."

"We bought books," Amy said.

"Glow-in-the-dark star books." Clair put a finger to her mouth. "Shh. Don't tell Octavia."

"She won't mind," I said. "She doesn't carry those books at her store. And she won't care if you borrow from the library, either. Reading is the important thing."

Amy scanned the office. "Where's Rocket?"

"He's getting a bath. I'll pick him up later and bring him over to your house."

"Okay, girls," Meredith said. "Time to go home, unpack, and let Aunt Charlotte do her work." She gestured with her thumb. "Matthew's in the wine annex. Are you going to be okay?"

"Fine. Promise."

With Jordan's origami heart tucked into my pocket, its presence a reminder of his steadfast love, I faced the rest of the day with calm assurance. Little upsets didn't bother me. Customers picking up their tickets for tomorrow evening's event made me smile. I assured each that there would be plenty of wine and cheese.

Midway through the afternoon, as I was reading a past issue of *Culture Magazine,* I got an inspired idea to pair chocolate and cheese for tomorrow's soiree: milk chocolate with a variety of Goudas, and dark chocolate with Cheddars, including Prairie Breeze Cheddar, an award-winning cheese made in Iowa with milk from Amish farms. Our event wasn't going to compete with the new candy store's event; most shops on Honeysuckle, like All Booked Up, had held their events on Tuesday. A pang of regret gripped me as I realized Dottie hadn't been able to participate. She'd planned to give out cake pops to any kid who came in with a parent.

Around dusk, Grandmère entered the shop with my grandfather. Each was holding a to-go cup from The Country Kitchen. *"Chérie,"* she said. "Have you seen the activity on the streets?" She stamped her feet to rid her boots of a dusting of snow before moving further inside. "It is *merveilleux, non*? So many tourists are visiting our fair city, and the locals are enjoying, as well."

"It is because of all the hard work you do to lure them here," Pépère said as he sweetly brushed snow off the shoulders of her wool cape. "You are the one who is *merveilleux.*"

She preened beneath his praise and popped the lid off her coffee, which turned out to be caffeine-free green tea. She tossed the teabag into the trashcan beyond the cash register.

"No coffee?" I said, astounded. She rarely made it through an afternoon without a good dose of caffeine.

"I am trying to cleanse my body."

"Really? Who convinced you to do that? Are you also going to give up your occasional gin fizz and chocolate?"

She scowled at me. I offered her a tasting of chocolate and the Prairie Breeze Cheddar from the sample platter I was creating.

She hesitated, then gave in. "One cannot live without chocolate." She hummed her appreciation.

I glanced around to see if Rebecca was near. She wasn't. She was helping Matthew set out champagne glasses in the wine annex. I put a finger to my lips and waved my grandparents to the far end of the tasting counter. "Tell me, Grandmère, how are rehearsals going?"

"I am pleased. Your Rebecca is quite feisty. If you are not careful, you might lose her to Hollywood."

"You think so?"

"She has the passion. Like Belinda Bell's daughter, who, by the way, is in town, did you know?"

"She's here?"

"*Oui.* She is in the diner *serre maintenant*" — Grandmère tapped the counter — "this moment, with a line of fans begging for autographs."

I cut a look out the front of the store. People, bundled up due to the weather, were streaming out of the diner onto the street.

"She is sitting with her mother and that man —" My grandmother tapped her head then mimed a long beard and bushy hair. "You know who I mean." She looked to Pépère, who shook his head, clueless. He had never been good at charades.

"Eddie Townsend?" I said.

Grandmère shot a finger at me. *"Oui."*

"How could you forget his name? He's on the city council."

"The age. It is creeping up on me."

I laughed. "Stop it."

"Alas, my memory fails me, but do not worry. Death will not get me for a long time." She leaned in. "*Chérie,* do you think Belinda and Eddie are dating?"

"Why would you think that?"

343

"The way they were talking. So intimately. Tête-à-tête."

Pépère chuckled. "You have love on the brain, Bernadette."

"If not love, then what?" She slipped her arm through his. "Could it be they are plotting something? Do they plan to overthrow me as mayor?"

I gaped. Did my grandmother have ESP?

"Come," Pépère said. "Enough of this chatter. No one will get rid of you, *mon amie.* No one will dare. We are going home."

"Wait," I said. But before I could warn my grandmother that she was right about people wanting to oust her from office, my grandfather shuttled her out the exit.

As the door closed behind them, I wondered about the powwow between Bell, Townsend, and Bell's daughter. What if they were meeting with Aurora for an entirely different reason? What if Aurora found out that Zach was now with Pixie Alpaugh? Had she come home to win him back? Maybe Bell and Townsend were trying to talk her out of pursuing him because . . .

Because why? Because they thought Zach was a murderer? Had they seen him outside the pub? Had they seen him chase after Tim? If so, why wouldn't they have told Urso by now?

Rebecca stole to my side and rapped me on the arm. "I see your mind working. What's going on?"

I outlined my theory.

Rebecca flicked a finger. "But you said Ray and Dottie were at the pub that night, and although Ray hated Zach, he only implicated Jawbone. Don't you think he would have at least mentioned seeing Zach if Zach had been there? Maybe Violet was wrong about seeing him in the parking lot. She didn't seem all that certain." Rebecca took a coupling of Gouda and milk chocolate and downed it in one bite. She didn't savor; she didn't show her approval. She licked her fingers and pressed on. "Let's forget Bell and the others for a moment and return to Jawbone Jones. Are you certain he's not guilty?"

"He has a pat alibi, corroborated by the Face It cell phone video."

She scoffed. "Did you consider whether the video might be fake?"

"Can a fake video include a time stamp?"

"I saw a thriller on AMC about a month ago in which phony date stamps were added to old photos. Anything's possible in this day and age. Tech-savvy people are the wave of the future."

Great. Not what I needed to hear.

"And while we're batting around theories," she said, "what about Ray? Did you ever figure out whether he had motive to kill Dottie? Did he have a life insurance policy on her? He'll inherit the business, I presume. Have you asked around about his finances?"

"Who would I have asked?"

"That bank clerk friend of yours. The one that likes really tart goat cheese."

"But what reason would Ray have had to kill Tim?"

"What if Ray's business is suffering? What if it's under water? What if Tim saw Ray getting a loan from someone, like a loan shark?"

"It's not illegal to borrow money."

"Or" — Rebecca took another cheese-chocolate combination; plop, swallow, move on — "what if Jawbone is Ray's lender?"

"Why are you so set on Jawbone being guilty? I thought you liked him. Do you have something against bald-headed men?"

Rebecca hesitated. She grasped a towel and twisted it into a knot.

"You do," I said. "Why?"

"Back when I was a girl, an older man, a bald friend of my grandfather's . . . he did a bad business deal with my grandfather. My grandfather wept. He couldn't believe a friend would use him. When the elders found out, the man was ejected from the community. Seeing a man with a bald head makes me think of him." She untwisted the towel; her eyes widened. "Whoa. I hadn't thought of that."

"What?"

"On AMC. That movie."

"Which movie?" I didn't mean to sound exasperated, but sometimes having a conversation with Rebecca could be like trying to restart a flooded car. Stop-go-stop-go.

"That movie by Hitchcock." She brandished two fingers. "Two men." She smashed her fingers together. "On a train."

"*Strangers on a Train.*"

"Right! What if —"

"Jawbone and Ray worked in cahoots with one another," I said, in sync with her stream of thought. " 'I'll kill yours, if you kill mine.' "

She clapped her hands. "Two people dead; two killers; twice as easy. Each killer would have an alibi for one or the other murder."

CHAPTER 32

Rebecca reached for another goodie from the chocolate-cheese platter.

I swung the platter away and said, "Uh-uh. No more chocolate. You're revved up enough."

"Spoilsport."

"Just watching out for you." I deposited the platter in the walk-in refrigerator and returned to the counter.

Through the picture window, I saw Aurora Bell sitting inside The Country Kitchen. She didn't look nearly as radiant and upbeat as she had the last time I'd seen her. Then I spied Urso squeezing past her and her admiring fans, and I wondered, number one, if I'd mentally summoned him the way I'd conjured up Zach Mueller outside the jewelry store, and number two, why he hadn't returned my calls.

I told Rebecca I'd return and hurried across the street.

Like Urso, I edged around the line of fans and entered the diner. The alluring scent of onion soup rich with Gruyère cheese made me inhale deeply. Ah, if only aromas could satisfy one's appetite, dieters would have a lot more success.

I caught sight of Bell, her daughter, and Townsend. All three looked on edge, but I couldn't focus on them. I spotted Urso sitting in a booth at the rear of the restaurant. Seated opposite him was Delilah. She was leaning forward, the light in her eyes so brilliant that I wondered if she'd been struck by a lightning bolt.

That was when I had a *duh* moment.

Urso was the one for whom Delilah had fallen. Again. They had dated a while back, but the romance hadn't taken off. Because both of them were strong-willed people, they had sniped at each other repeatedly, and in the end, Urso admitted he was still in love with me. Why were they back together now? Was it due to the season? Or was it because Jordan and I were supposed to have tied the knot this past weekend, so Urso finally found the courage to give up on me and move on? It didn't matter. I was too excited for both of my pals to care. Way back in high school, I'd believed they belonged together. Was I upset that neither felt they could tell me? Sure. But I'd get over it.

Delilah leaned forward and intertwined her fingers with Urso's.

Rather than interrupt — I wanted them to have a few stolen moments alone; I could share the latest theories concocted between Rebecca and me after I picked up Rocket at Tailwaggers — I retreated out the door, returned to The Cheese Shop, fetched Rags, and hurried to the north of town.

Rocket was delirious to see me. Had he really thought I wouldn't come back? He'd had a bath more than a dozen times since he'd become part of the family. What kind of pea-brain memory did he have? *Not nice, Charlotte.* I scruffed his neck and ears and assured him all was well, hitched him to his leash, and the three of us trotted outside.

For the first part of the walk to Matthew and Meredith's house, there were lots of people on the streets. Many strolled arm in arm. A few folks walking solo looked on with undisguised jealousy. During February, it seemed everyone wanted to be in a duo.

Not far from the house was a fenced dog park where Rocket liked to run free. He let out with three sharp yips and tugged me toward it.

"Hold on, fella."

The center of the park was grass and dirt; the outlying area was an oval-shaped path set up with benches. Though usually brightly lit by streetlamps, the park tonight was ominously dark. At least three lamps were out of commission. Grandmère had told me that the lighting system throughout Providence needed an overhaul. The weather could erode the wiring. It was on her list of things to discuss at the next board meeting.

Rocket barked and yanked again.

Although I was uneasy with the lack of foot traffic — as in, there were no people around; zilch — I said, "Okay, fine. I don't need Councilwoman Bell declaring you to be a yapping nuisance. Five minutes."

We entered the park, and I unhooked his leash. He dashed off. With Rags in tow, I meandered toward a bench. I dusted off a layer of snow, prepared to sit. Rags meowed, indicating he wanted me to pick him up. I obliged. "Have you been putting on weight, kitty cat?" I teased. He hadn't. I was diligent about his diet. No pet needed to be overfed.

He mewled again and rubbed his head against the underside of my chin.

"I know. You're hungry. We'll just be here a few —"

Bushes crackled. Footsteps.

I whipped around.

A figure in black — black jacket, black pants, black ski mask — sprinted toward me. I didn't recognize the eyes. He was about a half a head taller than me, maybe five-feet-ten. He aimed something at me. At first I couldn't make out what it was, but then it glinted. A knife. Nothing special, the kind often found in a kitchen. But highly lethal. Any professional or home chef owned something similar.

I backed up.

"Give it to me," my assailant grunted, voice low and altered. "Now!"

"Give you what?" My throat felt as dry as sand.

He lunged but didn't strike. "Your ring. Give it to me, or you'll regret it. Now!"

With Rags tucked in my arms, I struggled to wriggle off my engagement ring, which was a half-carat diamond bordered by two rows of smaller diamonds. Two thousand dollars retail.

"Hurry."

"C'mon," I urged the ring. Usually, in cold weather, the ring was easier to remove, but not tonight. *Of course, not tonight.*

"Faster," my attacker ordered.

I yanked the ring off, bruising my knuckle.

My assailant snatched the ring and fled.

At that moment, Rocket must have caught sight of him. Yapping, he barreled toward the stranger at full speed.

"Rocket, no!" I yelled.

But he didn't listen. He dove at the thief. He must have made contact, because I heard a human yelp, followed quickly by a canine yelp.

"No!" I shouted. "Somebody, anyone, help!"

The assailant scrambled to a stand and sprinted out of view. He must have darted through the bushes and leaped over the fence.

I raced to Rocket. He lay sprawled on the ground. "Rocket? Are you okay, boy?"

Before I reached him, he roused and lurched to his feet. He jogged to me and tucked his head beneath my outstretched hand while woofing an apology.

"No worries, fella. He didn't hurt me." Well, maybe my pride was hurt. I knew a few defensive moves. I should have used them, but at the time of the attack, I couldn't. Not with a cat in my arms. Not in the dark. I was lucky to escape unscathed. Rocket, too.

Hurriedly, I re-leashed him and we zoomed out of the park. Back to the lit street. Back to safety in numbers.

Who was the attacker? A tourist? One of the riffraff, as Prudence called them? Or was it someone I knew? I shuddered to think I might have been his specific target.

I recalled a faint whiff of whiskey. Jawbone Jones was an imbiber, but so were many others. Could it have been Zach Mueller? Did his mother tell him I suspected him of murder? Had he tailed me from The Cheese Shop? Maybe he saw me approach the diner with the intent of touching base with Urso. Maybe he thought I knew something that could implicate him. If so, why not kill me? He'd had a weapon. Was his intent to scare me into silence?

I paused. Why would the attacker carry around a ski mask? Possibly because he had stolen things or mugged people on more than one occasion. Ray claimed Zach was a thief. Did Zach rob me so he could pawn my ring? Why take the risk when the eyes of the law had to be all over him? Did he think he could scare me and prevent me from digging further into his motive for killing Dottie or Tim?

"This way, Rocket." Shakily, I steered him in a U-turn, and we hurried back to the diner to talk to Urso.

When I arrived, I peered through the

window. Urso wasn't in the booth where I'd seen him earlier. Remaining outside with the animals in tow, I poked my head in and beckoned Delilah.

She dodged the line of fans and exited. "What's up?" She rubbed her bare arms to warm her from the cold.

"I know about you and U-ey."

"Huh?"

"Don't act dumb. I saw you two. Entrenched in romantic conversation."

She reddened. "I was going to tell you —"

"I'm thrilled. Don't get me wrong. However, at the moment, I need to talk to him. I was mugged."

She seized me by the shoulders. "Are you okay? Are you hurt?"

"I'm fine. Where's U-ey?"

"The precinct."

I told her I'd be in touch and sprinted north with the animals.

When I arrived at the precinct, however, Urso wasn't there, either. He had left to deal with a fire at the movie theater. The clerk directed me to Deputy O'Shea. I was surprised that he was at work. I would have thought he'd have rehearsals, like Rebecca. The clerk, an old hand at performing at the theater, reminded me that my grandmother liked to rehearse one actor at a time so she could help the actor, or in this case actress, delve deeper into her emotional reality.

Deputy O'Shea's office was similar to Urso's, only smaller. Neat desk, file cabinet, Levelors on the windows. He looked healthier than he had the other day. His skin had color, his hair was combed.

Rising from his chair, he directed me to sit. He was receptive to my complaint. I replayed the scenario, and he filled out a report, which I signed. He promised to let local pawn shops know of the theft. He asked if I had a picture of the ring and whether it was covered by insurance. I told him I didn't care about the monetary value; I wanted it back because of its sentimental value.

"Are you sure you can't ID the thief?" he asked.

"I suspect it was Zach Mueller. He's about the right height, but there are so many in town about his size, including Jawbone Jones."

O'Shea's eyes brightened.

I said, "Do you know something about Jawbone that I should know?"

"No, ma'am."

"You don't have to hide anything from me. I know you've been investigating."

He frowned.

I assured him Rebecca hadn't said a word to me. "But I know the kind of person you are. You're like me. You won't rest until justice is served. Now, what have you learned?"

"I've been tailing Jawbone, keeping an eye out, hoping to see him trip up. He hasn't. He goes to work. He meets with his music partner. I think he knows I'm watching."

"I did detect a hint of alcohol on the assailant's breath."

"Perfect. I'll question him about his whereabouts tonight. Don't you worry. We'll solve this." O'Shea rose and asked if I was going to be okay.

I told him yes, but I wasn't. I was shaky. And mad. And determined to take more self-defense classes.

Chapter 33

Matthew and Meredith wouldn't let me go home after I dropped off Rocket. They demanded I sleep in the guest room. I was too tired to refuse. I sat on the edge of the guest bed with Rags tucked beside me, and I called Jordan; the call went immediately to voice mail. I told him what had happened and that I was safe; he didn't need to call me back. Then I lay back on the pillows. I barely slept a wink. Rags didn't do much better than I did, digging into me with restless regularity every few minutes.

Just before dawn, I returned with Rags to my house. The second I stepped out of the shower, I heard the doorbell. Once. Twice. Then someone pounded on the front door. Swell. I threw on my favorite mint green terry robe and while finger-drying my hair scurried downstairs. Rags trailed me. I peeked through the sidelight window and saw Urso and Jordan standing side by side on my porch. Jordan's eyes blazed with concern. Urso looked grim and stoic.

Feeling sheepish for no good reason, I slowly opened the door.

Jordan strode into the foyer and took me in his arms. "Are you all right?"

Urso stepped inside as well.

I pressed apart from Jordan and addressed both. "I was scared, but I wasn't harmed in any way." In fact the more I thought about the incident, I felt that other than taking my ring, the culprit's main objective had been to scare the pants off me. Did that mean the thief was Jawbone? He had taunted me at the winery. Was this another of his attempts to get me to back off asking questions? He had a confirmed alibi now. Why would he do that?

Jordan said, "Tell me what happened."

I recapped the attack then thrust my bare left hand at him. "He demanded my ring." I added, "And I forked it over."

"The ring doesn't matter as long as you're all right. We'll get another one. A larger one."

"I don't need larger."

Jordan looked as if he wanted to hug me again but restrained himself.

Urso said, "Deputy O'Shea tells me you

suspect either Zach Mueller or Jawbone Jones."

"How do you figure that?" Jordan asked.

"Height, weight" — I eyed Urso — "woman's intuition?"

Urso grunted. "Any distinguishing marks?"

"It was dark; he was wearing all black. Didn't you read O'Shea's report?"

"I did, but sometimes, hours after a crime, a victim remembers something more."

A *victim.* I hated that I was, yet again, prey to a criminal's whim. Guilt — no, *anxiety* — skated across my skin and gave me goose bumps. If my sheer brawn wasn't enough to protect me, did I need to learn to shoot a gun? Did I need a permit to carry? *No, never.* I would not become a nervous Nellie.

"Charlotte?" Urso said. "Do you remember anything more?"

"Nothing. I can't remember his gait, and he disguised his voice."

"Could it have been a woman?" Urso asked.

"I suppose." I tried to picture the attacker. Larger than me overall. Knife in hand. Barking out orders. "Rocket!" I blurted. "He attacked the person. He went for the calf with his teeth. There might be bite marks."

"Only if the dog was able to nip through the fabric," Urso cautioned. "Winter clothes are much thicker."

"Maybe Rocket left a bruise. Maybe the mugger is limping."

Urso smiled. "I'll assign this to O'Shea and Rodham."

"How're his wife and baby doing?"

"Super. They went home yesterday. Rodham's back on the job and handing out bubble gum cigars."

Jordan said, "Then you don't need Charlotte."

"I never said I did. On that point" — Urso glowered at me — "I know you're trying to help by investigating."

"I'm not investigating."

"What would you call it, butting in?"

"I didn't butt —"

"You questioned Belinda Bell." His tone was sharp and disapproving.

I lifted my chin. "She hated the noise Dottie made. She wanted to raise Dottie's rent. I went to Memory Lane to, yes, snoop, and I saw evidence that I thought was suspicious."

"What evidence?"

I told him about the pastry wrapper in Bell's shop. "Believing that Dottie and Tim's murders might have been done by the same person —"

"Why would you think that?"

"C'mon, U-ey, two murders inside of a few days. Are you going to tell me you're not thinking along the same lines?"

Jordan said, "I happen to agree with Charlotte."

"Based on what?" Urso asked.

Jordan smirked. "Woman's intuition?"

Urso groused and pointed at me. "Go on."

"Violet saw Belinda Bell outside the pub the night Tim was murdered. She was meeting with Councilman Townsend. What if Tim saw them together and figured out they were plotting to kill Dottie?"

"Plotting?"

"They've met together numerous times since."

"We saw them at the Bozzuto Winery," Jordan said.

"And you must have seen them at the diner with Bell's daughter, Aurora," I added.

Urso shrugged. "Maybe they're dating. This is the week of love."

"Prudence assures me they're not."

Urso glowered. "Prudence Hart? Have you drawn her into your investigation?"

I held up a hand to stop him. "Okay, if not Belinda Bell, who else do you suspect? Do you believe Zach Mueller's alibi that he was talking to Pixie Alpaugh? Violet saw the two of them . . ." I hesitated. "Well, she *thinks* she might have seen them in the parking lot that night. Zach and Pixie could have been planning to elope, and if Tim overheard them —"

"Charlotte, stop."

"U-ey, I care about this town, and I care about my friends and family. I know you don't take me seriously —"

"I do take you seriously."

"You do?" My breath caught in my chest. "Really?"

Urso rubbed his hand along the back of his neck. "Yes. It bothers me, but you're good at this. Mind you, you're better at selling cheese, but you do understand people, and you see through lies."

I took a moment to glow beneath his praise. "What do you know about Ray Pfeiffer's finances? Is his business suffering? What if he killed Dottie to get the insurance?"

Urso sighed. "I've checked. He didn't. They had no insurance policies. The pastry business won't sell for much. It would be different, of course, if he owned the building, but he doesn't."

"Which brings us back to Belinda Bell," I said. "She's the landlord."

Urso held up his hands. "Okay, got it. I'll check her out. No more theorizing."

Jordan spun me to face him. "Get dressed. It's time for you to take the day off."

"I can't. I've got the Lovers Trail event tonight."

"You can and you will."

Doing my best not to bristle, I said, "Don't manage me."

Jordan laughed. "Like anyone could. Please take the day off? I'm sure Rebecca can handle everything at the shop. We'll call your grandfather to help out, too."

"Half a day," I said.

"Deal. Anything to spend time with you."

"By the way, U-ey." I aimed a finger at him. "When were you going to tell me that you and Delilah are a couple?"

"They are?" Jordan said. "You dog."

"Yes. I caught them holding hands at the diner." I focused on Urso. "Did you think I would tease, taunt, and bring up the past?"

Urso worked his tongue around the inside of his mouth.

"I won't." I held up three fingers in a salute. "Scout's honor. I'm happy for both of you. It's about time. She'll make you laugh, and you could use some of that."

A smile tugged at the corners of his mouth. "Yeah, I could."

■ ■ ■ ■

The Ice Castle, an imposing edifice nearly a block long, was located near the mini-mall that held the grocery store and bank. The royal blue and white interior looked freshly painted. Around the rink itself, a matching blue stripe lined the guardrail below the Plexiglas window. In addition to ice-skating and hockey, on Sundays and only Sundays, the rink offered bumper cars on ice and birthday parties. The music piped through the overhead speakers varied from hour to hour: sometimes classical; at other times, like now, rock and roll. A rousing rendition of Bill Haley's "Rock Around the Clock" was playing.

While lacing up our rental skates, Jordan and I perched on narrow benches. The metal sent a chill through me. Despite my hyper-warm leggings, mittens, and three upper layers, I shivered.

"Are you okay?" Jordan asked.

"Fine." I finished double-knotting the laces and smacked my hands together, a dull sound thanks to the mittens.

"So, you didn't answer my question."

"I'm not following. Which question?"

"Perhaps it wasn't formal enough in a

note." He lowered himself to one knee and took my hands in his. "Charlotte Erin Bessette, will you marry me on May first?"

I yanked free of his hands and rummaged in the pocket of my parka. I pulled out the heart-shaped origami and spread it open. Beneath his question, I had written: *Yes!!*

He drew me into a hug and we kissed. When we broke apart, he said, "Unless, of course, we have occasion to get married earlier and the timing is right."

"You mean, elope? I couldn't. I want my family and friends . . . No." I shook my head emphatically. "Let's do it the right way. I'll get Tyanne on board."

"I've already alerted her. You have enough to cope with." He kissed me again. "How long has it been since you last skated?"

"A year. You?"

"At least a year. I'm sure my ankles will protest tomorrow."

I giggled. "I'm certain my thighs will."

Offering his hand, Jordan pulled me to a stand, and we tottered on the thick rubber mats toward the rink. We stepped onto the icy expanse and skated around the perimeter.

Jordan said, "You're pretty good."

I'd forgotten how much I loved to skate. As a girl, I'd skated in this arena — way before Ray Pfeiffer owned it — at least once a week. I hadn't done more than single loops or lutzes, but I'd loved to pattern dance, and I'd adored gliding with one leg in the air, arms wide. In addition, my high school boyfriend, who later became my fiancé, had played hockey. Long story short, he'd wanted to be the best player ever and had pleaded with me to play one-on-one with him. I would chuck a puck to him, and he would hit it into the goal. Occasionally, he would bodycheck me against the wall to steal a kiss.

"Charlotte?" Jordan said. "Did you hear me?"

I hadn't, but I was embarrassed to say where my mind had gone. Jordan held no affection for my ex. Neither did I.

"I'm proud of you for not fighting the thief," he said.

"If I had, I might be dead."

"Exactly."

"I think he wielded the knife purely to get me to obey."

"Which worked."

"Hey, do you think if I can come up with a visual image of the knife, the police could figure out who owned it?"

Jordan shook his head. "I doubt it, unless it was some unique hunting-style knife."

"It wasn't."

After a half hour of skating, I suggested we take a break.

The Ice Castle featured a work-a-raunt café, meaning *serve yourself.* As I perused the menu, I wondered if Paige Alpaugh had a hand in crafting it. Almost everything was a healthy snack: fruit, juice, raisins, protein bars, and nuts. Any sweet options were made with coconut or maple syrup; no processed white flour was used in any of the preparations. The one non-healthy item the café offered was hot cocoa.

We ordered two cups and took them to a white and blue Formica table. I wrapped my hands around the old-fashioned childproof mug to warm my hands. Sitting there, gazing at all the children with parents, a feeling of angst started to well up within me. I sipped and sipped until I'd finished the entire cup without really tasting a drop. I pushed the mug aside.

"Wow, you drank that fast," Jordan said. "Are you okay?" He looked at me with knowing eyes. "What's wrong?"

"Nothing. Let's skate some more." I lumbered to a stance, took my mug to a dish depository, and scuttled to the ice. Blades are never easy to walk on.

Jordan followed. In minutes, we were arm

in arm, skating the cha-cha to a song called "Telephone" by Lady Gaga. The words made me laugh. Lady Gaga didn't want to be bothered by her boyfriend's phone call because she was busy dancing.

"You're smiling again," Jordan said. "I like it."

"Was I frowning earlier?"

"Back there." He hitched his head. "Do you want to talk about it?"

"Truth?"

"Always."

"I'm getting old."

"You're thirty-hmm-hmm." He mumbled my age on purpose as he guided me in a twirl under his arm. "Big deal." He swooped me into a hold and skated me backward. One, two, three, cha-cha.

"We've never discussed it. I think I want children. Do you? What if I've passed my prime? What if I can't have any? What if I'll be a horrible mother?"

"Sweetheart —"

Ray skated up to us, edging to a stop and spraying up ice. An array of skates hung over his shoulder by the shoelaces. Often, he would change out skates for people who didn't pick the correct size the first time around. "Hey, you two. Lookin' good." He whacked Jordan on the arm. He spun around so he was skating backward, facing us. "Charlotte, I saw you do that last move." He wiggled his hips. "You've got rhythm."

I grinned. "That was me trying not to fall."

"Don't kid a kidder." He pointed at Jordan and me. "You two should come to the couples' skate on Saturday. There'll be prizes. The sign-up list is over —"

"Ray!" An older version of Dottie with her doughy features and unruly red hair called from an entrance onto the ice. Wobbly-kneed, she skated toward him. Two other similarly shaped redheads followed.

Ray grimaced. "Dottie's sisters. They won't leave me alone."

"They care," I offered.

"They hover. They want me to talk it out. Share my feelings. The oldest is a therapist." He rolled his eyes. "Like I could ever —" His voice caught. Creases dug into his forehead. "The younger one wants to take over the pâtisserie, but Dottie wouldn't have wanted that. It was her baby. Her sister will make a shambles of it. She's not a baker."

"Ray!" the eldest sister called again, beckoning him with an urgent hand.

"Come to the event Saturday," Ray repeated, then skated off to join his sisters-in-law.

Like a band of harpies, they latched on to

him and picked at him nonstop. I could tell Ray wasn't listening. His gaze veered to the right, as if he was searching for someone to save him. I could only imagine how lost he felt, without Dottie or children to comfort him. His loss made me think again about my dilemma. Did I want children? Did I want someone, in addition to Jordan, to love and cheer me as I grew older? Would I be able to find happiness without the *more* that comes with family? Would Ray?

CHAPTER 34

The activity through the afternoon at the shop was constant: slicing, arranging, double-checking napkins and wineglasses, setting out pads and pencils for customers to make notes at tonight's event. If we didn't provide the latter, customers could get snippy, claiming they wouldn't be able to remember one cheese or wine from the next. Notes were vital.

Amidst the furor, Rebecca apologized for having to run off to a dress rehearsal. Pépère, too. My grandmother couldn't do without him when it came to lighting and stage preparation. I waved good-bye with an easy spirit. All was in control. Nothing could go wrong.

Fifteen minutes before customers were set to arrive, a lanky guitarist set up in the wine annex. Matthew thought music would add texture to the evening. Accompanied by an acoustic piano to establish his rhythms, the guitarist set to work.

Tyanne sidled to me. "Ooh, isn't he good? I love romantic tunes." So far, the musician's playlist had included "Maybe I'm Amazed," "Still the One," and "Just the Way You Are." She offered a bowl that had been stuffed with gold-sprayed Styrofoam, into which she'd inserted cheese pops — like cake pops, only made with cheese. "Taste these, sugar. They're the perfect appetizers when moving around a soiree such as this. A customer doesn't have to linger over one cheese tray. My mother used to make them all the time. These are more gourmet than Mama's, of course. They're made with mascarpone cheese as well as a yummy Gouda, honey, dried cranberries, and sunflower seeds."

I bit into one and savored all the flavors and textures. "I want the recipe."

"Done. By the way, I love what you're wearing."

After skating, I'd hurried home to change into my favorite ecru sweater and chocolate corduroy trousers.

At that moment, Eddie Townsend entered the shop, his hair askew, his suit rumpled. He was rummaging in a black leather satchel that hung strapped across his chest. First one pocket, then another.

"Lose something?" I asked.

"My work diary." His words slurred together. His nose and cheeks were a ruddy red, which was a stark contrast to the whiteness of his beard. Had he had a wee bit to drink? "I keep notes on everything I say or do after six P.M." He tapped his head. "The mind isn't what it used to be."

Overindulging in liquor will do that, I thought. He was too young to have memory lapses like my grandmother.

"I don't want to forget anything I taste tonight."

"Don't worry. We have notepads for all the customers." I pointed him in the right direction. "Remember to try the chocolate and cheese combinations."

He thanked me and moved off.

Tyanne giggled. "Luckily this is a walking event. I wouldn't trust him behind the wheel of a car."

Jordan joined us and handed each of us a glass of sparkling wine. He looked so handsome in his jeans, white shirt, and blazer. I flashed on how he would look in his suit when we got married but pushed the image from my mind. May first would come soon enough.

"Which one is this?" I asked.

"The Schramsberg," he said. "I don't

think I need to taste any other."

I took a sip and agreed.

"By the way, the Thistle Hill Farm Tarentaise cheese on the tasting counter . . ." Jordan kissed his fingertips. "What a great pairing with that fig jam. People are devouring it."

"They should. It's organic and very carefully made."

A mixture of men and women entered the shop.

"There sure are a lot of singles here tonight," I said. Most of Matthew's wine tastings seemed to draw singles. I wasn't sure why. It wasn't like the wine annex was a bar, but I think tasting wine allowed singles to talk freely, about the nose, aroma, and flavor of a wine, perhaps making it easier to meet people than going to the pub and trying to engage in conversation while watching sports.

"Doesn't Violet look lovely?" Tyanne wiggled her fingers in Violet's direction. Violet, dressed in an orchid sweater and matching slacks, was standing near the arch leading to the wine annex. Her marshmallow hair was swept into a sexy updo. "Prudence or Sylvie must be stocking a lot more purple-colored items for Violet and that neighbor of yours." Everything my neighbor

Lois wore was a shade of purple. She'd even named her bed-and-breakfast Lavender and Lace.

"Say, is that Paige's daughter?" Tyanne gestured toward the entrance.

Paige and her eighteen-year-old daughter, Pixie, walked into the shop and paused. They looked similar, with their luscious manes of hair and their toothy smiles. Paige spotted Violet and waved, and then she steered Pixie toward her.

Right behind them entered Jawbone and Ilona. Jawbone acknowledged me with a wink. Why did a shiver of fear crawl down my back? Ilona eyed Pixie, who peeked over her shoulder as if to make sure her mother wasn't watching before turning back and smiling ever so slightly at Ilona. I thought of Rebecca's comment that Zach and Pixie were like Romeo and Juliet. Stolen moments. Missives sent via friends. Chance meetings. Had Zach done something dastardly to hide their secret from Pixie's mother?

"Charlotte!" Delilah walked in with Urso. Were they officially *out*? Hooray. No more keeping me and everyone else in town in the dark about their relationship. Delilah had dressed in a cheery red ensemble and looked almost diminutive tucked into Urso.

He'd wrapped his arm around her waist. Both radiated confidence.

I wanted to shout *Yay!* but showed a modicum of decorum.

Jordan and I joined them.

"Who's on duty?" I asked Urso. "With you here and Deputy O'Shea at dress rehearsal?"

"Rodham. Why?" He winked. "Got any hot new tips for me?"

Delilah elbowed him.

"I'm not joking," he said.

Matthew appeared carrying a tray of champagne glasses. "Hey, young lovers. Take two. Jordan, do you mind if I borrow Charlotte for a moment? I could use a hand."

"She's on the clock. Feel free."

I pecked Jordan on the cheek and followed Matthew. "What's up?"

"Help me pour and take a tray around," he said. People were huddling by the bar in the wine annex. "Let's even out the crowd."

I always found it funny how, at parties, people jammed in near the food and beverages. Completely empty, non-claustrophobic areas could be found if you simply edged away from the action.

While I made the first pass at handing out glasses, I caught sight of Ray Pfeiffer in his standard shorts and T-shirt — far be it from him to dress up for a cheese and wine event. He stood with Dottie's sisters, all of whom were dressed in their Sunday best. I sidled toward them to offer tastings. They were in the middle of a conversation.

"Pastry is not healthy," the eldest sister said. "Too much sugar and fats." She knuckled Ray on the arm. "Admit it. You feel the same way. I heard you and Dottie argue about it."

"We didn't argue."

"You're trim. You've got a regimen. I'm not sure our little sis" — the eldest gestured to the heaviest of the sisters — "should take on the bakery. Ray, what do you think?"

Ray's arms hung at his sides, hands gloved as they always were. One hand rubbed against his pocket, as if he itched to get whatever was inside. Did he need a smoke? Did he need to grab his car keys and hightail it away from his in-laws?

"Champagne?" I said, thrusting the tray toward them. "Actually, it's sparkling wine." I explained the difference.

Ray looked positively gleeful for the intrusion. He took a glass and moseyed away from the sisters, who continued to debate the value of keeping the bakery.

I resumed circulating and spied Pixie Alpaugh standing by herself, looking wistfully out the window at the street. Was she hoping to catch sight of Zach? I doubted he would pass by. He should be at work by now. I slipped up to her and said, "We have some non-alcoholic cider in the main shop."

Pixie whirled around. Tears streaked her cheeks.

"Are you okay?" I asked.

"My mother." She spit out the word. "She's so . . . stubborn. It's always got to be her way. *Her* schedule. *Her* rules. She doesn't care about anything I might be feeling."

I recalled my musings at the ice-skating rink. Did I really want kids? Did I want my child to hate me at the age of eighteen? He or she would; it was a given. To a teen, parents grew more and more stupid before they ever became smart again.

"What did she do?" I said. "Is it about Zach?"

Pixie's eyes widened. "How do you know about him?"

I tilted my head. "Word travels fast around Providence. Are you in love with him?"

She didn't answer; she didn't have to. Clearly, she was.

"Supposedly, you are his alibi for the morning Dottie Pfeiffer was killed. Is that true? He talked to you around seven A.M.?"

"That's right. We talked for a long time."

"Have you told Chief Urso?"

Pixie gnawed on her lower lip. Hadn't she spoken to Urso? If not, why not? Because her testimony would be a lie?

Matthew called my name and twirled a finger, indicating I should continue serving.

I signaled *one minute.* "You know, Pixie, my cousin has a friend who can check phone records. He could prove whether or not you were talking to Zach during the time you claim."

Pixie looked right and left, as if trapped.

I set the tray of drinks on a bistro table and edged forward. "Are you lying?"

"Okay, we only talked for a minute," she conceded.

I knew it!

"But that's because" — she looked around again — "my mother left the house, and I wanted him to come over."

"At seven in the morning?"

"We only get small windows of opportunity. Like I said, my mother has me on a short leash. She . . . made bad decisions when she was my age. She got pregnant — with me. My dad . . . he . . ." She hitched a shoulder. "My mom's deathly afraid I'll make the same bad choices. But I won't." She hitched a shoulder. "Zach came over, and we . . . I'm old enough. We do it safely."

I didn't need a graduate degree to know what *do it* meant. "Were you together last Thursday?" I asked. The night Tim was killed.

"How did you know about —"

I cut her off. "People saw you. Why did you and Zach meet in the parking lot at the pub?"

"I needed to make sure my mom's car was there." She smiled sheepishly. "Then we went back to my house to . . ." She let the sentence hang.

"You're wearing a ring on your left hand," I said. Pixie wore a lot of rings, but that one was special. It was a thin gold band with one teensy diamond on it. Nothing elaborate. Not the one the thief stole from me. "The other day at Sew Inspired, your mother figured out about you and Zach, didn't she?"

Pixie chewed her lip. "She was furious. When we got home, she slapped the walls and slammed cabinet doors. When I told Zach, he said he'd make it all better. He would talk to her. He would ask her for my hand, real official-like. He came over last night, but what did she do? Told him to leave." She snuffled with disgust.

Last night was when the mugger attacked me. "When was he there?"

"Around now."

"Dusk?"

She nodded.

"What was he wearing?"

"Beige trousers and white shirt. He was dressed for work. Why?"

"No reason." Zach couldn't have been the assailant that stole my ring; the timing was off.

Pixie crossed her arms over her chest and slouched. "My mom is such a grouch. I hate her."

I rested a hand on her arm. "No you don't. She's trying to protect you. All moms try to control their kids. Not just yours." Mine couldn't have, of course, but my grandmother, in my mother's stead, had been vigilant. I whispered, "Are you and Zach planning to elope?"

"What?" She scrunched her nose. "Why would you think that? No! We're going to take our time. He wants to go to chef school. I want to go to college. I've got brains. I want to run a corporation. We've got plans."

Kids and their dreams. I smiled. "Tell your mom that. Put her at ease. She's worried you'll run off."

The music stopped. I looked in Paige's direction. She had left Violet and was walking toward the wine cubbies with the guitarist, who had yielded his chair and guitar to Jawbone. Ilona stood beside Jawbone, encouraging him to play. He started by tuning the guitar. Then deftly, he launched into a soulful blues song, one I didn't recognize. Had he written it? Matthew was grinning; he, like I, enjoyed the blues.

I turned back and caught sight of Violet, who wasn't listening to Jawbone play the guitar. She was watching Paige and the guitarist forlornly, which made me wonder whether he was the guy that Violet liked. I turned back to Pixie. "Talk to your mom," I repeated, then retrieved my tray of filled wine flutes and headed to Violet.

"Need a refresher?" I asked.

Violet took a glass and set her empty on the tray. "Men!"

"Is your relationship floundering?"

"Let's just say it's on hold."

I looked at Paige and the guitarist again. He had a lopsided grin and an easy, sensual way about him. Paige was delighting in a story he was telling. Not far from them, Ray's sisters-in-law were still going at it. Ray, who was studying the tops of his shoes, looked like he wished he could escape and join the conversation with Paige and the guitarist or anybody else in the room, for that matter.

Violet said, "He promised he would be there for me. Always."

"Is he worth fighting for?"

"Definitely. But promises are never written in stone."

Matthew drew up behind me. "What do you think? Should we hire Jawbone on a regular basis?"

If he's not convicted of murder, I thought. But then, he couldn't be. He had a pat alibi. Or did he? I thought of my earlier conversation with Rebecca. Was it possible that Jawbone and Ray conspired to kill Tim and Dottie, each doing the deed for the other, and each, thereby, having a solid alibi? Speaking of alibis, I flashed on the encounter with the mugger last night. My first impression was that it had been Jawbone. If I questioned him about his whereabouts, would I be able to tell if he was lying?

I waited until Jawbone finished his song and returned the instrument to the guitarist, and then excused myself from Violet and approached him. "That was great."

"Thanks."

Ilona ambled up to him and kissed him passionately on the lips. "You're getting better with age."

He petted her cheek. "You should have sung along with me."

"Are you kidding? Not without a mic." She honked out a laugh and ran her hand up the back of his neck. His tattoo lengthened, and I caught the word *King.*

"What does your tattoo mean?" I asked. I'd never asked someone why he or she wore a tattoo, but I was curious. "Is it for Elvis?"

Jawbone's mouth stretched into a grin. "It's for B.B. King. When I was a teen, I fell in love with his music. 'The Thrill is Gone,' 'Sweet Little Angel,' 'Three O'Clock Blues.' " His eyes glistened with awe. "Beyond belief. That man rocked my world. That's when I officially changed my name from John to Jawbone."

"Why?" Did he have a record? Was he running from the law?

"I needed a cool name if I was going to own a club and play week in, week out."

"Is that why you wanted to buy the pub from Tim?"

"Who told you that? Not Mr. Nakamura. He promised to keep our deal —"

"You and Tim were overheard arguing a year ago," I said.

Jawbone ran his tongue along his upper teeth. "I imagine you also heard that Tim and I nearly came to blows. Tim wouldn't budge, the stubborn son of a gun, rest his soul."

"Do you still want to buy the place?"

"Sure. The nephews don't want it. It's on the market." He cocked his head. "Except mine's not the only offer on the table."

"Is Belinda Bell trying to buy it?"

Jawbone snorted. "Why would she want it? She hates that place and makes no bones about it."

"Maybe to demolish it?"

"Are you kidding me? Uh-uh, no way." Jawbone eyeballed Ilona. "Guess I'd better work harder to preserve a town treasure. Let's up the offer. Get Nakamura on the phone."

Ilona pulled her cell phone from her pocket.

"I've got two more questions for you, Jawbone," I said.

He gestured for me to continue.

"The morning Dottie Pfeiffer died, where were you?"

He hesitated. His eyes narrowed. "You don't think I could have had something to do with her death, do you? I barely knew the woman." When I didn't respond, he rubbed his chin. "In bed sleeping. Sundays I always sleep until noon. Anything else, Miss Detective?"

"I'm not a detective."

"I know." He lasered me with a dismissive look.

"Where were you last night around dusk?"

"Why?" He blew out a harsh stream of air through his nose. "Did someone else wind up dead?"

"No." Thank heavens.

"Let me ask you a question first," he said. "Are you Urso's official interrogator nowadays?"

"No."

His lip curled into a snarl. "Then tell him to man up and ask me himself."

CHAPTER 35

Jordan walked up to me, his head turned slightly as he watched Jawbone grab Ilona and march her out of the shop. "What was that about?"

I dodged the question, not wishing to reveal that I'd overstepped my bounds. What had I been thinking? "Would you like another glass of sparkling wine?"

"No." He nabbed my elbow. "Charlotte?"

"It was nothing."

"Jawbone looked ticked."

"Urso should pin him down on his whereabouts for last night, when I was attacked."

"Did you confront him?" Jordan asked, then sighed. "Never mind. I know you did. It's what you do." He ran a finger along my arm. "It drives me insane."

I smiled weakly. "I'm sorry."

"It's also what I love about you. How much you care." He pecked my cheek. "I'll

388

let Urso know. Speaking of which, when this ends, Delilah wants us to join her and Urso for a beer at the pub. Are you up for it?"

"I can't imagine anything more fun." I winked. "Well, maybe I can think of one thing that would be more fun."

A half hour later, after the soiree at The Cheese Shop ended and all the customers had left satisfied with the tasting as well as their purchases, Jordan, Delilah, Urso, and I walked to Timothy O'Shea's Irish Pub. Like the other night, the place wasn't hopping. The crowd was thinner; the music just as dour. How I wished there was rousing Irish music. It lifted one's spirits in two seconds flat. Perhaps, as good as Jawbone was as a musician, refashioning the pub into a blues place might provide a fresh take.

While we waited in our booth for a waitress to appear, Jordan suggested that Urso re-question Jawbone. When he explained why, Urso got ticked. I couldn't escape the table fast enough.

"I'm going to check on our drinks," I said.

Nearing the bar, I spotted Eddie Townsend sitting by himself at the far end. I flashed on what he had said at the cheese tasting earlier, that he couldn't remember things at night if he didn't write them down, which set me to wondering about how much he might remember from the night Tim died. A well-placed question or two was in order.

I slid onto the stool beside him. "How did you like the cheese and wine tasting?"

"It was nice." He was slurring his words even more than he had at The Cheese Shop.

"Did you keep good notes?"

"Sure did."

"I see you found your diary." I thumbed toward the black bound book resting on the counter between a tumbler of amber liquid and a bottle of Dewar's scotch.

"Yep." Protectively, he laid a hand on it.

"Do you have anything written in there for last Thursday?"

His gaze grew leery. "Why that d-d-day?" he stammered.

"You were seen meeting with Belinda Bell outside the pub."

"I was. Outside. With her." He glanced to his right. Looking for an escape route?

"How long did you meet?"

He flushed bright red. "Um . . ."

"Don't you remember? That was the night Tim was killed."

"Well . . ." He studied the napkin beneath his drink.

"Why don't you take a look?" I aimed a finger at his diary.

"I . . . I don't have to."

"Why not?"

His shoulders slumped and he sighed. "Because it's not in there. There's no mention of a meeting with her. I must have bumped into her outside the pub. That's all."

"When you met with Mrs. Bell two days later at the Bozzuto Winery, did she tell you that you ought to remember that meeting?"

"No. I mean, it's not like you're implying. She said she was with me, and see, I couldn't remember. I thought maybe that one time, I didn't write something down. But then the other morning, following a stiff cup of coffee, I realized . . ." He rolled his eyes. "It was a *zap* moment. Do you ever have those? Your brain goes *zap*. It's like a lightbulb clicks on. A moment of clarity." He lowered his chin. "I'm what some might call a functioning alcoholic. I do fine during the day, and then the night goes dark and so does my brain."

"Does Belinda know this about you?"

He nodded. "Most people do. My kids . . . they tolerate me, but I know they want me to change. And I want to change. I'm thinking of joining AA."

"I know a sponsor."

"You do?"

I nodded. "I'll get you his number."

He looked so hopeful that I thought he might hug me. He slouched and tapped his fingertips on his diary.

"When you had your *zap* moment, did you tell Belinda? Did she suggest that you meet at the diner? Did she try to persuade you that you were wrong?"

"No. Not exactly."

"Did she offer to pay you to lie?"

"What? No!" His voice wheezed with panic. "She" — he licked his lips — "is simply going to work on the city council, gleaning votes, to get a road project approved. One of my clients really needs it to complete a shopping mall. At the far east edge of Holmes County."

I put my hand on his arm. "Do you think you should tell Chief Urso your predicament?"

"Will I get in trouble?"

"I don't think so."

But now Belinda Bell — unless a new witness came forward to verify her whereabouts before she bumped into Townsend — was without a viable alibi for the time when Tim died as well as when Dottie Pfeiffer was killed.

I returned to the table with four beers and Eddie Townsend. After hearing the Realtor out, Urso excused himself. He had a councilwoman to see.

CHAPTER 36

The next morning, eager to hear news from Urso yet hearing nothing, I needed projects and lots of them. I devoted the morning to constructing the goodie basket for the Friday Lovers Trail giveaway, which Rebecca had smartly decided we should offer. I placed wedges of cheese, boxes of biscuits, jars of jam, decorative napkins, a bottle of sparkling wine, and a pair of red-rimmed flutes into the basket. By the time I was attaching ribbon to the arm of the basket, I was humming. After I picked the winning ticket and contacted the exuberant winner, I needed another project. Refacing cheese did the trick.

Rebecca zigzagged past me to tend to a customer. Under her breath, she said, "I'm so nervous about tonight. The lines are whirling through my head."

"I thought you didn't have to memorize them."

"I don't, but they're there anyway. And tears are brewing right here." She patted her chest. "I hope I can hold them back until the point when I'm supposed to cry."

"You have to. That's the job."

I glanced at the telephone on the wall by the register.

"Why the sour face?" Rebecca asked. "Who were you hoping would call?"

"Urso." I explained.

"I see. Sorry. I haven't heard hide nor hair from him." She rummaged in her apron pocket. "Will a note from Jordan brighten your mood? He swung by while you were in the office on the phone trying to reorder the French bread. He didn't want to disturb you."

I wished he would have. For the better part of an hour, I'd searched for a new baker. I finally settled on a bakery that was located next to the grocery store. The bread wasn't as delicious as Dottie's, but the sandwiches we offered would taste fine as long as I kept up the quality of the cheeses, salamis, and sauces.

"Here it is." Rebecca handed me a cream-colored envelope. "He drew hearts all over it. How sweet."

I opened the note and felt my cheeks warm. He wrote how proud he was of my accomplishments. He thought the event last night was, in a word, terrific. I hurried to the office to write a note saying how much I admired him but decided to call him instead.

He picked up after the first ring. "Hi, sweetheart."

"Thank you for the letter." We cooed for a minute, but then I went silent.

"Why else did you call?" Jordan asked. "Something is eating at you. Are you upset that I didn't break into the office and seduce you?"

I giggled. "No. I'm mad at U-ey." I told him why. In detail. When I finished, I said, "We're a team."

"No, you're not. Charlotte —"

"Don't."

"Listen to me. You and I are a team. Urso is a solo act or, at the very least, a team with his deputies. Not you."

"But you heard him. He takes me seriously. He values my opinion."

"Yes, he does. But he does not report to you. He'll bring you into his inner circle when he's good and ready and not before. You feed him what you have. That's your right and responsibility as a citizen. I am so proud that you do that much. It's more than most would do. But after that, you can't do anything except what you're really good at — running The Cheese Shop and loving me."

That night, the Providence Playhouse was packed. Every seat in the house was filled. I heard that a reviewer from Cleveland was also in the audience, a woman who could run hot and cold about the experimental choices my grandmother made as the theater director. I prayed she wouldn't skewer the show.

The lights lowered and I sank back in my chair, worrying my hands together, hoping that Rebecca would hold up under the pressure. She did better than that; she shone as an actress. She possessed a gift of honesty that made her delivery seem simple yet enlightened. The female lead in *Love Letters* grows from a quirky, funny ingénue to a jaded, sad adult. I wasn't sure Rebecca could pull off the second half of the play, but she did. Her voice lowered; her face lost its joy; her body sagged. O'Shea went through the same kind of transition. The audience called them to repeated bows for their performances.

Afterward, in the foyer, guests dined on the red-themed feast of paprika-dusted cheese pastry, watermelon kabobs, heart-shaped linzer cookies, and cranberry punch. Chatter among the attendees related to the theme of the play: how love can grow sour and not be all two people dreamed it could be when they were young and innocent.

"Psst." Delilah beckoned me with a finger. She stood against the far wall. Urso was nowhere in sight.

"Is U-ey working?" I asked.

"Yep."

"I was hoping he'd call and fill me in."

Delilah slung a fist into her hip. "If it makes you feel any better, he won't tell me much, either. I know he went to see" — she stabbed a finger in the direction of Belinda Bell and her daughter Aurora, who were standing near the far wall. Aurora still looked pale and tired. Was she ill?

Bell turned in our direction. Had she heard us? No, she couldn't have, not with her hearing problem, and yet she made a beeline for us. Aurora hung back, looking as if she'd like to blend into the wall. "Are you talking about me, Charlotte?" Bell said.

"No." *Liar, liar.*

"About my daughter, then?"

"No."

"You're gawking at us. Why?"

I wanted to say Delilah was, too, but why drag a friend under a moving bus? "Yes, I was staring. I was concerned about Aurora. She doesn't look well. And —"

"She's just dandy." Bell over-enunciated the consonants. "What else?"

"I was wondering whether Chief Urso talked to you about your alibi for the night Tim died."

Delilah cleared her throat with gusto. Was she trying to make me stop?

I wouldn't be deterred. "Eddie Townsend couldn't corroborate that you met for two hours. He had no notes in his diary. I believe you used him, given his propensity to forget, thanks to alcohol, to back up your story."

Bell deliberated, then sighed. "You're bound to find out from Chief Urso."

"Uh-uh," Delilah inserted. "Chief Urso won't tell anyone anything. He's as true as they come."

"Yes, but Charlotte seems to have a way of learning these things." Bell assessed me from head to toe. Her nose flared. Apparently I didn't smell very good. "You're earning quite a reputation, dear girl."

"I don't mean harm."

"I didn't imply you did. However, you seem to have a way of ferreting out the truth." She paused. "If you must know, and I trust you can keep a secret, I was consulting a private detective that night. You see, my daughter is addicted to a variety of pills. The stress of the job, the hours, the constant attention by the media is undoing her. Her physician prescribed the pills."

I could only imagine the cocktail Aurora needed to keep going: uppers, downers, and in-betweener pills.

"In addition," Bell said, "Aurora figured out how to get extra doses from other sources." Her eyes welled with pain. "If her producer finds out, she'll be fired, thanks to a substance abuse clause, and her career will be over. Someone, an Internet gossip, threatened to expose her. The woman claims she has photos and documents. The private detective is dealing with damage control."

I peered at Aurora, who was reviewing messages on her cell phone and texting responses, and I recalled how Tyanne said Tim wouldn't text. Words needed to be spoken or written, as far as he was concerned.

"Do you understand damage control?" Bell asked. "I couldn't reveal where I was that night. I couldn't let anyone know whom I was meeting. Utter confidentiality is vital to limiting the rumor mill gossip. I repeat" — she grabbed my hand — "I trust you will honor me with your silence."

"Did you give Urso the name of the private detective?"

She nodded.

"Then you have my word. I'm sorry for Aurora. I hope she beats the addiction."

"She has. But it will be a day-to-day battle from here to eternity."

Chapter 37

Later that night, I couldn't sleep. I needed to bake to work through the worrisome thoughts caroming in my mind. I pulled out the recipe Dottie Pfeiffer had given me for winter squash muffins and rooted through my refrigerator and pantry for the ingredients. The only thing I was missing was the squash. I had zucchini. It would make a dandy substitute.

Using my Cuisinart, I made the pastry dough. I chopped the zucchini into fine shavings. I shredded a half pound of Gouda.

While putting together the items included in the recipe, I worked through the suspects in Tim and Dottie's murders. *My suspects.* I didn't know if Urso had others.

I'd ruled out Belinda Bell. I'd also ruled out Zach. After Paige's daughter Pixie put him at her house for not only the time of Tim and Dottie's murders, but also for when I was mugged, I felt he couldn't be guilty.

Paige Alpaugh, despite her obvious abhorrence for Dottie and despite the fact that she might love to see Zach Mueller go down for that murder and, thus, remove the boy from her daughter's life, had pat alibis for both murders.

Ray Pfeiffer had an alibi for his wife's murder, and he had no discernible reason to want Timothy O'Shea dead.

Jawbone Jones had an alibi for Tim's murder; however, Rebecca had put that into question when she'd wondered whether the time stamp on the Face It video could have been altered. Jawbone had a weak alibi for Dottie's murder. He said he was sleeping. Granted, he had no motive to kill her — he barely knew her — but I couldn't stop thinking about the angle in the movie *Strangers on a Train.* Two murderers; two victims; two flawless alibis.

But if that wasn't the case, and everyone on my list was innocent, whom was I missing as a suspect? Did Urso have the killer or killers on his radar?

First thing Saturday morning, Jordan arrived at my door looking like a skater hoping to vie for gold at the Olympics. He was dressed in trim trousers and a snug sweater.

His handsome face was flushed with excitement.

"Are you hoping to win the couples' event at The Ice Castle?" I teased.

"Why not?" He smiled and the dimple that dented his right cheek deepened.

I swooned. "Me too." I opened my coat and showed him what I'd put on, a slimming ultra-long red sweater over leggings. I'd even donned sparkly faux ruby earrings.

He swooped me into a kiss. Breathless, we hurried to the car. I yelled to Rags that we would be back soon. He couldn't care less. He'd eaten a tuna breakfast and last time I checked was playing with his favorite ball of yarn in his bed.

By the time we arrived at The Ice Castle, a slew of people were entering. "Did we need tickets?" I asked Jordan.

"Got 'em."

"I love a man who thinks of everything."

"I love a woman who does the same." He nudged me at the arch of my back to move forward.

Ahead of us in line, I spotted Matthew and Meredith with the twins. Paige stood in front of them by herself. I searched for Pixie among the crowd and saw her hanging back at the fringe — with Zach. Perhaps Pixie had chatted with her mother after last night's event and convinced her that she and Zach were taking it slowly.

"Charlotte, sugar!" Tyanne yelled. She came up behind us while holding on to the hands of her two towheaded kids. "Are the twins here yet?"

I pointed. "They're way up there. See them near the entrance?"

"Will they save a space for us at a table?"

"I'm sure Clair will see to it."

I eyed Tyanne's son. He blushed.

The moment we were inside and had laced up our skates, Jordan headed to the concession stand to purchase a couple of cups of cocoa with the caveat that he expected the wait to be longer than a half hour.

"Don't worry about me. I'll warm up with a slow skate."

The skating surface wasn't too crowded yet. Most of the other participants were still donning skates or shedding parkas. The freedom I felt on skates was something I hadn't experienced in a long time.

After doing two languid laps around the rink, I glided to the center and did a series of turns. When I stopped, I was facing away from the concession stand. Outside the railing stood Violet, dressed in a pretty purple skating outfit, her marshmallow hair in pigtails. From this angle, she looked like a tall, lithe teenager. Her attention seemed to be on a group of people at the entrance squabbling over their tickets.

Ray, with numerous sets of skates slung over his shoulder by the shoelaces, was disputing the number of tickets handed to him by a large party of people. He shook his head and held up a finger, indicating that the group was one ticket short. A woman pleaded. A freckle-faced boy started to cry. That did it. Ray softened. He scruffed the head of the freckle-faced boy and gestured with his thumb, indicating the group could enter. They were so ecstatic that you'd have thought Ray had given them free tickets to Disneyland.

While watching them, Violet curled a tress of hair around her pinky in a coy fashion, and out of nowhere I flashed on something I'd said to Jordan about Rebecca's performance. During her audition, she had captured the character, with the right emotional catch in her speech and the loving look in her eyes. That memory was quickly followed by what the twins had said last Saturday night when they'd stayed with me. Amy had accused Clair of luring Ty-anne's son with those sexy eyes of hers. To illustrate, she'd batted her eyelashes and twirled her hair around her pinky.

Right then I was struck by another *duh* moment, the second in as many days: Violet *loved* Ray. Did he know? Was he in love with her? She was much younger. Had he found a love in her eyes that had waned in Dottie's? Violet had changed her lifestyle to make herself healthier. Ray said he no longer ate sweets or drank caffeine. Had Dottie's bad dietary choices plagued Ray? Had he grown tired of the fact that she regularly plied the town — especially children — with fats and sugar? Did the reality that Dottie couldn't ever have kids eat at him? Violet was vital enough to have a passel of children.

At the pub the night Tim was murdered, Paige had hinted that Violet was pregnant. Violet swore she wasn't. When she drew a pack of cigarettes out of her purse, I commented that only one had been smoked. At first she claimed it wasn't she who had smoked it, but she quickly revised her statement, saying she had. Just one. Had she lied? Had someone else smoked it? Ray, perhaps? Despite his health regimen, he hadn't given up that vice. I had seen him smoking when he was posting flyers. Had Violet met Ray on the sly? Had they talked, chatted, kissed . . . plotted to do away with Dottie?

"Sugar," Tyanne said as she skated up, kicking up ice shavings onto my leggings. "Are you okay? You look like you've seen a ghost."

"Better. I've seen the light."

"What are you talking about?"

"I think Violet and Ray killed Tim and Dottie." I supplied the basis for my theory. "The night Tim died, both Ray and Violet went out to the parking lot. What if they went out for a clandestine meeting, but the parking lot was a little busy. So they stole around to the back of the restaurant. Near the kitchen. What if Tim went outside for some fresh air and he heard Ray and Violet scheming to kill Dottie? What if he spied them in a passionate embrace?"

I took a deep breath and continued. "On Monday night, when I was at the pub with Delilah, I saw Violet there. She walked over to Ray, who was sitting by himself at the bar, and she stroked his arm. I'd figured she was consoling him, but if that were so, then why had she needed to comfort him again when they bumped into each other outside my shop a day or so later? And she stared at him longingly at our Lovers Trail event. I'd thought she was eyeing the guitar-

408

ist, but looking back, I know I was wrong. It was Ray."

"But, sugar, this is all conjecture. Do you have anything solid? Chief Urso will require facts."

I glanced at Jordan, who was still standing in the concession line, his back to me. "Notes!" I blurted, remembering Jordan's love letters to me. "Ray and Violet were passing notes."

Tyanne shook her head, not following.

"Stay with me on this." I skated in a circle to keep the blood flowing in my legs. "You know how Ray posts flyers for The Ice Castle on the kiosk in the Village Green? They're all done on blue paper."

Tyanne skated backward, nodding while listening. We made slow loops.

"The other day," I said, "when Violet was in the shop, she pulled out a note from her purse. It was for me from Jordan."

"Why did she have it?"

"She'd seen him tape it to the door. That's not important. What *is* important is that, at the same time, out came a bunch of other stuff, all tangled together. In the mess were a number of folded pieces of blue paper. Violet gave me Jordan's note and jammed the rest into her purse."

"So?"

"The paper looked like the same stock Ray uses for his Ice Castle flyers. What if Ray posts notes on the backs of his flyers for Violet to fetch, secret missives telling her where and when to meet? That way they would never have to exchange phone calls. They'd have no digital record of their affair. I remember seeing Violet in the Village Green on the morning Dottie was killed. She'd split from the group to peer around the kiosk, as if expecting to see Ray, or to see if there was a new note from him." I drew to a stop using my toe pick. "Come to think of it, I also remember spying a folded piece of blue paper tucked into her purse on the night Tim was killed."

"Go on."

"Not long after Violet fumbled with the bundle of stuff in the shop, I was followed to the park and mugged at knifepoint. What if Violet thought that I, catching her blunder, was onto her and Ray? What if she was the one who mugged me?"

"Sugar, the mugger took your ring."

"To confuse and misdirect me. I think Violet wanted me to believe the mugger was either Zach or Jawbone. The mugger reeked of liquor. Violet could have doused herself with it, like perfume. Granted, I can't be sure it wasn't Jawbone, because he won't tell me if he has an alibi."

"You asked him?"

"At the soiree Thursday night."

"You are too daring." Tyanne sighed. "And what about Zach? I assume you asked him, too."

"I found out he was with Pixie at her house, begging her mother's forgiveness." I rubbed my hands in front of me to warm my fingers. "If Jawbone had mugged me, wouldn't he have used a gun instead of a knife?"

Tyanne grinned. "Violet has a state-of-the-art kitchen at her inn filled with quality chef's knives."

"Exactly. And look at her. See how much slimmer and more muscular she is as a result of her diet? She's a good four or five inches taller than me. In the dark, in a panic, I could have mistaken her for a man. The mugger was dressed in black and wearing a ski mask."

Tyanne sneaked a peek in Violet's direction. "But you said the person who attacked you had a deep voice."

"Violet used a mannish voice when talking to a client the other day. I've done the same. Lowered my tone so I'd sound more authoritative."

"Even if Violet attacked you and killed

411

Dottie, she has a solid alibi for when Tim was killed. She was with Paige."

"Right. But what if Ray killed Tim?" I explained the *Strangers on a Train* theory.

Tyanne shook her head. "Everyone saw Ray and Dottie head home together that night."

"Yes, right after Tim sped away. What if Ray went out again? I never asked. I'm not sure Urso did, either. With Dottie dead, we can't confirm whether or not Ray stayed home with her."

"How would he have caught up to Tim?"

"I don't know. But if I'm guessing correctly, Violet must have killed Dottie, because Ray was at a service at the chapel in the ravine. Right after she did the deed, she joined Paige and the others by the kiosk."

"Hold it. Did you say Ray was at the chapel on Sunday morning?"

"Yes. The sunrise service."

"That's impossible." Tyanne dug the toe of her skate into the ice. She glanced over her shoulder and back at me. "Sugar, the chapel was being used by me. Well, not *me* technically. My clients. The out-of-towners. Talk about spontaneity! The night before, around nine P.M., they asked me to call the minister and pay him whatever he wanted for the event. We shut the chapel down at five A.M. Some parishioners gathered outside and watched the festivities, but I don't remember seeing Ray in the crowd."

"Mommy!" Tyanne's daughter yelled from across the rink. "Tommy pushed me."

Tyanne squeezed my arm. "I'll be right back."

I stood stock still, thinking back to when Ray had rushed into the pastry shop. He saw Dottie and dashed to her. He touched her face, her neck, her hair. At the time, I'd believed he was trying to save her. Had he been trying to mess with the crime scene? Had he killed Dottie, returned home, and changed from regular jean shorts and a T-shirt into all black so that he could say he'd gone to chapel? Except when he saw me he realized he was still wearing his gloves; they probably had traces of flour and Dottie's DNA on them. That was why he'd tried to help her. Immediately he accused Zach. He claimed jewelry had been stolen. Was that part of the plot? I recalled how Ray had pulled on his ear the entire time he was talking to me. Deputy O'Shea had done the same thing when auditioning, as if he hadn't believed the words he was saying.

I eyed Tyanne, who was busy with her children. I looked for Jordan; he was still in line at the concession stand. Above the stand hung a sign that read: *Go Team!*

Teamwork. Rebecca and I had guessed that Ray and Jawbone had worked as a team, but the truth was, Ray and Violet were the team players. Who had come up with the plan, Ray or Violet? Did it matter?

I spied Violet standing alone at the edge of the rink, searching the crowd. For a glimpse of Ray? Violet hoped to have kids one day. Had she and Ray killed so they could start building that family, sooner rather than later?

Violet looked my way. Her eyes widened. In them I saw apprehension. She raced toward the rear of the rink where skates and other equipment were stored. My cell phone was in the locker that Jordan and I had rented. I didn't have time to retrieve it and dial Urso. I called out to Jordan, but he didn't hear me. I didn't see a deputy anywhere in the vicinity.

Shoot!

I couldn't wait for help. I couldn't let Violet flee. I sped off the ice and tore after her, teetering on the blades of my skates as I galumphed across the rubber flooring. The double doors to the equipment room were always open. No room attendant was in sight. No skaters were standing in line waiting for equipment.

Violet skirted around the rows of shelving and disappeared down an aisle that held cascades of hockey sticks and helmets.

I went after her. A long narrow bench separated the passage. Separated us.

"Violet," I said. "Stop."

She spun around. "Ch-Charlotte." She stumbled over my name. "Fancy seeing you here."

The poet Robert Southey wrote: "Innocence is like a polished armor; it adorns and defends."

Except Violet didn't look innocent, or pretty. She appeared older. Not a teenager. Not even a fresh young woman. Her face had turned as pale as her hair. Her eyes, which were outlined heavily with purple liner, blinked rapidly.

I said, "You attacked me in the dog park."

"Are you nuts?"

"Someone held me up at knifepoint and stole my ring. My dog attacked the mugger." I peered at her calves.

She glanced down as well. A dark six-inch bruise was visible through the beige stockings. She gazed at me again, her eyes hard.

"You came after me because you thought I figured out about Ray and you."

"Ray and me? I don't know what you're

talking about."

"When you gave me Jordan's origami note, you fumbled with folded blue notes from your purse. Notes from Ray. You figured I knew they were love letters, and you panicked. You followed me to the dog park, and you attacked me. You wanted me to think the mugger was Jawbone or Zach. So I would go running to Chief Urso. To divert the investigation."

"This is crazy talk."

"There were other telltale signs, Violet. Both Ray and you implicated Jawbone in Tim's murder. That establishes that you were in the parking lot outside the pub at the same time."

"So?"

"On another occasion, you said that Ray didn't like Dottie's pastry. How would you know that?"

"I heard him talking one time. Big deal."

"You seemed surprised to hear that Ray was helping Dottie in her shop. Not just surprised. Miffed, come to think of it. In addition, there were the quick exchanges between you and Ray, in the pub and outside my shop. At first I thought you were offering him your condolences, but looking back, I remember how you touched him. Gently, lovingly." I tilted my head. "Tim saw you and Ray outside the pub that night, didn't he? He saw you in a tender embrace. Did he hear you plotting to kill Dottie?"

Violet drew up taller. She raised her chin in a condescending way and sniffed. "Charlotte, honestly, sweetie, you are letting this theorizing for the police go to your head. If you're not careful, your flock of followers will flee faster than a flurry of pheasants."

I bit back a snort. How long had she worked on that alliterative phrase? Ever since she'd assailed me in the park? "You're guilty, Violet. Even if you didn't kill Dottie, you are an accessory to murder."

"An accessory? But I didn't . . . Ray —"

"Shut up, Violet!" Ray stormed around the corner, skates clattering over his shoulder. "Don't say another word!"

CHAPTER 38

Ray strode down the aisle, the skates batting his chest. His gloved hands were clenched. His face looked harder than rock salt. His lips — I'd never noticed his mouth before — were thin and pulled back, baring teeth that didn't match. Some were brighter than others, as if he'd had some replaced. He must have played hockey, like my ex, and lost a few in on-ice battles. Had he been an enforcer? The muscles in his forearms flexed with tension.

I backed up, hands feeling behind me for balance. I rammed into the stand of hockey sticks. I clutched one with both hands. *Wrong, Charlotte. You need the weapon in front of you.* But if I tried to do that, wouldn't Ray or Violet hurtle toward me? *Teamwork.* I thought of Jordan. Had he noticed that I was missing from the ice? Had someone told him I'd called out to him? Would he come searching for me?

"You killed Tim, didn't you, Ray?" I said. "You left the pub that night, under the auspices of getting Dottie's overcoat — something you'd planned, I imagine, to grab a stolen moment with Violet. You two met around back, out of sight of people entering the pub. You talked about your plan to kill Dottie so the two of you could be together. When did you realize Tim overheard you?"

Ray didn't say anything for a moment and then shrugged. "When I heard him beat tracks away from us."

"You knew where he was headed: to find Urso. You knew where Urso was: at Jordan's bachelor party. You fetched Dottie, told her some cockamamie story about Tim arguing with Jawbone, then whisked her back to your house and dropped her off. Where did you tell her you were going?"

"To the store for coffee."

"Ray," Violet cried. "Stop talking!"

"But you don't drink caffeine," I said.

"Decaf. She bought the lie."

"Ray!" Violet warned again.

"Quiet!" he ordered.

I juggled the hockey stick to my right hand. I was perspiring. The grip felt slick and unmanageable, but I held on tight. "How did you catch up to Tim before he could talk to Urso?"

Ray snickered. "Bad luck for him, good luck for me. That old piece of junk of his, the truck he always bragged about being so reliable, stalled out along the way. I pulled up to Pace Hill Farm seconds after he did."

Wow. The irony of that made me wince. Tim had loved that truck and had trusted it with his life. I edged the hockey stick toward my hip. No sudden moves. I would only have one chance to swing. "How did you get Tim to go into the cheese facility?"

"I told him I just wanted to chat." Ray splayed his hands. Mr. Friendly. "A few minutes in private, I said, and we could clear up any misunderstanding. I told him Violet and I were joshing around. He didn't believe me. That's when I pulled out my gun."

It was the same scenario I'd fashioned when I'd suspected Jawbone was the killer.

"You own a gun?" I said.

"You bet I do. I stow it in the glove compartment of my truck. I transport a lot of cash to the bank on Saturdays. The ice rink is a cash cow. No two-bit thief is going to get the jump on me."

Was he packing now? Was his pistol anchored at the arch of his back? If I wielded the hockey stick, would he shoot me and flee?

"But Tim did get the jump on you," I said, vamping for time, hoping somebody would realize I was missing. "Inside the facility."

"Yeah."

"So you whacked him."

"All it took was one good blow to the back of his thick skull." Ray mimed the action. "He lurched forward and slammed into the vat. Out for the count."

That was when the button on Tim's shirt must have popped off.

"Then you hoisted him, unconscious, into the vat and unleashed the milk," I said. "Did you make sure he'd drowned?"

"You bet I did."

Violet gagged, but I didn't glance her way. Ray was the danger. Ray, with his meaty arms and powerful fists.

I pressed on. "Next, you raced away and called Violet. That was a risk, but you had to take it. You didn't have time to write a note on a flyer and post it on the kiosk."

Ray looked impressed. "You figured that out?"

"I sure as heck didn't tell her," Violet blurted.

"You told Violet to stay at the pub," I theorized. "Being with Paige gave her a solid alibi. Next, the two of you plotted to frame Jawbone. You'd seen him at the pub. He was

421

a good foil. Violet knew about Jawbone having the set-to with Tim. Perfect. Except his alibi held up and his motive was weak when it came to Dottie. So you needed another patsy. Enter Zach. How could you have known he'd have a solid alibi, too? He was sleeping with his girlfriend at the time Dottie died."

Neither Ray nor Violet said a word.

I inched the hockey stick forward, keeping it pressed against my leg. "Why didn't you ask Dottie for a divorce?"

"He did," Violet hissed. "She wouldn't give him one."

"Did you force Ray's hand, Violet? Did you say, 'Marry me, or else'?"

Violet eyed Ray with venom. "Dottie knew what was happening. She was losing him, but she dug in. She vowed she would never let him go. It was all her fault."

I gawped.

"If she'd granted him the divorce, we could have gotten married. I'd be pregnant by now. Dottie would be alive with that . . . that pastry shop she treasured. But no, Dottie had to have it her way."

"Violet, hush," Ray said.

"Don't hush me. You weren't in love with her anymore. She didn't take care of herself. She let herself go."

"Ray?" I said. "Did you ask Dottie for a divorce?" It was a common complaint in broken heart columns that some men would tell their lovers they wanted a divorce, but they never found the courage to confront the wife.

He nodded. "I did, but you know Dottie."

Knew.

"She could be a tough cookie. She looked soft around the edges, but she was all business. When she lost the baby, something inside her changed. She refused to try again."

"I heard she couldn't have children anymore."

"Nah. That wasn't true. She decided she didn't want one. She wanted *me.* Only me. Oh sure, we would give to the charities and she would volunteer, but she wanted me. She *needed* me. It became too much. I never had a free moment." He lifted his shoulders and dropped them. "When I went to the pâtisserie that morning, I begged one more time for a divorce, but she wouldn't grant it. She said, 'Over my dead body.' "

"And you obliged by shoving a Pace Hill Farm Gouda–filled pastry in her mouth and suffocating her."

Ray didn't disagree.

"Was that how you and Violet had plotted

to kill her?" I asked.

"Are you insane?" Violet said. "He was going to use arsenic. Dottie kept it in the shop to kill varmints."

"A pinch or two a day." Ray's mouth curled up. "Who'd have known a thing?" His lip caught on a tooth, which produced a vile-looking grin. "Killing her at the shop that day, sure, it was spur of the moment, but it was inspired, if I do say so myself. Tim, drowned in the cheese vat; Dottie, suffocated with the cheese pastry."

I shuddered.

"Ray, end this now. Kill Charlotte," Violet said. "She'll talk. You know she will. She'll spoil everything."

Was this how the first murder had come about, Violet prompting Ray to action? *Go after Tim. Get him.*

"Wait!" I blurted. "Dottie's brooch, Ray. Did you —"

"Shut her up, Ray!" Violet aimed a finger at me. "Do it now before anybody figures out where she is!"

"Ray," I said. Anything to steer his attention to me and not to Violet. "Did you steal it?"

"Yeah. What do you care?" Ray moved toward me. A skate on his shoulder bobbled. He glanced down as if the skate had given him a novel idea, and quicker than a whip, he removed a pair from his shoulder. Gripping the shoelaces, he swung the skates like a lasso.

In the nick of time, I drew the hockey stick in front of me and blocked Ray's attack. The skate wound around the stick like a ball struck in a game of tetherball. Ray tried to pull the skate free, but his efforts made the laces tighten. He released the set of skates.

The stick, with skates attached, was unwieldy, but I could still hoist it. I swung out. The shoe of a skate struck Ray on the side of the head. He careened backward. His knees struck the bench. He toppled to the ground and his head struck a locker with a *clack.*

"Ray!" Violet shouted, then she whirled on me. "You!"

She came at me with a knife — the same knife she'd used to mug me. Where had she been hiding it? Inside her slim jacket? I struck out with the skating shoe–hockey stick mess. The stick part hit her forearm. She released the knife; it fell to the ground. I ran at her and wrestled her backward into the stand of hockey sticks. She slid into a muddled heap.

At the same time, Jordan rushed into the

area — no cups of cocoa in hand, only an expression of grim determination. "Charlotte, are you —"

"I'm fine. Check Ray."

Jordan did. "He's breathing. He has a pulse. He's unconscious."

"How did you find me?"

"Tyanne said you'd disappeared. I called 911."

"Hands up!" a man shouted.

Jordan and I obeyed.

Umberto Urso strode down the aisle. Deputy O'Shea entered next. Both had guns drawn.

Chapter 39

For the remainder of Saturday, chatter in The Cheese Shop was loud. People stopped in to see how I was doing. Rebecca, Meredith, and Tyanne couldn't stop hovering over me. Every so often, Matthew threw me a look of compassion. His ex-wife Sylvie stopped in, claiming that she wanted to know if she'd won yesterday's cheese basket giveaway. Delilah brought me not one but two ham and pear grilled cheese sandwiches. Quigley, a local reporter, asked me for an exclusive. He was hoping the story would go viral on the Internet.

On Sunday — a week after Dottie was murdered; a week after Jordan and I were to be married — Jordan, who hadn't left my side until the police were finished questioning me, entered the shop carrying a huge bouquet of daisies. He looked incredibly handsome in a brown suit and cream-colored collared shirt. "For the hero," he said.

"I'm not a hero."

"Dottie and Tim have been avenged. Violet and Ray are facing charges. Dottie's sisters now have the heirloom brooch; they're selling the pastry shop, by the way. Zach Mueller was cleared. So was Jawbone Jones. And, this just in, Councilwoman Bell has given up trying to oust your grandmother from office."

"Why?"

"Because she's moving to Los Angeles to help her daughter through her rehabilitation. Hero."

"Heroine," I revised.

"What are you, a literary major now?" He kissed me on the cheek. "You look beautiful, by the way."

"I don't. I need a week of sleep, a facial, and a massage, not necessarily in that order."

"Beautiful. Glowing."

"Get out of here."

"I never lie."

I raised an eyebrow.

He grinned. "Occasionally, I obfuscate the truth."

I laughed, then took the daisies, placed them into a crystal vase filled with water, and set the vase by the register. "Now, my sweet man" — I leveled him with a gaze —

"what's this I hear about you buying the pub?"

"Who told you?"

"Quigley."

"O'Shea and the other nephews don't want it. I don't think Jawbone has a clue how to run a place like that. I've been thinking about making a switch. And Luigi has decided not to sell La Bella Ristorante." He slipped an arm around my waist. "Actually, I came here to talk to you about the prospect."

"What about your farm?"

"My sister wants to take it on." A year or so after Jordan moved to town, he covertly relocated his sister to Providence to protect her from an abusive husband. The man was now dead. End of story. "Jacky loved working it while I was away in November." When Jordan left town for the WITSEC trial, he had put his sister in charge of the farm. "She said tilling the soil suits her."

"I thought she was going to give up her pottery store and move to Los Angeles to become an actress." Back in October, she'd had a fling with a famous independent movie director.

"That relationship has ended."

"What about the negative publicity the farm will receive? A murder occurred on the property."

"She looks forward to the challenge." He took me by the elbow. "Would you mind walking around the pub with me and checking it out? You've got a better eye for space and décor."

"Ha! You're the one that used to own a restaurant."

"Years ago. I'm rusty."

"I'll meet you there after work."

"How about now?" He gestured to Rebecca. "Do you mind watching the shop while Charlotte and I go on an errand?"

"Sure," she said. "It's slow this morning with everyone in church."

My insides snagged. Weddings and funerals. Beginnings and endings. Life and death. I pushed the thoughts from my mind.

Jordan said, "We'll be back in less than an hour."

"Whatever." She shooed us away. "Go!"

Jordan guided me across the street and onto the path through the Village Green.

"What's with the indirect route?" I asked. I didn't mind. I was dressed for the cool weather.

"I thought we could use a dose of sunshine." He drew me close. We ambled through the park, pointing out other couples that looked as happy as we were.

Minutes later, Jordan opened the door to the pub and allowed me to enter first.

"Surprise!" more than thirty people yelled. Friends and family, all dressed for a party. Some were blowing party horns. Rice flew into the air and splattered my face and shoulders.

Front and center stood Tyanne with a Cheshire cat grin on her face. She rushed to me carrying what looked like my ecru wedding dress. "Hurry, sugar. We don't want to keep the minister waiting." She started to lead me toward the kitchen.

I gaped. "Minister?"

"I've set up the bathroom in the back to be our staging area."

"Our what?" I turned to Jordan, who had trailed us to the back of the pub.

He dropped to one knee and took my hand in his. "Charlotte Erin Bessette, will you marry me . . . today? Here, right now. In my new pub."

"Your . . ." I glanced over his shoulder and realized, for the first time, that the pub was decorated with white streamers, balloons, and daisies.

"I . . ." He paused. "All of us want to make good memories at the pub again."

Rebecca emerged from the pack carrying a bouquet of daisies and baby's breath. She thrust it at me. "Here you go."

"The shop."

"Closed for a celebration."

"You knew?"

"We're all in on it." She swirled a hand to indicate the rest of the party.

Grandmère and Pépère stood off to the side with Meredith, Matthew, and the twins. Delilah and Urso stood beyond them, as did Jacky and so many more friends. All were beaming.

Meredith broke from the group and ran to me. "I stole into your house and filched your mother's pearl earrings." She held out her hand. The baubles gleamed in the soft light.

Tyanne said, "I've hired the French horn player. He's standing by. Delilah's worked with the pub's chef to put your menu together. The winter salad with chocolate-dipped strawberries, the chocolate cheesecake, and, well, everything. And, sugar, we have butterflies waiting to be released."

Tears sprang into my eyes. I turned to Jordan. "Are you sure?"

"I've never been more sure of anything."

"I'm impulsive and curious," I admitted.

"And loyal and true." He tipped my chin up with a crooked finger. "Don't forget, I have a few faults."

"Not many."

"By the way, I brought you something blue." He withdrew a note from his pocket and handed it to me. "Open it."

It was a note in my handwriting — a note that I'd written a couple of years ago, thanking him for the first bouquet of flowers he'd ever brought me. It was our first love letter. I pressed it to my chest as a wealth of emotions caught in my throat. If only my mother and father were here to witness the occasion.

"Yes, Jordan Pace, I will marry you. Right here. Right now."

Everyone cheered. The band lit into my mother's favorite song. I swung around to signal my thanks and stopped, my mouth falling open. Jawbone Jones and Ilona Mueller headed up the band.

"I thought they played blues," I whispered to Jordan.

"Not today. They're good, aren't they?"

"Yes."

"Glad you approve. Now, get a move on, woman. Don't keep me waiting any longer."

We married.

The next day, after the coroner made official determinations as to the causes of death in both cases, which matched Ray's account — death by drowning and death by suffocation — Urso released Tim's and Dottie's bodies, and the families held funeral services, not just memorials.

At Tim's service, Tyanne's eyes brimmed with tears as she gave the eulogy. Deputy O'Shea followed her with an earnest speech. After Tim's body was laid to rest in the cemetery, Jordan closed the event saying how much Tim, a friend to all, would be missed. His voice caught three times during the talk.

Following the ceremony, Jordan and I took a contemplative walk.

The next day, we moved ahead with our lives and went on our long-anticipated honeymoon. Bliss.

RECIPES

CHEESE POPS
À la Tyanne
(MAKES 12)

18-ounce container mascarpone cheese
2 tablespoons honey
1/2 cup craisins
1/2 cup sunflower seeds
8 ounces Gouda, shredded, room
  temperature

Put all the ingredients into a large bowl and mix well. Using your hands, form the mixture into balls. Insert a white lollipop-style stick. Set the pops, cheese-side down and sticks in the air, on parchment paper and place in the refrigerator to harden.

When ready to serve, cut a piece of Styrofoam to fit into a serving bowl or basket. Cover the Styrofoam with a piece of parchment. Make 12 slits in the parchment. Shove the cheese pops, stick-side down, through the slits into the Styrofoam. Bring to room temperature and serve.

[**Note from Tyanne:** *These are so easy to make, even my children could do it. In fact, it's a fun activity for families. If you prefer, you can always substitute the craisins with raisins and the sunflower seeds with a nut of your choice. Pecans are my favorite. If you're not a Gouda fan, try another cheese that you like, for example, Monterey Jack, Cheddar, or Havarti. Savor the flavors!*]

MACARONI AND CHEESE APPETIZER
À la Timothy O'Shea's Irish Pub
(SERVES 4)

2 cups dried macaroni, cooked to tender (about 4–5 cups cooked)
4 tablespoons butter
1 clove garlic, chopped
1/2 teaspoon salt
1/2 teaspoon white pepper
1/2 teaspoon paprika
1 1/2 tablespoons cornstarch
3/4 cup milk
1/4 cup white wine
1/2 cup mascarpone cheese
1 cup grated cheese (equal parts Cheddar, Gouda, Monterey Jack)
1/4 cup bread crumbs

1/4 cup Parmesan cheese

Cook macaroni according to package directions. Drain and set aside. Pasta may be made a day ahead. *Note: Do not forget to drain and set aside. You do not want the pasta to be wet.*

In a large saucepan, melt the butter over medium heat. Add garlic, salt, pepper, paprika, and cornstarch. Cook about 1–2 minutes. It will boil and thicken. Stir constantly.

Add milk and wine, stir, and let boil to thicken.

Remove from heat and add mascarpone cheese and grated cheeses.

Pour sauce over drained macaroni. Stir well. Fill 6–8 appetizer-sized ramekins with the mixture. Top with bread crumbs mixed with the Parmesan cheese.

Turn oven on to broil. Set the ramekins about 4 inches under broiler. Broil for 5–6 minutes until crisp.

Serve hot.

*[**Note from Charlotte:** This is perhaps my all-time favorite comfort-food appetizer. It simply melts in your mouth. The wine adds just a hint of a kick! For a gluten-free option, which I make for the twins since Clair has to*

eat gluten-free, I use gluten-free pasta and gluten-free bread crumbs. Everything else is good to go! Enjoy!]

GOAT CHEESE COOKIES
Gluten-Free
(MAKES 36-48 COOKIES)

2 1/2 cups gluten-free flour (I like sweet rice flour with tapioca starch)
1/2 teaspoon baking soda
1 teaspoon baking powder
1/2 teaspoon xanthan gum
1/2 teaspoon salt
1 1/2 cups sugar
1/2 cup crumbled goat cheese, room temperature
6 tablespoons unsalted butter, melted
1/4 cup vegetable oil
1 large egg
2 tablespoons milk
1 teaspoon vanilla extract
1/2 cup of sugar for coating cookies

Preheat oven to 350 degrees F.

Line a baking sheet with parchment paper.

In a small bowl, whisk together gluten-free flour, baking powder, baking soda, xanthan gum, and salt. Set aside.

In a large bowl, combine the sugar, crumbled goat cheese, and melted butter.

Whip the mixture for 1 minute. Add in the vegetable oil. Stir. Add the egg, milk, and vanilla extract, and stir the mixture until smooth. (You might still see a few lumps; that's okay.)

Add the flour mixture and stir well. The dough will be soft but should be workable. If it's not, refrigerate the dough until it stiffens up, about 15 minutes.

Pour the 1/2 cup of sugar for coating cookies into a small cereal-sized bowl. Using your fingers, take a tablespoon of cookie dough, roll it into a ball, and roll it in the sugar to coat. Set the cookie on the prepared baking sheet. Remember to leave about 2 inches between cookies. They will spread.

Bake each batch for 10–12 minutes, until the cookies are just set and slightly cracked. DON'T overcook.

Cool on the baking sheet for 3 minutes, then transfer the cookies to a wire rack or paper towels to cool. Store the cookies in an airtight container for up to 1 week. They may be frozen if wrapped individually in plastic wrap.

[**Note from Charlotte:** *Goat cheese, like buttermilk, adds a delicate tang to these cookies, almost like lemon, which is a perfect balance for all the sugar. Trust me. They are chewy,* yet crisp.]

[**Second note from Charlotte:** *For regular cookies, substitute out the gluten-free flour with regular flour and omit the xanthan gum.*]

APPLE BACON GOUDA QUICHE
(SERVES 4-6)

1 pie shell (homemade recipe below, or store-bought, usually frozen)
1 green apple, pared and sliced into thin slices
4–6 slices of bacon, crisply cooked and crumbled
1 tablespoon brown sugar
1/2 cup sour cream
1/2 cup whipping cream
1/2 cup milk
1/2 cup mascarpone cheese (or cream cheese)
2 eggs
1/2 cup shredded Gouda cheese
1/2 teaspoon cinnamon, if desired

Heat oven to 400 degrees F. Bake pie shell for 5 minutes. Remove from oven and let cool. Reduce oven heat to 375 degrees F.

Arrange apple slices in cooled pie shell. Arrange crumbled bacon on top. Sprinkle with brown sugar.

In a small bowl, mix sour cream, whipping cream, milk, mascarpone cheese, and eggs. Mix in the shredded cheese. Pour the mixture into the pie shell on top of the apples and bacon. (The apples and bacon will rise in the cream. Don't worry.) Dust with cinnamon, if desired.

Bake 35 minutes until quiche is firm and lightly brown on top.

[**Note from Charlotte:** *If you need to eat gluten-free, either use a gluten-free pastry mix, a gluten-free store-bought pie crust, or substitute the sifted flour in the Pastry Dough recipe below with gluten-free flour. My favorite combo is sweet rice flour mixed with tapioca starch. Add 1/2 teaspoon xanthan gum to the mix. And make sure you roll out the dough between parchment paper for best flexibility. Gluten-free dough doesn't hold together as well as regular dough, but be patient.]*

Pastry Dough for Pie Shell

1 1/4 cups sifted flour
1 teaspoon salt
1/2 teaspoon white pepper
6 tablespoons butter or shortening
2–3 tablespoons water
1 egg beaten with 1 tablespoon water, for egg wash on pastry

Put flour, salt, and white pepper into food

processor fitted with a blade. Cut in 3 tablespoons of butter or shortening and pulse for 30 seconds. Cut in another 3 tablespoons of butter. Pulse again for 30 seconds. Sprinkle with 2–3 tablespoons water and pulse a third time, for 30 seconds.

Remove the dough from the food processor and form into a ball using your hands. Wrap with wax paper or plastic wrap. Chill the dough in the refrigerator for 30 minutes.

Heat your oven to 400 degrees F.

Remove the dough from the refrigerator and remove the covering. Place a large piece of parchment paper on a countertop. Sprinkle flour onto parchment paper. Place the dough on top of the parchment paper. If desired, cover with another large piece of parchment paper. This prevents the dough from sticking to the rolling pin. Roll out dough so it is 1/4-inch thick and large enough to fit into an 8-inch pie pan, with at least a 1/2-inch hangover around the edge.

Remove the top parchment paper. Place the pie tin upside down on the dough. Flip the dough and pie tin. Remove the parchment paper. Press the dough into the pie tin. Crimp the edges.

Brush with the egg wash. Bake the pastry shell for 5 minutes. Remove from the oven and let cool.

The Country Kitchen Diner Chicken Potpie
(Serves 4-6)

4 cups chicken broth (gluten-free, if necessary)

1/2 cup butter (one stick)

1 onion, chopped

2 large carrots, peeled and cut into thin rounds

1 celery stalk, diced

1 tablespoon dried parsley

1/2 teaspoon dried sage

1 clove garlic, chopped fine (if desired)

1 teaspoon salt

1 teaspoon freshly ground black pepper

1/4 cup cornstarch

1/4 cup heavy cream

3 tablespoons white wine

1 pound skinless chicken breasts, precooked and shredded

1 cup frozen peas

1 recipe Pastry Dough (see below)

[Note from Delilah: *Make pastry dough first and refrigerate, then precook your chicken breasts. To cook chicken breasts, I wrap them in foil and pop them in the oven at 300 degrees F for 35–40 minutes. Remove from oven and let cool.]*

Preheat your oven to 375 degrees F.

In a 6-quart saucepan, heat the chicken broth over medium heat for 2 minutes.

Meanwhile, in large stockpot, melt butter over medium heat. Add onions, carrots, celery, parsley, sage, and garlic. Sauté until tender, about 10 minutes. Add salt and pepper. Stir.

To the hot broth, add the cornstarch and whisk together until it thickens, about 5 minutes. Add the mixture to the vegetables. Stir in the heavy cream, white wine, chicken, and frozen peas. Bring to a boil then reduce to a simmer for 5 minutes.

With a ladle, fill 4–6 ovenproof ramekins or bowls with the filling. Place the ramekins on a baking sheet.

*[**Note from Delilah:** For the crust, you can use store-bought pastry dough, or you can make it from scratch using this recipe. For gluten-free, substitute your favorite gluten-free mix for the flour. I use a blend of sweet rice flour and potato starch.]*

Pastry Dough for Potpie

[**Note from Charlotte:** This recipe is slightly different from the recipe for the quiche pie shell, in which I use white pepper. All the savory quiche recipes I make at Fromagerie Bessette have white pepper in the pie shell. Without it, the pastry doesn't have quite the kick.]

1 1/4 cups sifted flour
1 teaspoon salt
6 tablespoons butter or shortening
2–3 tablespoons water
1 egg beaten with 1 tablespoon water, for egg wash on pastry
Kosher salt

Put flour and salt into food processor fitted with a blade. Cut in 3 tablespoons of butter or shortening and pulse for 30 seconds. Cut in another 3 tablespoons of butter. Pulse again for 30 seconds. Sprinkle with 2–3 tablespoons water and pulse a third time, for 30 seconds.

Remove the dough from the food processor and form into a ball. Wrap with wax paper or plastic wrap. Chill the dough in the refrigerator for 30 minutes.

Remove the dough from the refrigerator and remove the covering. Place a large piece of parchment paper on a countertop. Sprinkle flour onto parchment paper. Place the dough on top. If desired, cover with another large piece of parchment paper. This prevents the dough from sticking to the rolling pin. Roll out dough so it is 1/4-

inch thick. Using a biscuit round or mold (or be daring and go freehand), cut out dough large enough to cover the tops of the ovenproof ramekins, leaving about 1/2-inch hangover. Place each round on top of the individual bowls and crimp the dough over the edge.

Brush with the egg wash and — IMPORTANT — make 4 small slits on the top of each to let out steam. Sprinkle with kosher salt. Place the baking sheet with ramekins in the preheated oven. Bake for 15–20 minutes. Remove from the oven and serve hot.

[**Note from Delilah:** *This is perhaps the most scrumptious potpie I've ever made. The stew is savory and reminds me of cool winter nights, tucked in front of a fire.*]

TRIPLE-CHOCOLATE PUDDING
From The Country Kitchen Diner
(SERVES 6)

3 tablespoons unsalted butter
4 1/2 ounces semisweet chocolate
1 ounce unsweetened chocolate
1 cup sugar
1/4 cup cocoa powder
3 tablespoons cornstarch
1/8 teaspoon fine kosher salt

3 large eggs plus 1 egg yolk
1/4 cup heavy cream
3 cups whole milk
1 tablespoon espresso coffee
1 teaspoon vanilla extract
Whipped cream and shaved chocolate for
  topping (optional)

Melt the butter in a heatproof bowl or double boiler over a saucepan of hot water. The water should be simmering, not boiling. Chop the semisweet and unsweetened chocolate and add to the butter. Stir until melted and smooth, about 5 minutes. Remove the bowl or top of double boiler, and set the mixture aside.

In a medium bowl, whisk 2/3 cup of the sugar, cocoa powder, cornstarch, and salt. Add the eggs and egg yolk and cream. Stir. Set aside.

In a medium saucepan over medium heat, heat the milk and the remaining 1/3 cup of sugar until it is steaming. You'll see little bubbles around the edge of the milk. *Note: Do not overcook.*

Gradually stir half of the hot milk mixture into the sugar/cocoa mixture, whisking continually. Pour that mixture back into the saucepan with the remaining hot milk mixture. Stir continually and bring to a boil, scraping the sides of the pan. When the mixture starts to boil, reduce the heat and let bubble for about 30 seconds. It will thicken a lot!

Remove the saucepan from the heat. Have a sieve with big holes ready. Strain the pudding through the sieve into a medium bowl. Add the melted chocolate mixture, espresso coffee, and vanilla, and stir well.

Spoon the pudding into 6 dessert bowls. Cover each serving with plastic wrap. The wrap can touch the pudding surface. Pierce the plastic to let out steam. Cool the pudding to room temperature for 1 hour.

Refrigerate the pudding until chilled for at least 2 hours.

Remove the plastic wrap and top each serving with whipped cream and shaved chocolate.

[**Note from Delilah:** *This can be made up to three days ahead. How cool is that? And here's a cool tip that I learned from my dad. To shave chocolate, use either a vegetable grater or a knife instead of a cheese grater. These tools help make the chocolate look artistic.*]

ABOUT THE AUTHOR

Agatha Award–winning author **Avery Aames** loves to cook and enjoys a good wine. She speaks a little French and has even played a French woman onstage. And she adores cheese. As Daryl Wood Gerber she also writes the Cookbook Nook Mysteries. Visit her at averyaames.com.